THE COCKLES OF YOUR HEART

BY

JO HARRIES

DEDICATION

To all my family with much love.

ACKNOWLEDGMENTS

To my husband Ken for all his patience.

Chapter 1

By focusing her eyes on the horizon it was still possible to hold on to the belief that it was going to be the perfect day. The sun was already burning off the heat haze, its rays glancing off the sea in dancing ripples of light. Trying desperately to ignore the clamour on the road below, she became aware of someone calling her name and reluctantly forced herself to look down to where a few people were standing at the bottom of the steps.

'Good morning!' the man shouted. 'You certainly picked a good day for the wedding, I hope it all goes well.'

Bryony smiled and waved back. 'Thanks Tim, at least the weather's perfect, but why is there so much traffic along here?'

'Oh that,' he replied with a rueful grin, 'it's the return of the cockle pickers. Didn't you know they'd re-opened the beds in the bay?'

'No I didn't,' she groaned, 'so I expect this is going to go on all morning.'

Tim laughed. 'All weekend more like. It happened so quickly even the local lads have been caught out and nobody's been able to prepare for it; apparently it's absolutely chaotic on the jetty.' He raised his arm high above his head and gave a hearty wave before striding away to witness for himself the unusual goings on. When he'd walked a few paces he suddenly slowed down and called over his shoulder, 'You should have a word with your husband; he must have known what was happening.'

'Colin.' Of course he must have known, but he wouldn't have even considered the impact it might have on the wedding and he certainly hadn't thought to warn her. She stroked away the frown line forming between her eyes as she screwed them up against the glare. It was important to look her best today and that made no allowance for worry lines. Shielding her face with cupped hands, she turned to follow the line of slowly moving traffic. From where it could be seen emerging round the curve of the bay it stretched along the outer promenade, before passing directly in front of the hotel and continuing all the way towards the jetty.

The convoy was made up of mostly old and decrepit vehicles carrying sailing vessels of all shapes and sizes, and it was moving so slowly it was almost at a standstill. It didn't appear to be a problem which would be resolved before the arrival of the bridegroom's family, an event she'd been eagerly anticipating and which would now be completely ruined. She couldn't believe that after more than a decade of absence the cockle pickers were back in Merebank Bay, and despite the problems it would cause it was too late for her to do anything about it.

Groups of people were gathering but most of them hurried past the hotel with hardly a glance as they made their way towards the hastily set up checkpoints, from where altercations between drivers and officials could be heard. With a fixed smile she returned the greetings of passers-by, but she was racked with frustration and disappointment when the reality of the situation became clear. The wedding day of Ralph Portman's granddaughter had been hijacked by a pack of scruffy fishermen who were already drawing attention from what should rightly be the most important highlight of the year. She was so deep in thought she jumped when Ralph unexpectedly appeared at her side, but despite everything she greeted him with genuine affection.

'This is a bit of a turn-up,' he said. 'Did you know it was on the cards?'

'No,' she replied, 'and I'm afraid it's going to spoil everything.'

He was silent for a moment while he appraised the situation and the impact the unexpected turn of events would have on the wedding. 'I know it's not ideal,' he said at last, 'but I honestly don't see why it should make much difference, after all most of the guests are here already.'

'I know, but not Piers and his family, and I especially wanted them to be impressed when they drive up to the hotel. I'm not even sure they will be able to come to the front entrance and I can't bear to think what a terrible impression they'll get even if they can.'

Ralph nodded sympathetically. 'Yes, I can understand you feeling that but they've already been here before, and anyway I'm sure they'll be amazed at what you've done inside the hotel, and after all that's what really matters.'

She valued his advice above anyone's, but today all she wanted was sympathy and his pragmatic approach wasn't helpful. 'Try to stop worrying,' he said to her. 'I'm sure everything will be perfect. Now if you'll excuse me I must be off, I don't want to miss my constitutional even on a day as important as this.'

She watched him move effortlessly down the steps and turn to walk against the growing tide of sightseers. His progress was constantly interrupted by friends and acquaintances who greeted him warmly and tried to engage him in discussions, but somehow he kept up his chosen pace. The feelings of respect and affection towards him were genuine and mutually shared, unlike his son, who constantly shied away from responsibility and neither gave nor instilled respect. At the thought of him she spun round and hurried back into the hotel; he had some very pertinent questions to answer and she was determined to confront him immediately.

A few early risers were passing through reception but by some skilful manoeuvring she was able to reach the safety of the lift, avoiding unnecessary conversation. A swift half smile thrown in the direction of Justin seemed to achieve the desired effect of reassuring him he was still in her favour, although in truth she was still furious with him. As her deputy he should have been aware of any potential threat to the success of Amelia's wedding, and under normal circumstances he would have been on the receiving end of her fury. But things weren't normal and she was going to depend on his co-operation, both today and in the future.

As soon as she stepped out of the lift she could hear Colin snoring, thank goodness none of the guests were occupying rooms on this top floor. She paused outside Amelia's room but there was no sign of any movement, so she opened Colin's door and stood on the threshold of a room in disarray.

She tugged the cord until the blind reached the top of the window and the dark room was flooded with sunlight. Colin dived back under the duvet, his muffled complaints mercifully impossible to hear. When she made no reply he peered out like a mole emerging from underneath the ground, and his voice was self-pitying and mournful. 'Bryn, did you really have to do that?'

'Yes I did,' she replied, rounding on him and sweeping the bedding back to reveal his flabby body curled up in the foetal position, one which seemed oddly appropriate considering his childish behaviour. 'You've got some serious explaining to do.'

She turned away and moved round the room, picking up the clothes he'd strewn haphazardly on the floor the previous evening. Even in his muddled state he seemed to recognise the need for some sort of reaction, so he tentatively put his feet to the floor and stealthily worked his way round the bed to retrieve his dressing gown from behind the door. 'God, what have I done wrong now?' he muttered to himself before making another appeal to her better nature. 'Please Bryn, have a heart, I've got a thumping head.' Splaying his fingers across his red-rimmed eyes, he forced himself to turn and face her but he shrivelled under the glare of her undisguised disgust. Having achieved her aim of propelling him out of bed she lowered the blind enough to provide some shade in the room, but was careful not to hide the view outside.

'This time,' she told him, 'it isn't what you've done, it's what you haven't done. It's Amelia's wedding day in case you've forgotten.'

'There's no need to be sarcastic,' he replied indignantly. 'I'm well aware what day it is.'

'But do you also know,' she asked, ignoring his jibe, 'that Merebank is being invaded by hordes of marauding cockle pickers who are threatening to ruin her wedding day?'

Through the fog of his hangover he remembered snippets of conversations and meetings but the details remained lost. 'I did know it was being discussed,' he said sheepishly, 'and if I remember rightly it was actually agreed, but honestly Bryn I had no idea it was going to be this weekend.'

Bryony found her anger draining away with the familiar sense of frustration and resignation taking its place; it was too late to expect anything else from him now. Standing at the window looking down on the disruptive jam of ugly traffic snaking its way past the building, she sagged with resignation. 'Oh Colin, you're absolutely useless,' she sighed. 'What is the point of being on the local council if you can't use it to your family's advantage when we need it?'

Colin joined her and despite everything, he watched with interest, although for once he seemed sensitive to her feelings. 'I see what you mean,' he conceded, hoping to keep on the right side of her, 'but I don't see why it should affect the wedding very much.'

She sank onto a chair. 'If only you'd warned me we could have told Piers and arranged for them to stay somewhere overnight. I really wanted everything to be perfect.'

'As I'm sure it's going to be,' Amelia said, tying the belt of her negligee as she entered the room. Her long blonde hair framed her face in a tousle of curls, and although she exuded a sexuality Bryony had always craved for herself, she hoped the hairdresser would be able to tame her daughter's locks for the wedding. 'I heard you mention Piers' name, is something wrong?' Amelia asked.

Bryony leaped up and embraced her. 'Of course not,' she said, 'it's just that there's a lot of traffic out there and I'm worried Piers and his family might have trouble reaching the hotel.'

Amelia's laugh swept away the tension in the room. 'Oh, you mean the cockle pickers?' she said airily. 'That's no problem, surely?'

'It is, according to your mother,' Colin complained, 'although how she thinks I personally can influence the Department of Inshore Fisheries I have no idea.'

Bryony ignored him but she was puzzled by Amelia's knowledge of what was going on. She was still in her nightclothes and, as far as she was aware, hadn't yet stepped outside the hotel. 'Never mind that for now,' Bryony said, turning to Amelia, 'how do you know about the cockle pickers?'

'Louisa told me,' Amelia explained, 'when she texted to let me know where she is.'

Bryony reminded herself it was Amelia's wedding day but even so she struggled to hide her irritation. 'What do mean, to let you know where she is? She's your bridesmaid and she's staying here, you know where she is.'

'Well yes, in a way, but at the moment she isn't exactly on the premises. Anyway there's nothing for you to worry about, but I must go and phone Piers to let him know what's going on with the traffic.'

Bryony was galvanised into action; there was no way she wanted Amelia and Piers being in touch with each other before the ceremony, and although she had a sneaking feeling they probably already were she preferred to keep up the pretence. 'I'll ring his mother,' she said, pushing past Amelia, who suddenly found herself flattened unceremoniously against the door frame. 'Sorry sweetheart,' she said, hesitating just long enough to see Amelia turning towards her father who was sitting dejectedly on the edge of the bed.

'Don't worry, Dad,' she told him. 'It will all turn out to be a storm in a teacup.'

Colin, who was relieved to be at least temporarily let off the hook of his wife's displeasure, replied with feeling that he never failed to be surprised how much Bryony could get into a teacup when she felt so inclined, but all he wanted at the moment was a strong cup of tea with plenty of sugar. Bryony told him in no uncertain manner to make his own cup of tea as he had everything provided in the room and could drink tea to his heart's content.

'I think I'll ring down and ask for breakfast to be sent up,' he replied, 'apparently that's what the wedding guests are getting. I am the father of the bride after all, so I think I deserve a little bit of luxury.'

Amelia laughingly had the last word. 'Dad,' she said, before running back into her room and closing the door, 'you're incorrigible.'

Back in her own room Bryony took a deep breath to calm herself before trying to contact Phoebe, who unfortunately was unavailable as she was busy preparing for their imminent departure. Piers' father Thomas took the call and assured her they wouldn't allow anything to make them and especially their son late for the wedding, and he was confident they would have no trouble negotiating an alternative route to the hotel which would avoid any potential hold-up. Far from being put out by any possible inconvenience it may cause them, he seemed genuinely fascinated by the cockle picking in the bay, which he'd been watching with interest on the television. At the end of the conversation she was left with a feeling he'd been amused by her concern, but nevertheless he'd inadvertently given her an idea with his unexpected reaction to the events in the bay. From now on she would turn it to their advantage and instead of apologising, she intended pointing out the uniqueness of what was happening. With a sense of relief she began to feel more in control again.

It was almost time to go down and meet Greg so she took some time with her appearance and she was surprised to find her hand was shaking. It was important to remain calm, especially in front of Amelia and Greg, so she gave herself a little confidence boost by dabbing on a tiny spot of the fine fragrance chosen especially for today.

Most of the guests would still be in their rooms but already some were out and about, and she wanted Amelia to see the floral decorations while it was quiet. It had been an inspired suggestion by Ralph to close the hotel to paying clientele and offer hospitality to the guests who would be travelling to Merebank for the wedding. At first she'd been very reluctant to relinquish the income usually generated on the last weekend in September, but once she'd embraced the idea she'd thrown herself into it with fervour and planned and designed like she'd never done before.

She looked up to her father-in-law, who was everything she admired in a man. Effortlessly suave and innately dignified, he'd always treated her with respect and encouragement. If only Colin had inherited a modicum of his father's strength of character and the entrepreneurial spirit of his ancestors, how different her life would have been. She'd never loved him; a mild admiration for his enthusiasm for life when he was young was the best she could summon up, but she did love the money, the hotel, and the status that marriage to him had brought, and it would be very hard to give it up. One thing she would be eternally grateful for was that the rogue gene which made up Colin's character hadn't resurfaced in his offspring.

Amelia breezed into the room. 'Hi Mum, are you ready?'

'I am,' she replied, 'but before we go anywhere will you please explain as briefly as possible where Louisa is?'

'Oh it's quite simple really,' Amelia explained. 'She and Damian met last night when they were all having a drink together, and apparently they hit it off straight away. They've gone for a walk on the beach and will be back soon.' She sighed. 'I think it's lovely if my oldest friend and my bridesmaid become an item at my wedding.'

Bryony found nothing remarkable about the budding romance but her interest perked up with the realisation that the young man involved was the son of Marie, her own closest friend. She was very fond of him and found him rather quiet and thoughtful, which made his present behaviour rather out of character. Surely they both knew their responsibilities were to the bride and groom and it was irresponsible to disappear on the morning of the wedding. A thought suddenly struck her. 'I was under the impression Louisa was involved with someone,' she said. 'Isn't it Piers' boss?'

'Oh, that's all over,' Amelia explained, 'she finished it ages ago, but apparently he's not happy about it and has been a bit of a pest. Unfortunately he and his wife are coming tonight so I hope he doesn't make things difficult for Louisa.'

The probability of a successful businessman showing himself up at a wedding, especially in front of members of his staff who were also invited to the evening celebrations, was so ludicrous Bryony almost laughed out loud, but she said nothing and kept her thoughts to herself. Amelia's loyalty to her friends was absolute and she may take it as a slight to Louisa.

'It's all a bit mysterious, this meeting with Uncle Greg,' Amelia said. 'We're going to be seeing each other all day.'

'There's nothing mysterious about it,' Bryony replied, 'it's simply because he hasn't seen you for a while and you know what weddings are like, you never get the opportunity for a proper chat.'

'I'm not complaining,' Amelia said, 'I absolutely love him to bits, you know that.'

'Yes I do, and he loves you,' Bryony said quietly.

They'd walked down the first set of stairs and as they reached the landing where the two flights joined before descending into the reception hall, Amelia stopped and gasped. 'Mum, this is glorious,' she breathed. 'It's absolutely fantastic.'

Bryony nodded in delight, revelling in Amelia's reaction, which was everything she'd hoped for. It had cost an astronomical sum to persuade the florists to start in the very early hours of the morning, but it was worth every penny for the satisfaction of knowing the wedding guests staying in the hotel would see it like this when they first came downstairs. The Portland Arms Hotel had been transformed into a wedding venue which she was certain would surpass even the highest expectations of the most discerning guests.

She found herself unconsciously slowing down when they neared the wine bar, as a feeling of unexpected nervousness spread through her body and Amelia, who had linked her arm through her mother's, felt the tremor and asked if she was feeling alright. Bryony shrugged it off, saying it was nothing more than a shiver of excitement, but for a fleeting moment she was tempted to use it as an excuse to leave and return to her room. Giving herself a mental shake, she allowed Amelia to draw towards the bar where they were meeting Greg.

Amelia was delighted when she saw the bottle of pink champagne resting in an ice bucket and the bowl of sugar-frosted strawberries on the table in front of Greg, who was already there when they arrived. He handed them both a glass of champagne and Amelia's face lit up with pleasure as she dipped a strawberry into the bubbles before enthusiastically popping it into her mouth. 'It's a bit early for this, but what the hell? It is my wedding day after all.'

Bryony felt a tinge of jealousy and regret for not having planned this herself, but it was typical of Greg to be so thoughtful and she may as well enjoy it.

'You look radiant,' Greg said to Amelia, 'and remarkably calm. Isn't all the fuss getting to you just a little bit?'

'Not really,' she told him, 'I never wanted all this, as you know.' She looked at Bryony with a smile. 'I only went along with it to please Mum but I must admit it is turning out to be quite good fun.' Acknowledging the greetings and good wishes of the people filling up the room, she beamed at Greg, who'd played such an important part in her life and raised her glass to him. 'I want to drink a toast to us all,' she said, 'to happy families.' Greg began to protest, pointing out he wasn't strictly a member of the family, but Amelia refused to hear. 'You are to me,' she said, 'and anyway you are my godfather, which is almost the same.'

'Well it's very nice of you to say so,' he replied with feeling.

'I know it's none of my business,' Amelia said, 'so tell me if I'm interfering, but you two were an item at one stage weren't you?'

Bryony could feel the colour draining from her face but Greg seemed unperturbed by Amelia's curiosity. 'Well, we were engaged for a time but you already know that, it's never been a secret,' he replied.

'I know,' Amelia said, 'but I've sometimes wondered what went wrong and why you split up.'

'Bryony chose your dad instead, it's as simple as that,' Greg told her.

Bryony cringed, willing Amelia to stop, but for some reason she seemed determined to carry on delving into their past. To her surprise Greg appeared completely unruffled and willing to satisfy her curiosity, even when she asked him jokingly, 'Is that why you've never married?'

Greg laughed out loud. 'No Amelia, I don't want to spoil your romantic fantasies but I haven't spent my life pining for what might have been.' Smiling broadly, he added, 'I live in hope, that one day I'll meet the right person.'

Bryony couldn't believe how easily the words tripped off his tongue; he must know how hurtful they were to her, but she consoled herself that he'd been left with no choice if he was to protect Amelia from the truth, especially today of all days.

'Maybe you'll meet someone on your cruise,' Amelia suggested with a smile, and he nodded and lifted his glass.

'Let's drink to that,' he proposed. 'A new life with Piers for you, and a rich widow for me.'

Bryony joined in the toast, avoiding Greg's eyes. When she'd agreed to arrange this get-together it had seemed the perfect start to the weekend, but nothing had prepared her for this and she didn't know how to change the topic of conversation without sounding churlish. When Amelia seemed ready to persist she lost her patience. 'Why are you suddenly bringing this up now?' she demanded.

Amelia shrugged. 'I don't really know, but I suppose it just seems a good time now that I'm getting married myself. I don't suppose we'll have many opportunities for cosy chats like this in future.'

'You make it sound as if you're going away forever,' Bryony said, 'but it's your own life you should be concentrating on, not ours.'

Amelia, obviously recognising her mother's discomfort, was instantly contrite. 'Sorry,' she said, 'I didn't mean to upset you.' She looked at her watch. 'I really must go and join the girls so I can make a start on all my beauty treatments, otherwise I'll look a wreck on my wedding day.'

'You could never look anything other than beautiful to me,' Greg said, 'with or without make-up, but before you go I want to give you something.' He drew an envelope from his pocket and handed it to her. Tentatively she took it from him.

'Am I allowed to open it?' she asked.

Greg nodded. 'It's up to you,' he replied.

Sliding her finger under the flap, she opened it and peeped inside. 'Oh no,' she whispered, 'it's another cheque. I can't possibly accept this, you've already given us our wedding present and a very generous one it is too.'

'This isn't a wedding present, it's just something I want you to have, to do whatever you want with. Travel the world with Piers, put it towards a property, anything you like. I've sent the same to Hugh and told him there are no strings attached.' He gave a wry smile. 'I suppose that means it will go towards his orphanage but that's fine with me.'

Amelia slipped the cheque out of the envelope and her eyes widened in surprise. 'It's a lot of money,' but before she could say anything else he affectionately waved her objections away.

'It's a pleasure,' he replied.

They all stood up and she turned to hug him tightly. 'You know I love Dad very much, but somehow you've always felt like a second father to me. I think that's what I was leading up to with all my questions.'

Greg looked at her, his eyes filled with fondness. 'And you're the daughter I never had,' he replied. Bryony's heart thudded against her ribs as she watched and listened to them. Stepping in quickly, she briskly reminded Amelia she should be on her way as her bridesmaids would be wondering where she was, and she told her she would follow as soon as she'd finished her drink.

Amelia blew them both a kiss and smiled broadly in response to the medley of good wishes which followed her from the room. In the split second when all eyes were on her daughter, Bryony's hand briefly brushed Greg's, which she was surprised to find was gripped tightly by his side.

Chapter 2

Stuart was adjusting his steps to Marie's slower pace, but he couldn't disguise his eagerness to reach the jetty where the fishermen were going down onto the beach to launch their fishing craft into the sea. It was a spectacle rarely seen in the bay and Marie knew he wouldn't want to miss out on seeing it for himself, especially as it would enable him to contribute to the inevitable discussions which were sure to take place in the future. She sympathised with his feelings because under normal circumstances she too would have been interested, but today wasn't a normal day, it was her goddaughter's wedding day, and the impact of the disruption could be quite detrimental.

She was certain Bryony would have had no idea this was going to happen, and would probably be in a state of panic. As one of the few people who stood any chance, however slight, of calming her down, she felt it was her duty for Amelia's sake to go over and at least try to help. A group of Stuart's friends were already leaning over the railings holding an impromptu meeting to discuss the interesting developments, and she knew he would be more than happy to join them.

'If you don't mind I think I'll go across and see

Bryony,' she said. 'I'd like to have a look at the floral decorations before there are lots of people milling about everywhere.'

Stuart was more than happy to comply but his nonchalant reply didn't fool her for a second and she colluded in the pretext that he was doing it simply for her benefit. They agreed to meet at the Sands café for lunch following Marie's intended visit to the lifeboat shop on her way to the café. Stuart remembered he'd planned to have a game of bowls with his friend Russell but he thought he'd give him a ring and tell him to join him here instead.

'In that case,' she told him sternly, 'don't forget to keep your phone switched on to let me know when you're at the café.' She looked at him quizzically. 'You have got your phone with you, I presume.'

Stuart nodded vigorously while surreptitiously checking his pocket. She couldn't help smiling at his barely disguised look of relief as he located his mobile in his shirt pocket and patted it to reassure himself it was really there. Suddenly, out of nowhere, something careered into her legs and she found herself almost pole-axed and thrown headfirst into Stuart's arms, almost knocking him over. Regaining her balance and pulling away from him, she saw his face cloud over with anger as he began to remonstrate with a boisterous puppy and the young boy struggling to gain control of it. Several times he succeeded in grabbing the lead only to see it slip from his fingers before he was able to hold on tightly, and all she could do was stand there while the dog wove himself between her feet. The boy's father was hurrying towards them encumbered by a folding chair, wind break, and several bags strewn around his body. He was full of apologies and dropped everything to unwind the lead from round Marie's ankles, where the dog had managed to entwine it in its excitement. By the time the harassed mother arrived pushing a buggy, Marie was looking into the moist brown eyes of a very apprehensive boy called Sam, who despite his ordeal was abstractedly trying to flatten down the curls which were springing loose from the constraints of copious amounts of hair gel.

Suppressing a smile, she lifted her head and was met by a severe expression on the face of his father, who was almost a mirror image of the boy but who had obviously given up the fight with his hair by having it cropped in a shorter style. She did her best to reassure them no harm had been done, and although at first Stuart was less forgiving he quickly saw the funny side of it and joined with Marie in making light of the situation. Sam was told to apologise before the family continued on its way, and although dire warnings to the dog could be clearly heard by Marie and Stuart, it continued to strain the lead and Sam's arm, oblivious to any threats of potential punishment.

Marie left Stuart and walked on until she reached the path leading over the downs towards the promenade, where The Portland Hotel imposed its presence in elegant style. The Portland family had been instrumental in founding the resort and the current owner Ralph had continued the traditional role of benefactor and supporter of local businesses. She'd grown up to respect the family's position but her friend Bryony had coveted the wealth and prestige which went with it. When the unexpected opportunity to marry into it had presented itself she'd caused quite a stir with the speed with which she'd broken off her engagement to the very eligible Greg Robson, to become the wife of the local buffoon, Colin Portland. Bryony had very few friends and sometimes Stuart had questioned why Marie stood by her despite the way she took advantage of her loyalty. It was something she often queried herself but today they were celebrating Amelia's marriage, and that meant supporting Bryony in any way she was able.

At least the weather was perfect, which was a bonus considering the time of the year. The town had been settling down for its winter slumber when the weather forecasters widely reported a September heatwave which was expected to benefit the western side of the country, including Merebank. Marie knew many of the hoteliers and proprietors of bed and breakfast establishments were already packing for the mass exodus to warmer climes abroad, but they'd shaken out the clean linen and flipped the vacancy signs in the windows to advertise the availability of rooms, and shopkeepers had quickly re-erected spinners bedecked with buckets and spades, balls, and windmills. Merebank was waking up again and Marie loved it. At the sound of footsteps hurrying behind her she stepped to one side to let the people pass, but felt a rush of pleasure when she saw it was her son Damian with a girl by his side.

'Hi Mum,' he said before giving her an affectionate hug. 'Where are you off to?'

'I'm just popping in to see Bryony, but more to the point where are you going?' She made no attempt to hide her interest in the attractive girl by his side and Damian decided to get the introductions over quickly.

'Mum this is Louisa, and Louisa, meet my mum.'

Louisa held out her hand and smiled at Marie, who returned the greeting before turning questioningly back to Damian.

'We're on our way back to the hotel,' he explained, 'although hopefully we won't see Bryony immediately as we are absent without leave, as you might say.'

'Well you are an usher so they'll expect you to be there,' Marie replied, looking with undisguised curiosity in Louisa's direction. 'Are you a friend of Amelia or Piers?' she asked without preamble, and Louisa's face lit up.

'Oh, I'm a friend of both but I'm also a bridesmaid today, I'm happy to say.'

Marie looked from one to the other in disbelief. 'What on earth are you doing here? Surely you should be at the hotel supporting Amelia and Piers.'

Damian smiled. 'Stop panicking, Mum. Louisa's been texting Amelia who knows exactly where we are and she's fine with it. Anyway we're on our way back now, and don't forget, Piers isn't even here yet.'

Marie still wasn't convinced and urged them to get back as quickly as possible. 'Amelia might be blasé about it but I'm sure Bryony won't be. She's got enough to worry about without you adding to it,' she said firmly, 'now off you go, you've got important duties to fulfil.'

Damian suggested they all walked together but she declined and shooed them away. 'I'd rather walk at my own pace and I don't want to delay you so go on, get a move on.' Watching them walk away to approach the hotel hand in hand she allowed herself a little smile; it was a while since he'd looked so happy and he deserved something better than the heartbreak his last girlfriend had given him.

The traffic was almost at a standstill, making her progress over the outer promenade easier than usual. At the entrance to the hotel she walked beneath the archway of flowers and made her way up the steps and into the foyer, where she was greeted enthusiastically by Ralph's nephew Justin.

'Good morning Marie,' he said, walking towards her. 'How are you today?'

'I'm fine thank you,' she replied with a smile, but she stood and slowly looked around in amazement at the transformation of the hotel interior. 'It's beautiful isn't it?' she remarked. 'I must admit I'm a bit surprised, I thought Bryony might have...'

Her voice tailed off as a voice from behind her interrupted. 'Might have what?'

She turned to see Bryony, who seemed to have appeared from nowhere as there'd been no sign of her when she'd entered the hotel.

'Come on now,' Bryony persisted, 'what did you think I might have done? I'm intrigued.'

'Well,' said Marie reluctantly, 'I was a little bit afraid you might have gone over the top with the decoration, but this is all so tasteful.' She paused and glanced around. 'You could almost say understated.' She laughed at the very idea and turned to look at Bryony. 'Understated and Bryony don't often go together, you must agree.'

Bryony took her arm. 'Understated? I don't even know the meaning of the word, but I'm really pleased you like the decorations.'

She began to draw her towards the lift but Marie

held herself back. 'Where are we going?' she asked. 'I'm meeting Stuart soon so I really can't stay long.'

Bryony kept a firm grip and pressed the button of the lift for the top floor. 'We're heading to my bedroom,' she said. 'I've got something important to tell you.'

Marie had had no reason to visit Bryony's room for several years and she was intrigued by the changes which had all Bryony's hallmarks. It was obvious she'd made it her own and it no longer fulfilled its original function of an overspill guest room. She walked around it, touching the luxurious bed coverings and elegant furniture before picking up and sniffing one of the expensive bottles of perfume on the dresser. 'I must say you've got yourself a very nice little hideaway here. Do you use it much?'

'Officially it was meant to provide somewhere for me to sleep when I'm working late but I find I'm staying here more and more. The other two rooms on this top floor are still used as overspill so aren't as luxurious, but if you think this is nice you should see Ralph's penthouse suite.'

'I have seen it, I came to the party when he moved in. He deserves it though, after putting in a lifetime of service to the business.'

'Of course he does,' Bryony snapped. 'I wasn't inferring he doesn't deserve it and I certainly wasn't suggesting I begrudge him anything.'

Marie pulled back, surprised by the sudden change in Bryony's attitude; she certainly hadn't intended to sound critical and couldn't help wondering what had triggered the sudden outburst. 'I wasn't suggesting you did,' she replied. 'Why are you being so defensive? Is something wrong?'

'I'm not,' Bryony said, 'you're imagining it, and no, there's nothing wrong at all.'

'In that case forget I said anything,' Marie replied. She knew Bryony well enough to recognise when something was amiss but she also knew there was nothing to be gained by pressuring her, she'd simply have to wait until she was ready to confide in her. Sometimes it was better to be kept in the dark and avoid the pitfalls of trying to give advice or offer help. 'What do you think about the cockle pickers?' she asked in an effort to change the subject, but as soon as the words were out she realised she'd probably made a mistake in choosing a contentious subject. Surprisingly Bryony seemed remarkably unfazed and casually shrugged her shoulders.

'I wasn't too happy when Justin told me,' she said, 'and I must admit I did give him a bit of a hard time at first, but I expect him, as my deputy, to keep his eye on the ball and be aware of things like that.'

It didn't take much imagination to figure out the dressing-down Justin would have received but Marie was quite confident he was used to Bryony's outbursts and would have taken it in his stride. What was more puzzling was Bryony's laid back approach to the diversion outside the hotel, but she decided to let the subject drop in an effort to keep the peace. Before she could attempt to stop her she saw Bryony deftly opening a bottle of champagne and fill two glasses, one of which she handed to her and the other she lifted to propose a toast.

'To friendship,' she said.

'To friendship,' Marie repeated with a smile, 'and

love of course.'

'Love! You've never said you loved me before,' Bryony exclaimed.

Marie chuckled. 'Not us, silly. Amelia and Piers.'

'Ah yes, Amelia and Piers, how lucky they are to be starting their married life with the one they love.'

'Isn't that what most people do?' Marie said, drinking deeply of the superb wine. 'I think it's quite customary to marry the one you love.'

'Is it?' Bryony said. 'Lucky them.'

Marie sat on the bed and stretched her legs, enjoying the effects of the champagne and the wonderful way it eased the pain in her back. 'We all make our own choices,' she dared to say, 'including you. No-one forced you to marry Colin after all. Mmm... this is lovely. Anyway, what's this important news you've dragged me here to tell?' she asked.

Bryony topped up their drinks but as she moved away to replace the bottle she remarked as casually, as if they were discussing nothing more important than the menu for the wedding breakfast, 'I'm leaving Colin.'

Marie gulped a mouthful of champagne and nearly choked as the bubbles exploded and fizzed in her throat and nose. 'Is this some kind of joke?' she spluttered, taking the tissue Bryony was handing to her.

'No,' Bryony said. 'I am deadly serious.'

'But why? Has something happened?'

Bryony stared at her with exasperation. 'Oh come on Marie, I can't believe you're asking me why I'm leaving Colin, after all you believed I was mad to marry him in the first place. Believe me, all the reasons you gave then still hold true, only more so.'

'Maybe, but you've lived with them all these years and done nothing about it. You haven't answered my question. Has something happened to bring this on?'

Bryony went over to stand silently looking out of the window, and once again lifted her glass, but this time it wasn't to propose a toast. Instead she indicated something outside. 'I suppose it's that,' she said. 'Life, people living their lives in the way they want to.' She turned to Marie. 'I feel as though I've been treading water all these years and now I want to experience new and exciting things. I'll never be able to do that with Colin, he thinks he's being adventurous if we choose a different hotel in Madeira every year.' She sighed. 'I can feel life beckoning me and I'm determined to follow. It's really bizarre,' she said, 'when we were young it was Colin leading a crazy life and Greg who was the quiet one. Now it's changed and it's Greg who's going on exciting holidays and Colin can't be bothered to do anything unless I force him to. Did you know Greg's going on a Mediterranean cruise in a couple of days?'

'I knew he was going away but didn't realise it was this week,' she replied.

'Yes, he planned it so he didn't miss Amelia's wedding.'

'Well of course,' Marie said, 'he wouldn't want to miss it. He's very fond of her, as we all are of course.'

For a few moments the room was quiet and Marie waited expectantly for Bryony to enlarge on what she'd told her, but she remained standing deep in thought with her eyes once more fixed on the view outside the window. 'Are you leaving Colin for another man?' she asked.

'You always were perceptive,' Bryony retorted, but turning to see Marie's angry face she quickly changed her tone. 'I'm sorry, I didn't mean that, but I can't say any more at this stage, I just wanted you to know what I'm planning so you'll be in the picture and be prepared when it happens.'

Marie didn't feel prepared; once again she was being given half a story, just enough to pique her curiosity but falling very short of a full confidence. Not that it made any difference, Bryony had always used her as a sounding board but never welcomed advice even when she'd asked for it. In this situation Marie wouldn't know what to say, she'd always been aware of the unconventional terms of the marriage but had believed Bryony had come to terms with it and enjoyed the benefits it brought. 'You'll be giving up this life of luxury which you always craved,' she said, 'and you can't pretend you haven't enjoyed it. After all, it is the reason you married Colin in the first place.'

'I know, but it doesn't seem so important anymore and all the things that seemed so glamorous when I was young are boring now. I'd rather be cruising round the world than attending stuffy official functions with Colin.' Picking up the bottle, she placed it within reach before sitting in the chair to face Marie. Her voice was uncharacteristically pensive. 'There is one thing that bothers me. I don't want to hurt Ralph because he's been so good to me.'

Bryony's earlier comments about Ralph were suddenly making sense, and Marie understood the concern behind her words. Ralph undoubtedly relied on her for the smooth running of the business, and this could plunge it into chaos.

'You may not want to,' she pointed out, 'but this is going to hurt him, not to mention Hugh and Amelia.'

'I know but I'm not going to stay with Colin simply to avoid hurting other people, and before you say anything at least I've waited until the kids have got their own lives sorted out. I know you're shocked and probably thinking all kinds of harsh things about me but it's been easier for you.'

Marie reeled with indignation; this was priceless even coming from Bryony, who seemed to have an ability to always feel sorry for herself. 'How do you make that out? What's been easier for me?' she demanded.

'You're happy,' Bryony insisted, 'at least you have a happy marriage.'

Marie stared at her in disbelief. 'Maybe we're happy because we got married for the right reasons instead of material gain like you, but we've had our problems as you well know. Stuart's business going bust wasn't exactly a walk in the park...' Her voice faded away, she still found it hard to discuss it without feeling a strong sense of disloyalty to Stuart and Bryony wasn't the most sensitive person where other people's problems were concerned. 'Why do you always presume you're the only one wishing for something more exciting in her life? Do you honestly believe you are the only person in the world who feels she's missing out?' Bryony stared, and shaken by her own outburst Marie shifted uncomfortably. One thing was certain, she'd drunk far too much alcohol so early in the day. 'You don't have the monopoly on boredom you know,' she added with a touch of defiance.

'Well, well, you do surprise me,' Bryony said. 'Here was I believing you were a happily married woman.'

'Oh for goodness' sake don't get all dramatic,' Marie protested. 'Of course I'm happy, but that doesn't necessarily mean I don't sometimes wish for something more out of life. That is absolutely no reflection on the state of my marriage. Anyway, it's you we're supposed to be talking about, not me, so don't change the subject. When are you proposing to tell the family of your decision?'

'I'd rather not say until I'm ready to do it.' She topped their glasses despite Marie's half-hearted attempt to refuse, but her willpower was slipping away.

'That's fine with me, I'd rather not know anyway. It isn't easy having to keep other people's secrets.' She looked straight into Bryony's eyes and the question she was determined to ask hung in the air between them. 'I know it might not be the ideal time for me to bring this up but I need to know. Have you told Colin and Greg about...?'

A sudden flush bloomed on Bryony's chest and neck and her face darkened. 'No I haven't,' she replied, 'and I have no intention of doing it now. For God's sake why have you brought it up after all this time?'

'I just think you owe it to them, especially with what you're planning to do.'

'I owe them nothing, and the time has long passed when I could have said something for it to have made a difference.'

'Well I believe they have a right to know, but I suppose as usual, what I think will have no influence on what you do.'

Bryony was scared and wary. 'You're not going to tell them, please tell me you won't say anything.'

'No, it isn't my place to say anything. Don't worry, your secret is safe with me.' Shaking her head, she looked into Bryony's stricken eyes. 'I must say it is a secret I wish you hadn't burdened me with, but I suppose I am left with no choice.' Looking at her watch she saw with a shock it was much later than she'd thought. 'I must be off,' she exclaimed, 'I'm supposed to be meeting Stuart.' She pulled herself upright and tottered towards the door but Bryony took hold of her arm to steady her.

'You meant what you said didn't you? You promise you won't say anything.'

'I promise,' Marie said.

'It's going to be a lovely wedding,' Bryony said, 'I've made sure of that, but in a way I can't wait for it to be over because I'm so excited about tomorrow.'

Marie nodded and pointed to the dress hanging on the wardrobe. 'I presume that's your wedding outfit, it looks lovely.'

Bryony lifted it down. 'Yes, I'm really pleased with it, although I did have a few doubts at first.'

'Why? You must have liked it otherwise you wouldn't have bought it in the first place.'

'I know,' Bryony agreed. 'I love the style of it, and it fits like a glove. Look, it's a demure three-quarter sleeved dress suitable for the mother of the bride, but when you take off the bolero it transforms into a sexy cocktail dress.' Twirling the hanger around, she nodded in appreciation. 'It's just the colour I'm not sure of, despite Jerome convincing me it complements my blonde hair.' She put the dress back and examined her reflection in the mirror. 'Do you think this longer bob suits me? I was persuaded by the hairdresser that it would look better under a hat.'

'Oh Bryony let's go, you know it's too late for any opinion of mine to make any difference now.' She walked unsteadily down the corridor and after locking the bedroom door Bryony hurried after her into the lift.

'What colour are you wearing?' she asked.

Marie leaned against the side of the lift and replied tipsily, 'It's green to match my eyes.' She eyed herself in the mirror on the opposite side. The alcohol had eased the pain in her back but although she certainly felt better than when she'd arrived, it wasn't reflected in her rather unkempt appearance.

'Your eyes aren't exactly green,' Bryony said, peering at her.

'They are at the moment,' Marie replied, 'with envy. You've got all this and a tall, handsome lover waiting for you if you give it up.'

'*When* I give it up,' insisted Bryony. 'You're drunk,' she added with trepidation, 'please promise me you won't say anything.'

'I already promised didn't I? Stop worrying.'

Before leaving the hotel to go in search of Stuart she asked Justin for a drink of water under the pretext of needing to take medication, but when he gave her a knowing smile she gave up all attempts at pretext. Feeling rather foolish she allowed him to accompany her down the steps where she assured him she was only mildly tipsy and quite able to take care of herself.

Unable to rid herself of the feeling that Bryony was keeping something from her, she tried to recall what she'd said about being excited about the following day. Something didn't quite make sense but she just couldn't put her finger on it. Maybe when her head cleared she'd be able to figure it out, but there was a buzz about Bryony that even the prospect of Amelia's wedding couldn't account for.

She was undecided whether to try and locate Stuart or briefly call in at the lifeboat shop. Checking the time she chose the latter, on the assumption that having cancelled his game of bowls he would have switched on his mobile and so he'd contact her when he was ready. If she didn't get a call before leaving she'd ring to tell him to make his way to the café.

Bryony's revelation was spinning around her head. Her impetuosity and self-confidence had often led her to streak ahead with plans made more in hope than certainty, but there was so much riding on the outcome of her intention to leave Colin. The impact would affect those closest to her, who also happened to be Marie's dearest friends, and she hoped for all their sakes that it would turn out satisfactorily. Feeling uneasy about the way she'd shared her own feelings of dissatisfaction with life she decided the time had come to get things back into perspective. Instead of harbouring disgruntled emotions it would be more productive to bring a bit of adventure back into their lives. The truth was they were happily married and the trouble didn't just lie with Stuart, and she must make sure he knew that.

The late summer sun had beckoned lots of visitors to the resort, eager to take the opportunity of relaxing in the fresh air before the mellow September climate gave way to the blustery winter weather. Walking along the flat promenade she was able to enjoy the view of the undulating grassy downs on one side, and the beach, which was accessed by steps and winding paths set at intervals along its length, on the other side. The beach was filling with families separated by wind shields, marking out territories guarded by an ever-increasing proliferation of flag-topped castles, and young, ardent sun-worshippers lay on towels rubbing sun cream into pink-tinged bodies.

She stood for a moment to watch a local boy drawing admiring glances from a group of girls obviously taken by his tanned physique. Adam was an enterprising young man and during the summer season he offered sunbeds and deck chairs for hire, and with the help of his younger brother he walked the donkeys sporting jaunty straw hats on their heads and children on their backs, up and down the well-trodden path. Lifting a reluctant child onto a donkey he jangled the bells round its neck until the little girl forgot her fear and her peals of laughter made everyone around her smile. Adam glanced up and saw Marie watching him. She returned his enthusiastic wave and cheery greeting before moving on towards the shop.

The downs were already scattered with older couples or families engaged in sporting activities, which brought back vivid memories of the times she and Stuart had enjoyed with their children. Until recently she'd rarely considered the prospect of getting older but recently aches and pains had brought it into sharper focus, and the pain in her back didn't help.

The gift shop was already doing a thriving business and although she'd promised Stuart not to get drawn in to help she couldn't resist starting a quick inventory of the shelves, before going into the back for new supplies. Empty spaces couldn't bring in revenue and the lifeboat service needed all the funds it could get, as she well knew. Claire and Bridget were working at full stretch but at the first sign of a lull she went into the tiny space adjacent to the store room to make them all a cup of tea.

'Have you heard from Russell?' she asked Claire. 'Stuart was hoping to have a game with him but got waylaid by the cockle pickers.'

Claire nodded. 'Yes, Russell went to join him but now he's gone to pick up something from home before he comes to meet me here. He didn't say where Stuart was going. Haven't you heard from him?'

Marie shook her head and checked her mobile. 'It's not switched on so I can't even leave him a message.' She sighed in exasperation. 'I don't know why he keeps doing this, all he has to do is leave the thing on. Never mind, I'll make my way down to the café, he's bound to be there.'

The café was busier than usual with the influx of visitors enjoying the unexpected heatwave and families who were attached to some of the fishermen, but there was no sign of Stuart amongst them. Every member of staff was busy chasing the orders and clearing tables, but she and Stuart were regular customers whatever the season, so when Billy the affable and rather rotund owner caught sight of her, he semaphored that Stuart hadn't been in. After signalling her thanks she turned and began to go in the direction where she thought he would probably be. It was a fairly short walk and although it would mean retracing her steps she took great pleasure in having some time to herself to soak up the welcome warmth of the sun. Passing the various benches and shelters dotted en route, she slid a glance towards each one to check if Stuart was there, but she wasn't surprised by his absence until her destination came into view.

There was no special reason why this particular shelter had become their favourite, but they both liked its unusual pseudo-Edwardian design topped by the unusual gently concave sloping roof constructed of black-painted cast iron with red and gold embellishments. This gave the impression from a distance of an oriental temple, totally at odds with everything else around it but it was perfectly placed just far enough along the promenade to be easily accessible, and it offered wonderful views over the estuary. With its central position it had become their regular place, providing a sun trap in warm weather and shelter from wind and unexpected squalls in winter. Sometimes at the end of the day they lingered on to watch the spectacle of the sun setting over the western horizon as it illuminated the sky and turned the sea crimson before slowly dipping from view.

'I thought I'd find you here,' she said, 'but we were supposed to be meeting at the café.'

His brows drew together with concentration. 'Oh dear. I'm sorry, I just automatically drifted here.' Choosing not to bring up the touchy subject of the advantages of mobile phones she slid the newspaper to one side and sat down beside him.

'How was Bryony?' he asked. 'Was she getting herself into a flutter as usual?'

'No, she was surprisingly calm,' she told him. 'Everything seems to be going to plan, but she's very organised of course.'

Stuart nodded. 'That's true but it doesn't always result in her remaining calm. She's a bit of a firecracker, that one.'

Marie nodded and resisted the temptation to tell him what Bryony had in mind for the future; it was difficult enough for her to come to terms with the potential fallout without having to explain and defend them to someone else. It wouldn't be the first time if it all went horribly wrong simply as a result of Bryony's mistaken belief in her own infallible power to make things happen.

In an uncharacteristic public show of affection Stuart leaned over and kissed her. 'You know I'll always look after you, don't you?' he said. 'No matter what happens I'll always look after you.'

Tightening her grip, she held his hand firmly in her grasp. 'I know you will,' she told him, and a frisson of the love they'd shared over the years passed between them. Feeling the tears begin to well, she turned her head and gently released his hand.

Stuart eased himself away, and trying to hide his emotions he began rummaging around in his bag looking for the binoculars. 'I'm just going over to the rail to take a look at the oyster catchers and waders; they seem a bit agitated by all the goings on up there,' he explained gruffly.

'Alright love,' she replied, and as he walked away to focus on the birds in the distance Marie remained gazing at the horizon while she allowed a few tears to flow. After a few moments she determinedly pulled herself together and sent a loving smile to her husband when he turned to give her a wave.

She watched as he trained the binoculars in the direction of the birds the very moment an undulating wave of black and white flashed across in front of him. A flock of oyster catchers rose and swept over the estuary before turning as one to settle on the sandbanks in a cacophony of incessant piping and rippling noise. He was gently turning the wheel of the binoculars and she'd learned just enough from him to know he was trying to pick out the orange red of the beaks which were undetectable in flight and which distinguished them from the other smaller species found on this coastline. Her knowledge was sparse but Stuart's enthusiasm was catching and she'd picked up little bits of the things that most interested him.

This dissatisfaction with life had sprung up unexpectedly as her birthday was approaching, but she was determined to shake it off before she made them both miserable. She must tell him about Damian's new lady friend; that would cheer him up.

Chapter 3

Tom forced the bag of baby things into the corner of the boot and wedged the picnic basket between the buggy and cricket bat before slamming the door shut and locking it. Anything else Sharon decided was essential for a day's outing would have to be squeezed into the car around the children. Checking she wasn't within hearing distance, he tried his mobile again but Danny's number was still unavailable. Where the hell could he be and why wasn't he answering his phone? Returning to the house, he found Sam watching television and shouted at him to go upstairs to finish getting ready. Glancing swiftly around he switched the set back on again and changed channels to catch the local news. He was just in time to see a reporter giving an update on the situation in Merebank. The place looked in a state of upheaval and dire warnings were being issued to anyone thinking of making the journey to the bay with the intention of making some easy money. He didn't hear Sharon enter the room and jumped at the sound of her voice.

She was standing in the doorway with Lily slung on her hip. 'Why are you watching that?' she demanded suspiciously.

'I thought I would try and catch the weather forecast,' he replied, 'but I think I've missed it.'

He felt the full force of her glare. 'Tom, don't you even think about it, and before you start denying it I'm not stupid. You're interested in that item about cockling aren't you?'

'No I'm not; I'm only concerned with our day at the seaside, it's pure coincidence that we happen to be going to the place which is making the news today. Now I'll just go and finish packing the car if that's alright with you.' He switched off the set and moved towards the door but Sharon blocked his way.

'After your accident you promised me you would never take any more risks.'

'I know and I'm not doing.'

'You'd better not, Tom. I mean it.' She moved aside to let him pass but he could feel her eyes following him, so instead of going to the garage to try again to make contact with Danny he walked over to the car. Sam was sitting on the back seat engrossed in a game on his phone, and he sighed heavily and didn't look up when Tom asked him if he'd cleaned his teeth.

'Course I have, Dad,' he replied indignantly, and to convince him he opened his mouth wide and thrust it into Tom's face. 'There,' he said triumphantly, 'can you smell the toothpaste?'

'OK, that's enough,' Tom laughed, 'but what about Rusty? Have you got everything he'll need for the day?'

'Mum will do that.'

'Yes I know she will, but she's already got more than enough to think about without adding the dog to it.' Before Sam had time to refuse Tom opened the car door. 'Come on son, remember what you promised when you wanted a dog. Now go and get his food and bowls and make sure you bring a big bottle of water, it's going to be hot today.'

Muttering under his breath, Sam returned to the house and Tom went round the corner to the garage. Sharon would be occupied for a few minutes making sure Sam didn't forget anything so that should give him just enough time to make a call.

Keeping alert to the possibility of anyone approaching, he moved around, randomly picking things up from the accumulated clutter. He would need to give some kind of explanation for being there if Sharon came looking for him, but he had no idea what excuse he could give and there was no time to think of one. Getting no response from either of the mobiles he decided to risk calling Rick's home number, but after a few words with one of his kids who told him Dad went out very early, he ended the call and quickly switched off his phone. The chances of Sharon overhearing were too high so he would have to wait until the opportunity arose later in the day to try again to contact them. Listening for any sign of movement, he thought he detected light footsteps on the path but after waiting a few seconds he decided to risk it and go back to the house.

He knew Sharon needed help to fix the dressing on her arm; he'd covered the wound earlier with a piece of lint stuck down with tape but it was only a temporary job and it was difficult for her to wrap a bandage using only one hand. The wound was getting bigger and more inflamed and the dressings they had were no longer big enough to cover it. She was looking in the first aid box, moving things around, but she seemed distracted and worried.

'Let me do that,' he said, and she sat down and rested her arm on the table while Tom removed the lint and replaced it with a sterile dressing before securing it with a bandage. He performed the task as gently as possible but she winced with pain. 'I'm so sorry about this,' he said, his voice thick with emotion.

Sharon stood up and took his hands in hers. 'It wasn't your fault,' she replied. 'Look Tom, I know you're stressed but we'll come through this, I know we will.'

'I hope so,' he muttered, and began to turn away but Sharon reached out to hold him back.

'We will survive,' she said firmly, 'but only if we're honest with each other and stick together.' He glanced away, unable to look into her eyes. It cut through him like a knife when she tried to be so brave and forgiving while he felt useless and humiliated. Putting her palm on his cheek, she turned his face towards hers. 'Tom,' she said gently, 'I heard you on the phone in the garage; I don't know who you were talking to or what you were discussing and I don't want to know, but last night you were very interested in the item on the news about cockling and you were watching it again just now.' He tried to interject but she stopped him. 'No, don't deny anything, just promise me you are not getting involved in that.'

He looked her in the eyes and said, 'I promise I am not intending to go cockling.'

'Right,' she said, 'let's get this show on the road.' Picking up a light cardigan, she pushed it into her bag. 'I'll have to wear this when we get there otherwise this bandage keeps slipping down.'

'Won't you be too hot? The forecast is for a heatwave today.'

Sharon shrugged. 'Probably, but I don't have much choice, it will be even worse if it gets the sun on it.'

Ben had come in and was watching. 'I want one,' he said. 'I want a plaster on like you.'

Sharon crouched down to explain that he didn't have a cut on his arm like Mummy so he didn't need a plaster. When his lip began to tremble, Tom opened the box again and took out one of Ben's favourite dinosaur dressings and very carefully placed it on Ben's arm. 'There you are, now you're just like Mummy,' he said, and Ben ran off proudly.

Tom lifted Lily from her rocker and carried her as they walked together towards the car. 'I saw you hesitate when Ben asked for a plaster,' he said. 'Was that because we don't have many left?'

Sharon nodded. 'Yes, and they're not on this week's shopping list so we can't afford to waste them.'

Tom had seen Sharon's little book where she kept lists of necessary everyday items which needed to be bought every week, with a separate section at the back for more occasional purchases. He knew it was the only way she could keep track of their outgoings but his insides churned at the thought of what she was being forced to do. 'What a state we're in,' he said, 'when Ben is denied a plaster when he wants one. When Sam was small we covered him in blue teddy bear plasters if he asked for them, and never even thought twice about it.'

'It doesn't matter,' Sharon said.

His voice was bitter. 'It does to me,' he replied.

He struggled to keep his mind on the road and the bickering from Ben and Sam didn't help his concentration, but when Sharon commented on his short temper he knew he'd better be careful not to arouse her suspicions. Yesterday he'd managed to delay their planned trip to the coast by telling her he was helping Danny repair his motorbike, and although she wasn't too pleased and the kids were disappointed, he'd promised to make it up to them today. Shouting his head off wasn't going to achieve that and it ran the risk of Sharon wanting to know what was wrong, so he took a deep breath, opened his mouth wide and burst into song.

'Dad, do you have to do that?' Sam complained, but Ben laughed and tried to join in and soon everyone was singing along. Lily, who'd been about to fall asleep, made her displeasure at being disturbed all too obvious, and when Sharon leaned over to give her a dummy she caught her arm on the seat and her face contorted with pain. With gritted teeth she forced herself to keep smiling, determined that nothing was going to spoil the enjoyment of the day, but Tom was aware of her grimace and he tried to fight off the rising feeling of helplessness and shame. If only he could have carried out his plans at least it would have helped to boost their finances a bit, but the news last night and again this morning had convinced him it would be absolutely stupid, to say nothing of being positively dangerous.

Danny had reacted angrily to his decision and Tom had a horrible feeling he might try to convince Rick to ignore it, but without Tom they could do nothing. Danny didn't have a clue about sailing; he'd never been interested and hadn't even been bothered to learn the basics on the rare occasions when Tom had persuaded him to join him on the water, and Rick knew even less. Not that he himself had much experience, and the dinghy had been stored away since before he got married. Floating down the canal or the calmest stretch of the river didn't exactly constitute the best practise for venturing out into the unknown territory of an estuary with tidal waves. The sea was an altogether different ball-game, as the presenter had pointed out, and no matter how good the money was he couldn't take that risk. He just wished he could get rid of this feeling in the pit of his stomach.

Sharon had made her feelings very clear after his fall from a roof while working for a cowboy builder, and she'd made him promise never to take any more risks. Although he'd meant it at the time he was getting more and more desperate to find a way to make some money to provide for his family. He couldn't believe how quickly the advantages they'd made for themselves after buying a house on the new estate were suddenly under threat. What had happened to his pride at achieving good grades at the technical college and the satisfaction of constant employment with a reputation for reliability and excellent workmanship in everything he did? The high standard of living they'd enjoyed until the financial crash caused the building project he was working on to be abandoned; it had slipped away, and he would never forget his horror when he'd found himself unemployed and claiming benefits.

The only work he'd been able to pick up was labouring and odd jobs for bosses who had no regard for health and safety and only paid the minimum wage. That came to an abrupt end when he had the fall from a roof and ended up in hospital, and Sharon had been distraught and extracted the promise from him never to put himself in danger again.

Struggling to cope with the situation, he'd almost reached breaking point when Sharon came home one day with a bag of food which she reluctantly admitted was from the newly set-up food bank in town. His rage had known no bounds at the thought of her having to sink her pride in order to feed the family, and he was only slightly mollified when she told him she'd met several of their friends there. When she'd described how they'd all been trying to slide in unnoticed he was consumed with anger at what they'd been reduced to through no fault of their own.

A chance hearing on the radio about the money to be made on the cockle beds had seemed too good to miss, and when he'd put it to Danny and Rick they'd both agreed. No-one mentioned the potential fallout facing them from their wives after the event, but they all secretly hoped that the sight of a wad of money would soften the blow. Monday was earmarked as the first opportunity for them all to get away, the main reason being it was a day none of them had to make the soul-destroying visit to the Job Centre to sign on. The dinghy was in need of some serious repair work and he'd come up with the ruse about helping Danny with his motorbike.

Sharon's reaction was predictably volatile but she calmed down when Tom convinced her of the necessity to get the bike back on the road to enable Danny to follow up an offer of some temporary work. Tom crossed his fingers at the lie but told himself it was partly true, at least the bit about the work. Last night after seeing the news and hearing the warnings about the dangers involved, he'd contacted Danny, saying he was calling the trip off, but Danny had refused to listen despite Tom's determination. 'It's my dinghy and my decision,' he'd hissed down the phone to Danny.

'It's my wife and my family who are hungry!' Danny had shouted back, before Tom hastily cut him off when he heard Sharon approaching. Seeing the news again this morning had scared him to death but neither Danny nor Rick were answering his phone calls and he didn't know what else he could do. The only hope he had left was that Rick would be more sensible and refuse to go, but if he was honest he didn't hold out much hope of that happening.

All he could do now was to make the best of the day and hope at least one of them would see sense before it was too late. The prospect of visiting his favourite place started to calm him and for the last few miles of the journey he reminisced with Sharon about the happy days they'd spent there, both separately as children and then together as teenagers and adults. He also remembered the days with his friends when they'd hopped on a train to Merebank to spend the day playing beach football before going down the coast to enjoy an evening's entertainment at the livelier resort, where there were bars and amusement arcades. Somehow the place made him feel secure and comfortable and he hoped it would be the same today.

Although they arrived at Merebank early morning the car parks were already full, and the only parking space Tom could find was on a side street a short walk away from where they hoped to settle. While Tom unpacked the car Sharon admired the small well-kept cottages, with their hanging baskets overflowing with an abundance of greenery and flowers. It was obvious by the matching and blending of colours that the residents had worked together to co-ordinate the display and the finished effect was delightful. She went to read a small sign displayed at the end of the street which announced them the winners of the local 'Small Town Flowers in Bloom Competition: Individual Street Category', which in Sharon's opinion was well deserved. The children were getting impatient and Rusty was desperate for exercise after the journey, so she hurried back and picked up one of the bags and slung it over the buggy. Tom had poured some water for the dog but Rusty was too impatient to be off to show any interest in it, so Sharon poured it away and put the bottle back in the bag.

'You'd better behave yourself today,' Sharon instructed the dog, 'otherwise you'll be in big trouble. Here Sam, you take hold of his lead and whatever you do, don't let go of it.'

Sam bristled with indignation. 'I am capable of holding a lead mum,' he muttered.

It took only a short time to finish unloading the car and soon they were walking along the promenade searching for the best place to settle down. Sam wanted to go on the beach but Sharon insisted the grassy area was best for them all, but promised he could explore with Ben and their dad later. While Sam was momentarily distracted the lead slipped from his hand and Rusty ran away as fast as his legs could carry him, only coming to a halt when he ran into the legs of a middle-aged lady. Fortunately she saw the funny side of the situation and by the time Sam and Tom, who was hampered by all the things he was carrying, reached her, she was well and truly tied up. Tom felt as if he'd die with embarrassment as he tried to untangle the lead from round her legs and he couldn't wait to get away once he'd achieved it. By the time Sharon arrived on the scene order had more or less been restored and they were soon on their way again. Sam's head drooped disconsolately when Sharon scolded him but Tom urged her to go easy.

'Don't be too hard on him,' he said, watching Sam trying desperately to keep control of Rusty, 'after all it's the dog that needs training, not the boy.'

'I know, but it doesn't do any harm to remind Sam he needs to concentrate on what he's doing.' She looked back over her shoulder to where the couple were still standing. 'They remind me of my mum and dad,' she said, 'only maybe a bit younger and trendier.'

The woman was wearing loose-fitting linen trousers with a sleeveless patterned top and the man, who was several inches taller, wore chinos and a light green polo-necked shirt. His white socks and sandals contrasted sharply with her strappy sandals and brightly coloured painted toenails. Sharon sheepishly waved back as they caught her looking at them but she was too late to stop Tom from glancing round. 'Yes you're right, they do,' he agreed. 'They were very understanding I suppose,' he added generously.

Sensing the lads were getting impatient he decided it was time to stop and make a decision about where they were going to settle. 'Come on, this will suit us fine,' he said, dropping his things on the grass before going back to manoeuvre Lily's buggy up the slope. Soon the rug was in position, Sharon's folding chair opened, and the wind break providing shade for Lily was securely fixed into the ground. As soon as the wickets were set up the boys were eager for their long-awaited cricket match to start.

Tom had deliberately walked in the opposite direction to the jetty but he was fully aware of the activity further along the bay and he was determined to make his way there sometime during the day. It would have to be done without Sharon's knowledge, which he knew wouldn't be easy but he was hoping to find an excuse to take the boys along there. In the meantime he had an important cricket match to take part in, so Sam was put into bat first and Tom bowled his first ball of the day. Sharon made sure the parasol on the buggy was shading Lily before she settled herself on the chair and picked up her magazine. Her arm was stinging under the cardigan she'd had to put on, and when she raised her arms to sweep her hair back into a pony-tail the stretching made it even worse. Positioning her body in the shade, she reached her legs out to where they would catch the sun and felt secretly pleased to have lost the extra weight she'd gained when she was pregnant. It was the only plus side to giving most of the food to Tom and the children so she might as well make the most of it. She settled herself down to enjoy this precious time with her family at the seaside. The trials and tribulations befalling celebrities in their glamorous lives and depicted with great detail in her glossy magazine only kept her interest for a short time before her eyelids drooped and she fell into a light slumber.

Chapter 4

Bryony left the salon shaking her head in despair. The perfect day she'd planned for months was slowly disintegrating before her eyes, and worst of all it was slipping out of her control. It had started with the phone call from Hugh to say he wouldn't be able to make the wedding, and despite all her pleas he'd been insistent the emergency at the orphanage meant he had to stay to sort it out. It was incomprehensible that anything in a ramshackle orphanage on the other side of the world could be more important than his sister's wedding, but he'd remained adamant and Amelia hadn't helped by assuring him she was fine with his decision. The cockle pickers had arrived on the scene, and to add insult to injury a bridesmaid had gone missing.

Amelia was unperturbed by both Hugh's decision and the potential fallout from the cocklers, but Bryony had detected a slight concern regarding the tension between Paul Sheridan and Louisa, which in turn made her very apprehensive. She wished she'd taken more interest when Amelia had tried to explain the situation earlier but she had the distinct impression there was more of an opportunity for trouble than she'd first thought. She still didn't believe he'd cause a scene but then who knew how any man would react on seeing himself replaced by a new and much younger rival?

Looking around for Greg but seeing no signs of him, she followed the discordant sounds coming from the direction of the function room. Today it would double as the setting for the ceremony before being completely changed in time for the evening disco and party, so she hurried across to make sure all her instructions were being carried out. She wasn't surprised to find Colin trying to make his contribution but succeeding only in making matters worse. She'd given both the group and the DJ carte blanche to set up their equipment as they required, the only proviso being that everything was hidden behind the floral displays during the actual marriage ceremony. This was obviously proving to be a cause for dispute and as she approached she heard Colin advising the group leader to ignore her instructions and position themselves in front of the displays. 'Is there a problem?' she asked, ignoring Colin and directing her question to the men who were erecting their separate pieces of equipment on each side of the room.

'Sorry about this, Mrs Portland,' the leader of the group said, 'but the acoustics will be affected if the speakers and instruments are all behind a bank of flowers, added to which there isn't much room behind here.'

For the first time that day Bryony felt laughter bubbling up inside her as the man peered at her through the flowers. Struggling to contain herself, she explained that she had arranged for the large urns to be dismantled when the room was being cleared in preparation for the evening entertainment. 'So whatever you do,' she instructed them, 'do not put anything in front of them. You will have all the unrestricted space you need, when you need it.' The men breathed audible sighs of relief and Colin set about helping to carry and lift things for them, completely undeterred by what had just happened.

Bryony could feel a headache coming on so she went to the office and took a couple of painkillers. Realising that all she'd had were a couple of strawberries washed down with champagne, she decided to get something to eat as soon as possible; it would be quite a time before the wedding food was served. She approached Justin and Ellie who were standing together absorbed in the reams of paper which covered the desk. He was reading out names as she crossed them off the list in front of her, and it took a few seconds before Ellie looked up to acknowledge the person standing in front of her. Slightly flustered at the sight of her boss, she apologised for keeping her waiting. 'It's understandable today,' Bryony assured her, 'but in future remember the customer always comes before administration, necessary though that may be.'

'I will,' Ellie replied, her composure regained, 'we were just trying to ensure everyone had been served breakfast.'

Bryony knew it had presented a logistical nightmare for the kitchen staff, who were working to a tight schedule preparing the canapés and wedding breakfast. As the dining room had been taken over for the wedding it had been decided to serve breakfast to the guests in their rooms. Wishing to maintain standards, Bryony had wanted to offer the full choice of breakfast but Luke, the chef, had pointed out the inherent problems involved and suggested there would be sufficient food provided during the rest of the day. He'd also pointed out there were snacks on offer in the bars during the day for anyone who wanted them. When Ralph entered the discussion he tended to agree with Luke and she'd reluctantly backed down, but now she saw the benefit of it. Not that she would admit it to anyone. 'Has everyone been served?' she asked Ellie, who looked back at the sheet in her hand.

'Yes, all except rooms 26 and 28 who have a "Do not disturb" sign on the door.' Her lips began to curl up into a smile but Bryony ignored it as she tried to remember the occupants of the rooms.

'Aren't those where the groomsmen and ushers are?' she asked.

'They are, Mrs Portland,' Justin replied, giving her the full title in the presence of others, 'but I expect even they won't be too long before rising.'

'If they are they'll forfeit breakfast,' she said. 'I suggest you give them a call and tell them in no uncertain terms that breakfast will be served immediately or not at all.' Shaking her head, she added, 'It's typical of young people to give no consideration to others.' Already having learned that one of the ways to placate Bryony was to appeal to her vanity, Ellie left Justin to his phone calls and complemented her on the floral decorations.

'I would never have believed this could be achieved,' she said, her voice full of admiration. 'Justin and I were saying we would love to get married here, but of course we could never afford it.'

She turned to Justin who replaced the receiver with a grin. 'Job done,' he said. 'Breakfast is on the way.'

'You would get staff discount,' Bryony told Ellie. 'I'm sure we could come to a mutual agreement acceptable to us all.'

Ellie's eyes lit up. 'Oh, do you think so? I know it wouldn't be as grand as this but it's always been my dream to have my reception here.'

Justin was more reticent and urged caution. 'Don't get carried away, Ellie,' he warned her. 'We will have to do a lot of sums before we can even consider it.'

Their reactions strengthened Bryony's belief in their suitability as prospective proprietors of the hotel; Ellie was full of enthusiasm and ideas which complemented Justin's more considered and practical approach. She wondered how he would take the news of his imminent elevation to being promoted and she believed it could turn out to be instrumental in Ellie being able to fulfil her dream. She leaned over the desk and said in a low voice, 'I decided to use our own occasion to promote the hotel as a wedding venue. Hopefully when people see what can be achieved they will want to book us for their own marriages. Now that we've been registered and are able to hold the ceremony here, we need to find a subtle way to spread the word and what better way to publicise ourselves than to show what we can provide?'

Justin nodded. 'I get your point, but unfortunately only today's guests will see all this,' he said, indicating the transformed reception hall.

Glancing round and dropping her voice even lower to deter eavesdroppers, Bryony said, 'Not a word to anyone but I've given the photographer instructions to pass some of the photographs to the local paper, especially the ones showcasing the hotel. It will be the best publicity we could wish for.'

Justin was quietly digesting her words and when he grasped the meaning of what she'd said his face fell. 'I thought Amelia didn't want any publicity in the paper,' he said in a voice so low she could hardly hear him. 'In fact she told me to make sure the reporter doesn't get into the building and I promised her he wouldn't.'

'Then you don't have a problem and you can keep your promise to Amelia, because he won't even try to come in here; he's going to get all he needs without any of the effort. Like I just told you, I've instructed our own wedding photographer to give some shots to the paper.' Bryony pulled herself upright with a satisfied smile and tapped the side of her nose in a secretive gesture. 'No-one needs to be any the wiser,' she added, 'this is just between us.'

Justin wasn't convinced. 'I still don't think Amelia is going to be very pleased to put it mildly,' he said, 'but at least it won't be my problem.'

'That's quite right,' Bryony agreed, knowing in fact it would be, 'and by the time the pictures appear in the paper Amelia will be far away enjoying her honeymoon; the last thing on her mind will be the appearance of a few photographs in the local rag.' Turning away from them, she scanned the room which was filling up with people who were all enjoying the luxury of relaxing in their chosen ways; some were sitting reading the newspapers, others were making their way to the coffee lounge, and the more active were leaving the hotel to enjoy a stroll on the promenade. There was still no sign of Greg so she left Justin and Ellie to deal with the request of one of the guests, and went in search of him.

Chapter 5

Ben was an inadequate fielder who didn't respond well to his older brother's instructions to run faster or catch the ball. Sam looked over to his mother. 'I don't know why you can't play with us,' he said moodily. 'You're really good at this and you always play with us.'

Sharon looked flustered. 'Not today,' she replied, 'I've already told you.'

'But why?' he pleaded.

'For one thing I'm too hot,' she told him, 'so don't ask again.'

Sam was past taking notice, and oblivious to his father's glowering expression he struck the cricket bat with force into the ground. 'If you're too hot why don't you take your cardigan off?' he mumbled.

'Leave your mother alone,' Tom said firmly. 'If she doesn't want to play and she says she is too hot that's the end of it.'

Sam turned away and took his place in front of the wickets, waiting for Tom to resume bowling. Both boys were beginning to lose interest and muttering about being starving hungry, so when Sharon asked if anyone was ready to eat there was a unanimous decision to have an early lunch. Tom shook out the brightly coloured picnic cloth to spread on the ground while Sam and Ben placed toys and food-filled containers at the edges to stop them flapping. Tom didn't point out that for once there was no breeze to lift the cloth when he saw the serious way they approached the job in hand. He was soon sinking his teeth into Sharon's corned beef and piccalilli on white bread sandwiches and was surprised to find how hungry he was, but it had been an early start to the day courtesy of Lily's inclination to wake at dawn demanding to be fed. Sam tucked into his favourite potted beef sandwiches while Ben devoured a whole packet of crisps before he was spotted and told in no uncertain manner by Sharon that no biscuits would be allowed before he'd eaten at least one sandwich. The boys drank the diluted orange juice while Tom and Sharon had mugs of tea from the vacuum flask.

Lily began to nuzzle her mother and before her cries reached a crescendo Sharon began to feed her, a carefully placed muslin sheet discreetly placed over her shoulder. She dreamily watched the group sitting close to them and was fascinated by the kaleidoscope of colour created by the saris of the women, who were busily engaged in chatter and constantly providing for the demands of the children. The men wore a mix of traditional clothing and trainers and the children and young people's attire was completely westernised. They were all engaged in different kinds of games but some were involved in a game of cricket, and Tom wondered aloud if it might be possible later to ask if Sam could join them to give him the chance to have a decent innings.

Sam and Ben soon became bored with inactivity, prompting Tom to produce his surprise. Pulling a twenty pound note out of his pocket he announced that Grandma had given it to him so they could all go to the café on the beach for a drink and a cake. The whoops of joy left no room for doubt as to how much they loved the idea, and when Sharon suggested they wait until a bit later, she was shouted down. He pretended he hadn't seen the dirty look she'd thrown in his direction but he supposed he should have checked with her first.

When they were starting the laborious job of packing their belongings and deciding which they could leave, one of the men in the nearby family suggested they left everything in place and they would keep an eye on them. Tom hesitated, pointing out the possibility of being away for quite a while, but Sharon readily accepted their offer and soon they were walking along the promenade towards the Sands café. Finding a table on the veranda, Tom was able to tie Rusty to a nearby post just below them and they all looked closely at the menu. Ben wanted an ice cream but Tom was still hoping to take the boys to the ice cream van as an excuse to walk past the jetty, so he refused, stressing that Grandma had stipulated drinks and a cake so that was what they must do. Sharon looked puzzled and pointed out that his mother wouldn't mind what Ben had, but she shrugged her shoulders when Tom insisted and took the boys to look at the display of cakes and cookies near the counter. Rusty lapped at the water in the bowl provided by the owners before settling in the shade where he could watch all the activity surrounding him.

When their order had been taken Sam and Ben

went onto the patch of sand nearby and started to build castles, which Ben took great delight in knocking down. 'This is lovely,' Sharon said, 'and a real treat. I didn't know your mum had given you some money.'

'Well that was the idea,' Tom said, 'she wanted you to have a surprise.'

'It's kind of her,' Sharon said. 'We never go out and treat ourselves anymore.' Tom watched as she eased her arm and stroked the dressing with her fingers. 'Oh, this is really beginning to sting now. I think it's getting worse but maybe it's only because of the heat.'

Tom shifted uncomfortably; he wanted to tell her how he felt but sometimes he simply couldn't find the right words. 'I'm so sorry, Sharon,' he said. 'I feel so ashamed and I wish you'd never got hurt.' She reached over with her good arm and placed her hand over his.

'It isn't your fault, Tom,' she said. 'It's just circumstances and a bad patch we're going through. I've told you we will get through it, we've just got to be strong.'

'I know,' he replied, 'but no matter what happens I'm taking you to the doctor's on Monday, that arm needs attention and I don't care how much you object.'

Sharon shook her head. 'You know what he's like, he'll insist on reporting it and then we'll be in even worse trouble.'

'I don't think it can be any worse than it already is. I could kill that bloody man.'

'Don't say things like that, it frightens me.'

They were interrupted when Ben hobbled up the

steps with his hand covering the plaster Tom had stuck on earlier. 'My arm hurts and it's coming off,' he whimpered.

Tom tried to keep a straight face. 'I don't think so, son,' he said. 'Your arm looks quite firmly fixed on to me.' Heeding Sharon's warning look, he lifted Ben onto his lap and tried unsuccessfully to stick it back on again, but Ben scampered off and jumped into the sand to join Sam and the group of boisterous children. Tom watched the two boys rolling around in the sand but he curbed his instinctive reaction to stop them. 'I still say I don't know how anything could be worse than what's happened to us,' he said, 'but at least they're having a good time today.' A shadow crossed Sharon's face. 'What is it?' he asked. 'What's the matter?'

'I can't help wondering,' she said, looking down, 'how you feel about Lily.'

'You know how I feel, I love her.'

She raised her eyes. 'When I first told you I was pregnant you didn't want her and you were very angry with me.'

'I was angry, very angry, but not with you. I just felt helpless, we were barely coping ourselves and the prospect of another mouth to feed was the last straw.' He was stunned. How could she not know how much he loved his own daughter? 'Sharon, believe me, I love Lily,' he told her.

'I know,' she said. 'I do believe you.'

The waitress arrived with their order and Sam and Ben rushed headlong up the steps and onto the veranda towards the table. Rusty, fuelled by the excitement, responded by trying to follow them and when his lead slipped off the post he ran up the steps and propelled himself like a rocket between the legs of the waitress. The tray upended, drinks went flying, and chocolate chip cookies spun through the air like flying saucers.

Tom completely lost his temper and told them they were leaving immediately; there would be no cakes or drinks for any of them. He pulled out the note to pay for the spilled food but the owner of the café came over to insist on replacing everything free of charge. One glance at Sharon's ashen face and the look of disappointment from the boys made him relent, but not before insisting they all sit quietly at the table until they were finished and ready to leave. He saw the woman at the table next to them slink away but one or two parents with young children threw them sympathetic glances, grateful that this time it wasn't happening to them.

By the time they returned to their place on the grass, the boys had lost interest in playing cricket and Tom suggested he would take them down to the boating lake to try out the paddle boats, followed by the ice cream he'd promised them earlier. Sharon was ready for a spell of peace and quiet and readily agreed. Lily was still asleep but showing signs of movement so with luck she might just grab a few moments before she had to feed her. 'You go,' she said, 'I'll be fine.

The boating lake and ice cream van were located beyond the jetty, which gave him the opportunity to see what was happening now that most of the vehicles had left or were standing empty, waiting the return of the fishermen. After they'd been on the lake and Sam and Ben had finally reached the beginning of the queue and chosen their ice creams, Tom guided them to a bench where they happily sat down.

'You stay there,' he instructed them. 'I just want to take a closer look. I won't be minute.'

'OK,' they chorused.

Tom read the notice with growing alarm; it was full of dire warnings of the need to be aware of the tidal flows, weather conditions, and safety precautions. Tom had overheard there hadn't been much checking done and the knot of fear in his stomach tightened. After once again trying unsuccessfully to contact Danny and Rick, he rang his mother.

'I have no idea where he is,' she told him. 'He was supposed to come with Amy and the children but it seems he's developed a sudden interest in sailing and he's gone fishing somewhere with Rick.'

'Do you know where they've gone?' he asked fearfully.

'I have no idea,' she replied. 'Amy knew nothing about it until the last minute so she's come on her own with the children, but she isn't very happy and I don't blame her.'

Tom tried to keep his voice light. 'Tell him to ring me when he does get in touch.'

'I will,' she replied. 'Anyway, how's your day going? Are the boys having a good time?'

'They're having a great time, filling themselves with ice cream as we speak.'

'Give them my love.'

'I will, and don't you worry.'

'Why should I be worried?' his mother demanded.

Tom thought quickly; what an idiot he was. 'No reason, I just thought you sounded a bit worried that's all.'

'Annoyed, not worried. Now get back to your family.'

Sam and Ben had joined him at the rail. 'Say hi to Grandma,' he said, holding the phone close to them.

'Hi Grandma, bye Grandma!' they shouted in unison.

Tom breathed a sigh of relief. At least he could explain away a reason for speaking to his mum if the boys mentioned it to Sharon, which they undoubtedly would.

'Come on you two rascals,' he said. 'I'll race you back to your mum.'

The boys took up the challenge and as always he held back until Sam reached Sharon with Ben following on behind. Rusty showed his pleasure at their return by nearly pulling the buggy over, and Tom vowed that the first thing they were going to concentrate on in the immediate future was training the dog.

Chapter 6

Marie watched Stuart replace his binoculars in the leather holder and lean over the railing to watch something on the beach below. 'What's caught your attention?' she asked when she joined him. 'I saw you having a chuckle to yourself.'

Stuart pointed to a group of teenagers further along the beach having a game of handball tennis. 'The lads are obviously very competitive but they are all so busy posing for the benefit of the girls they're missing the easiest of shots. Was I ever like that, I wonder?'

'Now let me think,' she said, focusing on the girls who were indeed watching with interest. 'Were you a poser? That's a difficult thing to answer but I suppose I should know better than anyone as I was there most of the time. It's funny you know but...'

'Come on girl, spit it out, I'm dying of curiosity here,' Stuart said.

'Well all I can remember is that you did make quite an outstanding figure in your Speedos.'

'You brazen hussy,' he laughed, 'you shouldn't have been looking.'

'It was hard not to,' she spluttered, 'but I'm not complaining so don't be too hard on those boys down there. Oh dear,' she said, 'what great times they were.'

'Luckily we've had lots more since then, and at least we've got plenty of memories to keep us going. It's the things that are happening now that are the problem. I've already forgotten when I arranged to meet Russell for our next game of bowls, if I don't write it down I'm hopeless. The joy of getting old I suppose.'

'It's better than the alternative,' she replied with conviction. 'Come on, we'd better go and have our lunch before we run out of time. I hope it's a bit quieter than earlier, it was packed out when I went to look for you.'

The rush had died down and they were able to find a seat outside on the veranda. It took no time to choose what they were going to order, they knew the menu off by heart, but today the promise of a lavish wedding breakfast had to be borne in mind. Marie tried not to be irritated by the arrival of a young family but the seating area here was quite restricted and she had to pull her seat in to make room for them behind her. Fortunately the table she and Stuart were sitting at was at the end of the veranda, away from the steps where the children were running up and down and adding to their dog's excited yelps. The muffled sounds of a young baby were detectable in between the louder noises but after a few soothing words from the mother and severe admonishments from the father to the boys to be quiet, things settled down. She concentrated on the conversation they'd just had about happy times when their own children were young, and told herself to stop being so grumpy.

When their order arrived she tucked into her sandwich with pleasure and for a time she gave Stuart her undivided attention, putting the distraction of the family out of her mind. Lacking the time for their customary second cup of tea, Stuart put the crockery back on the tray and went over to the counter to pay the bill. She was just about to join him when her attention was caught by a snippet of conversation between the young couple sitting behind her. She couldn't help overhearing and what she heard filled her with fear on behalf of the woman and her children, but then the conversation was interrupted when all at once pandemonium broke out. The dog had broken free and careered up the steps and into the legs of the waitress who was delivering the family's order, sending everything crashing about. The father's anger erupted and both children burst out crying. Billy and another member of staff rushed over to help the waitress, so unable to be of any assistance in the confined space she quickly made her exit. Stuart joined her round the side of the building and when he went to the gents' she hurried to a nearby seat and took out her phone.

Her hand was shaking as she made the call, but her daughter Debbie answered straight away and listened intently as Marie spilled her worries to her. 'Mum, calm down,' she said. 'Start at the beginning and tell me exactly what you heard.'

Marie tried to explain. 'I can't say exactly, it was difficult to hear properly but I want to tell you while it's fresh in my mind. They were a young family and the husband was apologising for causing a bad wound on her arm that was very painful. She tried to reassure him and said it wasn't his fault, it was down to circumstances and it had only happened because he was stressed. Then when he said he was taking her to the doctor's she refused because she said the doctor would report it and they'd be in even worse trouble than they are already.' Marie kept her eyes on the café to make sure Stuart wasn't on his way back. 'Then he said he'd been very, very angry when she'd got pregnant with the baby as she was just another mouth to feed. Oh Debbie, I'm so worried he might be going to hurt the baby as well.'

'Look Mum, I know it's upsetting but there's nothing I can do, we don't even know where they live.'

'Oh but I do,' Marie said. 'Have you got a pen? I'll try to remember it. Yes, here it is.' She'd heard the youngest of the boys talking to his new friend just below where she was sitting, and when they were proudly showing off their ability to repeat their address if ever they got lost she'd realised it was a place she was familiar with. 'Have you got it?' she asked, after repeating the address.

'Yes,' Debbie replied. 'Mum, that's in my area.'

Marie could now see Stuart approaching and knew she would have to be quick; he would tell her she was mad to interfere but she'd never forgive herself if she did nothing. 'I know,' she said quickly to Debbie, 'that's why I rang you. Will you be able to do something?'

There was a silence and for a second Marie thought she'd been cut off but then she heard her daughter speak. 'Mum are you absolutely certain about this? I don't want to follow it up if there is any doubt.'

Marie was already beginning to doubt herself but it was too late to go back now. 'I'm only telling you what I heard,' she said.

'Alright,' Debbie replied, 'as long as you're certain, it will be investigated.'

Marie hurriedly stuffed the phone back into her bag.

'Who was that?' Stuart asked, taking her arm.

'Only our Debbie ringing to say she hopes we have a nice time at the wedding. It was a poor signal so we couldn't have a proper conversation.'

'Perhaps as well, otherwise you could have been on for hours. Now let's go and get our glad-rags on in readiness for this wedding.'

*

Marie sat through the ceremony with tears in her eyes and a very heavy heart. Trying to concentrate on the words spoken by the couple and listen to the soaring music, she still felt weighed down by her actions earlier. She'd been so sure of what she'd overheard and it had seemed like the only possible course of action, but now she was having terrible doubts which were spoiling her enjoyment of the day. The temptation to confide in Stuart was very strong but it would only help if he agreed she'd done the right thing, and there was a distinct possibility he wouldn't. She kept going over and over the conversation; there was no denying what she'd overheard, and no matter how hard she tried she couldn't arrange the words in a different way. But still, she was unsure.

When Debbie had qualified as a social worker dealing specifically with children at risk, she'd told them of so many tragic cases and emphasised the need for people to report any worries they may have concerning a child. That was what she'd done, reported a concern, and who else better to look into it than her own daughter? At least this way it would mean it wouldn't go any further if her fears were unfounded.

Concentrating on Amelia and Piers exchanging their vows, she watched Colin proudly giving his daughter away. For some reason her eyes were drawn to where Greg was sitting looking on with pride, and not for the first time she felt sorry he hadn't been lucky enough to experience being a father himself. When he glanced over to smile at her she felt herself going warm with embarrassment but she told herself he couldn't read her thoughts, it was simply a moment of shared joy in their goddaughter's happiness.

Amelia looked stunning in an off-the-shoulder beaded dress which defined her lovely figure before falling into a small train around her feet. There was no veil on her head but her hair was loosely coiled and expertly dressed with gems which shimmered with every move she made. Piers was immaculate in his morning suit and his good-looking face was filled with love as he made his vows with his bride. Having fulfilled his duties, Colin went to sit by his wife's side and Marie noticed an almost imperceptible movement by Bryony to keep a small distance between them. Glancing round to check if anyone else had noticed, she was relieved to see that without exception the attention was exclusively on the bride and groom.

When they all stood for the hymn she couldn't help glancing over and comparing the two men who'd remained good friends despite both loving the same woman. Greg had retained his physique fairly well, aided no doubt by his height, and he was still handsome with a good head of fair hair; no longer blond, but then he had turned fifty. Stuart was shorter and already had a well-formed paunch, and unfortunately for him he hadn't inherited his father's hair pattern, his forehead was definitely getting higher. He still retained his impish sense of humour and despite all his weaknesses she had a very soft spot for him. He took part in the proceedings with a beaming face, totally oblivious to what was going to happen, and she felt a surge of sympathy for him.

*

The canapés and champagne were served in the large conservatory at the side of the hotel and she and Stuart mingled with old friends, some of whom they hadn't seen for years. Many of them had met their partners at university and followed careers away from home, sometimes leaving Marie with thoughts of missed opportunities, but that had passed and now she was happy to spend the rest of her life here. The craving for something to break the routine of her life was a recent occurrence but she'd found herself unsettled even more by Bryony's desire to grab all she could get out of life. That was all very well for young people like Damian and Amelia, but what about the generation heading for their half century?

'That's a very serious face,' Colin said, approaching her with gusto, 'and your glass is empty, we must remedy that immediately.'

Marie protested as he took her glass with one hand and replaced it with a full one with the other. 'I've already had too much to drink on an empty stomach; this is my third glass and it is far too much bubbly for me to cope with and stay in control.'

Colin found this highly amusing. 'Who said anything about being in control? It's a wedding and we're here to enjoy ourselves.'

Glancing round for a means of escape from the well-meaning efforts of Colin's attention, she saw Greg and Stuart walking in her direction, and by the expressions on their faces she guessed the appeal in her eyes hadn't gone unnoticed. Colin as usual was totally oblivious to the possibility of having outstayed his welcome, but she felt a sudden rush of affection for him. Deep down she knew he was a kind-hearted man but for some reason he was like a lost soul. Maybe with someone else he would have taken more of an interest in the business but Bryony had never loved him or given any encouragement, so he'd found solace in the drink which he'd grown accustomed to in his youth. With Greg and Stuart he was totally at ease and he greeted them with genuine pleasure.

'Isn't that right?' he asked as they approached.

'Whatever you said, I totally agree with,' Greg replied magnanimously.

'I was telling Marie we are all here to have a good time, it's a wedding and that's what you do,' Colin repeated. 'Anyway,' he said, pointing to Greg and Marie with his glass, 'if anyone should enjoy themselves, it's you two, you are Amelia's godparents after all.'

Greg turned to Marie and nodded. 'We are indeed, and very proud we are too.'

Marie lifted her hand to respond and to her surprise Colin once again exchanged it for a full one, but before she had time to resist she was startled to see the one being replaced was already almost empty.

'This is slipping down far too easily,' she said, 'but I must say the effects are very therapeutic.'

'Be careful you don't overdo it,' Stuart cautioned, 'you know what you're like when you drink too much.'

'I don't actually,' she giggled, 'I can't remember. But I must say I'm beginning to feel very good.'

Stuart looked ruefully at Greg. 'She's well on her way already and the day has only just started.'

'Speak for yourself,' Marie said. 'My day started this morning drinking with Bryony in her room.' She hiccoughed and Stuart put on a mock expression of despair.

'Heaven preserve us,' he groaned. 'Greg, would you keep an eye on Marie for me? I've just seen an old mate over there and I'd like to go and catch up with him but I can't really take her over like this.'

Greg was highly amused but Marie objected strongly. 'I may be tipsy but I'm quite capable of taking care of myself.' Stuart nodded and she pretended she hadn't seen the knowing look which passed between him and Greg.

'I have to admire Bryony sometimes,' she said to Greg as she watched Stuart walk away, 'it takes some doing, organising an event like this.'

'You did the same for Debbie when she got married, that was a lovely wedding,' Greg pointed out, but Marie wasn't convinced.

'Oh, but it wasn't half as grand as this,' she protested, 'and there were nowhere near as many guests.'

'Maybe not, but then not many people have the

advantage of owning a hotel to commandeer for a weekend like Bryony has been able to do. Don't put yourself down, Marie, you are just as capable as your friend.'

Marie looked around the room, taking in the beautiful decor and luxurious furnishings and a long, deep sigh escaped her lips. 'It is really lovely, this place, and I don't think Bryony realises how much she'll miss it when she leaves Colin.' She saw Greg's surprised reaction but somehow she couldn't contain herself. Anyway, there was nothing to worry about; she wasn't telling him anything he didn't know already. 'Oh, I know she'll still be involved with the business but it won't be the same as owning all this.' Sweeping her arm in an arc she saw the glass tilt, swirling the champagne dangerously close to the brim. Greg swiftly stepped back in an effort to protect his suit.

'Whoa there, steady on,' he laughed, and she sipped some more of the wine to reduce the danger of spilling it. Greg was looking at her closely but his voice was deceptively casual. 'What do mean about Bryony leaving Colin?'

She shook her head in a vain attempt to try to clear it but all she succeeded in doing was to make the room spin a little faster, so without thinking she grabbed Greg's arm to steady herself. 'Oh I'm so sorry,' she said. 'I'm not supposed to say anything, well actually I'm not supposed to know anything really.' She could feel herself swaying. 'Oh dear, I think I'd better sit down.'

'I think we'd both better sit down,' Greg replied, leading her to a chair and pulling one near it for himself. 'Can I just clarify something?' he asked. 'Has Bryony told you she's leaving Colin?'

Marie nodded. 'Yes, she has.'

A deep frown brought Greg's brows together. 'Did she say why?' he asked.

'Not in so many words, but it didn't take much working out and she didn't deny it when I guessed it was you.'

'Did she say when she was planning to do it?'

Marie tried to remember but it was all a bit hazy. 'Not exactly, but I somehow got the feeling it was probably going to be this weekend.'

'I see. Would you mind not mentioning this to anyone else?' he asked.

She gave him her word. 'Don't worry, my lips are sealed,' she assured him. 'I'm sorry Greg, I shouldn't have said anything but it's the double whammy of medication and drink, and although it's made me a bit giddy, I'm not so far gone I don't know what I'm doing.'

He looked doubtful but smiled fondly. 'I'm pleased to hear it. What's the medication for, is it your back?'

'Yes but it's nothing serious, I strained a muscle lifting a heavy box at the shop. I'm waiting to start physiotherapy and hopefully that will sort it out, but I'm ashamed to say I've let it get me down and I've turned into a grumpy old woman. Poor Stuart, I must have made his life a misery these last few weeks.'

Greg tried to reassure her. 'Knowing Stuart I feel sure he'll cope,' he said.

'I suppose so, but life's too short to just simply

have to cope and I'd like to make it up to him somehow.'

'Lucky man,' Greg said with feeling.

'You wouldn't think so if you'd been with me for the last few weeks, I've been a nightmare to live with.'

Greg smiled at her. 'I very much doubt it.'

'Hello you two,' Stuart said as he approached them. 'Thanks, Greg, for keeping Marie company. I hope you've had a nice chat.'

'We've certainly had an interesting one,' Greg told him.

Chapter 7

Irritation was swelling inside her like a balloon that was about to burst. There had been no provision made for the whole wedding group to leave the hotel to reassemble in public view on the downs of all places. Whoever had made the suggestion that the Victorian fountain provided the ideal backdrop for the photographs of a very modern wedding deserved to be shot, in her opinion. Not that anyone seemed to be asking her opinion, which made it even more indefensible. Amelia and Piers were so laid back about everything it was almost becoming an irritation. Colin was a complete waste of space as usual and Ralph smiled indulgently in Amelia's direction the whole time.

She could have borne all that if only Greg had shown some understanding, but he was in a strange mood. When she'd taken the only opportunity to tell him she'd have some important news to tell him later, he'd looked more irritated than pleased. Puzzled by his response, she'd hesitated just long enough to allow a member of staff to interrupt and the moment to ask him why was lost. Opportunities for private conversations were proving hard to find but she looked forward to the evening when they would be able to get some time together to discuss their future.

For the moment she had another pressing problem to resolve, and it was quite literally a pressing problem. She'd worked out fairly accurate calculations of the small distances she would be required to walk during the day which had been the deciding factor in her choice of shoes, but she hadn't taken into consideration the possibility of trekking over to the fountain. Walking along the path was proving difficult and painful in the gorgeous but gravity-defying heels and her mind vacillated between trying to walk slowly and gracefully or trying to speed up to get it over with no matter how she looked. Piers' parents had accompanied her until they'd chosen to take the shorter route over the grass and when they'd turned to beckon her to follow them she'd nonchalantly waved them away. The forced smile relaxed into one of pleasure and relief at the sight of Greg walking towards her with his hand outstretched in a gesture of assistance.

'You look like a damsel in distress,' he said, gently taking her arm and linking it to his. 'Those shoes are definitely not made for walking.'

'They weren't meant to be walking,' she told him, 'coming out here was never on the agenda.'

Greg laughed. 'Well, you've got to admit it looks like it's adding a whole new dimension to the day and everyone seems to be enjoying themselves, especially Amelia and Piers. I think you'd better go with the flow, as the young ones say.'

Bryony paused at the edge of the grass which lay between them and the group mingling around the fountain. 'These shoes cost a fortune and they've been dyed to match my outfit, if they get ruined it will be impossible to replace them.'

'You look beautiful,' he said, 'from top to toe, but today is about enjoying your daughter's wedding. Forget the shoes, throw caution to the winds and let's go.'

A small group of people had gathered to enjoy the unexpected spectacle of the wedding party and recognising several acquaintances amongst them, she returned their greetings with a smile and regal wave of her hand. The photographer appeared to have abandoned any attempts to persuade members of the family and guests to form traditional groupings and was pointing his camera in all directions. Amelia encouraged him to take informal shots and Bryony reacted spontaneously by contriving to place herself and Greg in his line of vision. It would be lovely, she thought, to have official photographs of them together, and she could picture them in the future reminiscing about this special day. When everyone had been assembled for the final photograph Greg edged closer to her but she swallowed the bitter taste of disappointment with the realisation that he was more interested in a couple who were standing watching. 'Who are they?' he asked out of the corner of his mouth. 'They look vaguely familiar, but I can't quite place them.'

Bryony followed the direction of his gaze. 'I think it's Piers' boss Paul Sheridan and his wife,' Bryony replied. 'They don't look very happy do they?' She was filled once again with a sense of foreboding about the possibility of him making things difficult for Louisa, but she told herself she was becoming paranoid. 'I hope they cheer up before this evening,' she said to Greg, 'they're coming to the dance.'

Greg nodded absentmindedly. The man was certainly behaving very oddly. He'd been staring in the direction of Amelia and the bridesmaids to the exclusion of everyone else, and was totally oblivious to the obvious distress of his wife. Abruptly turning from her, he began walking away, making no attempt to wait as she vainly tried to catch up with him. Despite his attention being focused on the unhappy couple Greg caught a movement out of the corner of his eye, and when he turned and saw Damian solicitously leading Louisa away he remembered something Amelia had previously mentioned about Louisa having ended an affair with Piers' boss. If that was correct, judging by the man's demeanour he was still smarting from it. Greg hoped he wouldn't cause any trouble and spoil the happiness Louisa was so obviously finding with Damian. Looking back towards the Sheridans he saw she was trying to keep up with him as he marched swiftly away from her. 'Poor girl,' he remarked absentmindedly. 'She's very attractive and certainly doesn't deserve to be treated like that.'

Bryony inched away. 'How can you make an observation like that? You don't even know them. And don't you think you're getting a bit carried away?' she added. 'She's hardly a girl.'

'That's true I suppose,' he acknowledged with a smile, but to Bryony's chagrin he added, 'nevertheless she is very attractive.'

Suddenly the proceedings were rudely interrupted by the arrival of a boisterous puppy running excitedly amongst the guests, jumping up with complete disregard for the chaos he was causing. Luckily they all seemed to find him cute and amusing, which gave the photographer ample opportunities to catch the happy spontaneity of the moment. He assured a doubtful Bryony that the puppy wouldn't feature in any of the resulting photographs but she was relieved when, with some assistance from Greg, the dog was finally back under the control of its irate owner.

The group began to break up to make their way back to the hotel led by a triumphant Colin holding aloft the bottle of champagne and a glass, which appeared to be constantly full despite him continually drinking from it. Bryony turned away in disgust and hung back to have a word with Bill Jackson, the photographer from the local paper. She'd become aware of him taking photographs for some time, even encroaching on the wedding photographer's patch occasionally, but she had to treat him with care to achieve her goal. Approaching him with the air of a fellow conspirator she told him she hadn't forgotten their agreement and she'd make sure the wedding photographer passed some pictures from the reception inside the hotel. Bill Jackson slung one of his cameras over his shoulder. 'Oh, you don't need to bother yourself about that now, Mrs Portland,' he said, returning her smile. 'I've got more than I need already, this has proved a fantastic backdrop and that puppy added an unexpected diversion so I was able to get some spontaneous reactions.'

Bryony was devastated. 'But I thought you told me it would be a small coup for you to have access to some indoor shots, and I was hoping to get some publicity for the hotel.' Reluctantly she found herself adding ingratiatingly, 'I'll make it worth your while.'

His mind was obviously already on the next

assignment as he packed his bag and to her irritation he started to walk away from her. 'I must go,' he called over his shoulder. 'Thanks for the offer but I want to get down to the jetty, that's where all the newsworthy activity is going on.'

She remained standing, alone and frustrated; the publicity for the hotel as a venue for marriage ceremonies was a major feature of her plan to convince Ralph of her ongoing commitment to the hotel. All she would have to do then would be to demonstrate how she envisaged her new role as an events and financial adviser. Her spirits lifted when she saw Greg, who, sensing she wasn't following him, had turned and begun to retrace his steps and was walking towards her.

'Is it those shoes again?' he asked, but she shook her head as she held out her hand to him. His gentle concern touched her and the worries about the business were temporarily forgotten. She could barely conceal her feelings but the moment for revealing her plans would come later.

Chapter 8

Tom was glad to get back to their space on the grass. The visit to the café hadn't turned out to be the special treat his mother had intended and it had left him feeling wound up and tense. Sharon was doing her best to put a humorous slant on what had happened but he could find nothing funny in the situation. It had simply been a humiliating experience and he was relieved to be away from it. They would somehow have to find a way to tell Mum how nice it had been without going into details, but the kids were sure to spill the beans. The family who'd kept an eye on their things was sitting around enjoying a rest and a drink but soon the children were jumping up impatiently, urging the adults to join them in another game.

Shrugging with good humour, most of the men stood up to take part and they invited Tom and the two boys to join them. Encouraged by Sam and Ben, he agreed and soon they were enthusiastically engaged in a far more interesting game than they could ever hope to have with just the three of them. Sam and Ben fell about laughing when he was bowled out for a duck by a far more proficient bowler than he'd encountered for many years. He took up his position as a fielder, determined to hone his skills before taking part in the local game arranged back home for the end of the season.

Just as he was about to execute a spectacular catch he was distracted by hearing Sharon calling to him, and he watched the ball roll away while an exultant youngster scored several runs. This caused even more hilarity and he wondered how much humiliation he would have to endure before the day was out. His annoyance at Sam's uncontrolled laughter quickly evaporated and he made his mind up to concentrate on improving his game. He set out to impress rather than be a source of merriment.

Sharon told him she was going to look at a bride over by the fountain and he watched her pushing the buggy over the uneven grass with Rusty by her side. He was filled with a rush of love for her and remembering what she'd said in the café, he realised he didn't tell her often enough. Showing his feelings didn't come easily to him and since losing his job he'd even lost interest in sex, which was previously unheard of and difficult for her to understand. If only he could get a job at least he wouldn't be on a short fuse all the time and normal life could be resumed.

After a few more attempts he was able to demonstrate some of his skills and he began to enjoy himself so much he was put out when everyone stopped playing to look over towards the wedding group. From where he was standing his vision was restricted but when he realised some of the well-dressed people were backing away from an energetic animal, his stomach clenched with apprehension. 'Dad, it's Rusty!' Sam shouted, confirming his worst fears. Sprinting as fast as he could, he saw the dog jumping up with excitement and bounding out of reach when anyone tried to grab hold of him. When the dog heard Tom's voice he responded by circling the group chased by two gleeful little girls. He could hear Sharon calling his name over and over again but it was only when one of the men helped to corner him that Tom was able to grab Rusty's collar.

'Thanks a lot,' he said to the man, 'I don't think I would have caught him on my own. Will you tell everyone I'm really sorry?'

'Of course,' the man replied, 'don't worry about it, there's no harm done. Actually it was quite a funny diversion and provided some good photo opportunities.' Tom nodded gratefully and standing hot and dishevelled, he scanned the horizon to check Sam and Ben were safe before walking over to Sharon.

'How did that happen?' he asked, and to his surprise she burst into tears.

'Lily started crying and while I was lifting her out of the pram the lead slipped out of my hand. I'm so sorry. Everything's going wrong today.'

'No it isn't,' he said firmly, hoping and praying it was true. The fear that was niggling away in his head didn't bear thinking about, and there was no way he could tell her about it. Hopefully by the time they got home, or even sooner if he was lucky, it would all be sorted and he would know they were safe with Sharon being none the wiser.

'It's been good in so many ways,' she said as they walked back and saw the boys laughing and playing with their new friends. 'I'm just feeling very tired, it's been quite a day.'

'It has and not least because of this little pest. You are in for some serious training when we get home,

Rusty. We're not having any more of these capers, I'll tell you now.'

*

No sooner had Tom started the car than Ben announced he needed the toilet. 'I asked if anyone needed the loo,' Tom said crossly. 'Why didn't you tell me when I asked you?'

Ben's voice wavered. 'I didn't want to then.'

'There's no point arguing,' Sharon pointed out. 'If he needs to go he needs to go.'

Tom turned off the engine and looked around. 'There are no public toilets around here so I'd better take him and try and find some.'

Despite her weariness Sharon scanned the area with the practised eyes of a mother of young children. 'No, you stay here,' she said. 'I'll take him in that pub just down the road, we won't be long.'

Tom watched and waited until Sharon and Ben were safely across the busy road and Sam was again immersed in a game before he pulled out his mobile. Impatiently he tried several times to get a response from his brother before reluctantly contacting his mother again. Having little time, he cut out the usual niceties and asked her directly if she'd heard anything from Danny. Her reply was unusually succinct. 'No, we haven't and we are getting worried because no-one has been able to get in touch with either Danny or Rick. Have you any idea where they were going, because you seem very interested in what he's up to?'

'No, Mum,' he told her. 'He didn't tell me what he was doing today. We're setting off now so I'll see what I can do when we get home, so don't worry.'

'That's the second time you've said that to me today so now I am worried. You'd better be telling me the truth, Tom.'

'I am Mum, honestly,' he replied, crossing his fingers, but he really didn't know what Danny and Rick had done today, he only suspected it, and there was no point in adding to his mother's worry. Despite all that he was pretty sure now that they'd defied him, and the only explanation he could think of as to why they'd decided to come today was because they knew he'd have no way of stopping them. 'I must go now, we need to set off,' he said, 'and...'

His mother interjected, 'I know, I mustn't worry. See you soon, Tom.'

'Shit,' said Tom.

'You're not supposed to swear,' Sam piped up from the back seat.

'Shut up Sam,' Tom replied crossly before getting out of the car to help Sharon, who was approaching with Ben. When they were all securely fastened in Sharon exhaled and said happily, 'Right, let's get this show on the road.'

'Dad said a rude word,' Sam mumbled without looking up from his screen. Sharon looked questioningly at Tom, who managed to control his annoyance.

'It was only mildly rude,' he said, 'and you shouldn't tell tales, young man.'

'Just saying,' muttered Sam, his attention once more firmly fixed on reaching the next level of his game.

At the first set of traffic lights Sharon slipped her

arm from her cardigan before tentatively easing the injured one free from the other sleeve. Touching it gently, she could feel where blood had seeped through the bandage and the pain and the burning sensation surrounding the area where it had spread further down her arm was getting worse. 'I think it's stuck to the dressing,' she said quietly. 'I'll have to dampen it when we get home before I can put a new one on.'

Tom's reply was heavy with emotion when he remembered the painful experience earlier. 'I'll do it for you, but can you wait until the kids are in bed?'

'Of course,' she replied. Sharon lightened the mood by changing the topic of conversation and they all joined in flicking through the memories of the day. 'It's been good hasn't it?' she said. 'And it didn't cost us a fortune. I know it wasn't funny at the time but the look on everyone's faces when Rusty ran into the waitress was absolutely priceless.'

'To say nothing of the wedding party when they were interrupted by an uninvited guest,' Tom added. 'Some of them seemed a bit toffee nosed and very precious about their wedding finery.' His laugh disturbed Lily, who made her usual response by making popping sounds as she energetically sucked her dummy. 'Go on girl, give it some welly,' Tom said encouragingly.

Sharon grinned. 'The man who helped you catch Rusty was very pleasant,' she said.

Tom agreed. 'Yes, he was very posh but he seemed a nice enough chap.'

'I thought he looked very smart,' Sharon said.

'Oh, you managed to see a lot for someone who

was supposed to be so upset. Well I believe I'll have to keep my eye on you in future.'

'Stop teasing,' Sharon said archly.

Tom loved it when Sharon got a bit uppity but he decided against provoking her, he recognised the signs when she was tired and didn't appreciate being mocked, even in fun. 'At least he did something positive, unlike all the others who just stood around,' he said, 'and I agree it was hilarious but even so, we must make sure we do something about training Rusty otherwise he's going to get out of control.'

'He's already out of control,' Sharon pointed out, 'but he's pretty cute all the same.' She closed her eyes and Tom let her rest, at least it would give her a little time to prepare herself for the small matter of getting three children ready and settled in bed. He guessed she was looking forward to the time later in the evening when they would be sitting together quietly, eating a pizza in front of the television. He hoped for everyone's sake that nothing would disturb their peace.

By the time they arrived home Lily was crying for a feed, Ben was asleep, and when Tom carried him inside he lolled about and wouldn't co-operate in getting ready for bed. Sam complained he was hungry and couldn't find his football kit for school the next day. 'Let's get organised,' Tom suggested wearily. 'Sharon, you sit down and feed the baby, I'll get Ben to bed. I don't think there's any point trying to get him to eat anything, and you, Sam, have a shower and I'll make you some supper.' Sam began to protest but Tom cut him short. 'You'll have to find your own kit, you are old enough now to sort your things out so don't bother your mum.'

'But I don't know where they are,' wailed Sam. Tom was quickly running out of patience; he desperately wanted to make contact with Danny and had little interest in the whereabouts of a missing football strip. Unfortunately Sam hadn't perfected the art of assessing his father's moods and didn't know when to stop. His shoulders slumped as he made his way towards the door and mumbled, 'I don't know how I'm supposed to know where Mum's put it.'

'Hang on a minute,' Tom said. 'If you put it to be washed you know exactly where it is, where your Mum always puts your clean clothes. If you left it in your sports bag I presume it will still be there.' Sam went back upstairs muttering under his breath, and Tom suppressed a smile despite himself. At ten years old Sam was already showing signs of adolescent behaviour, God knows what he would be like in a few years' time.

When the children were finally settled in bed Tom washed his hands and collected everything together in preparation for attending to Sharon's arm. Sorting out the children had caused it to bleed even more, which made the removal of the dressing easier but he sucked air between his teeth when he saw how bad the wound was.

'Despite what you said, I'm taking you to the doctor's tomorrow,' he told her. 'I don't care what the consequences are and you can object as much as you like but we are going.'

Sharon began to protest. 'You know what Dr Henderson is like, he'll insist on reporting the landlord and then I'll be out of a job.'

Tom placed his finger on her lips. 'Then let him report him,' he replied, 'we'll deal with that if it happens.'

Sharon was weary with the constant battle of trying to care for the family and the pain was obviously getting her down. He could see she was fighting back the tears and as he took her in his arms she leaned against him and wept. 'Tom, what are we going to do?' she asked.

'We'll manage,' he replied, 'I promise.'

'But how? We're not even managing now and it can only get worse.'

He tried his best to reassure her but actually he had no idea himself how they were going to get through when things just seemed to be getting worse and worse. 'I don't really know but we will. I've heard there's some work going in Leeds where they need experienced builders, so that means it will be decent pay.'

'Leeds? That's miles away!' Sharon exclaimed. 'You can't go to work there.'

'Beggars can't be choosers,' Tom said.

'Is that what we are now, beggars?' Sharon asked, but before Tom tried to correct his slip of the tongue, the phone rang.

Tom snatched it up. Sharon could hear his mother's voice and she soon realised it wasn't a social call when she heard it growing louder and angrier. The words were jumbled and he was struggling to make sense of them. 'Mum, calm down. What's the problem?' he shouted down the phone at last.

'What's the problem?' she repeated, her voice rising.

'The problem is your brother and Rick have gone with your dinghy to Merebank Bay to join the cockle pickers. Why did you put such a stupid idea in his head? He can't sail a dinghy and he can barely swim.'

'I didn't know he was going,' Tom insisted. 'We thought about it but I decided against it. They must have made a decision to go anyway without telling me.'

'Well now they're missing,' she told him. 'We don't know what's happened to them.'

Tom was stunned and could barely get his words out. 'What do mean, missing?'

'There are two men who went fishing who they think are trapped out there.' Her voice rose again. 'Oh, it's on the news again now. I'm going. You'd better get watching it too.' Before he'd put the phone down Sharon had already turned the television on.

They listened with mounting disbelief as the reporter gave details of the drama as it unfolded in Merebank Bay following an unexpected decision to open it to allow cockles to picked once more. Unfortunately news had quickly spread via social media, and people from a wide area had been attracted and had taken advantage before the regulations could be enforced. The emergency services had already been called out several times but two men who'd been reported being seen in difficulty had not returned, and despite searches being carried out near their last known sighting, they hadn't yet been found.

A long and detailed account of the dangers facing inexperienced men undertaking this specialised activity emphasised the need for stricter regulations and greater caution on the part of individuals. The tragedy of a few years ago when many Chinese immigrants had lost their lives in Morecambe Bay should be a salutary lesson to everyone concerned, was the opinion of a spokesman from the local fisherman's fraternity. 'It involves more than simply going out and collecting the cockles,' he pointed out, 'knowledge of the tides is essential, both the timing and the way and the speed they turn. Some of these people have no conception of what is involved and can't even handle the vessels they're in.'

Sharon had been sitting white-faced and silent during the report and she didn't move while Tom made the return phone call to his mother.

'How do you know it's our Danny?' he asked her. 'They haven't named the missing men yet.' She sounded much calmer now but this unnerved him in a way her anger hadn't.

'Neither of them has rung or made contact with anyone. Amy hasn't heard a thing and that's most unlike Danny, he's never off his phone normally. We only know what they intended doing because apparently Rick told his wife and apparently she had no idea of the implications or what it involved until she heard the news.' Her voice dropped and he knew she was struggling to speak. 'Apparently a fisherman overheard a man calling out and he was sure he was shouting the name Rick.'

Tom thought he was going to be sick. 'I'm sorry Mum,' he said, 'I'd called it off because I realised it was going to be too dangerous but they obviously decided to go ahead without me. I'll try and find out what I can and I'll call you back.'

'Do that, son,' was all she said, but he knew the

time for recriminations would come later.

Sharon walked towards him, crying. 'You were going to do it, weren't you? Despite all the promises you made, you were still going to do it. Despite nearly killing yourself falling off a roof you were going to do another stupid, dangerous thing.' Clenching her fists, she thumped them repeatedly into his chest and he stood unflinchingly waiting for her to vent her anger, because although everything he did was for her and the kids, he accepted the truth of what she said.

Her arms dropped to her side and she looked at him sadly. 'At this moment I hate you, Tom, because you've lied to me and despite everything you said you were going to put your life at risk again.'

He was devastated and without thinking he reached out to hold her close but she stepped backwards and he grabbed her arms and gripped them tightly to stop her moving away. Her scream of pain filled the room and she cried out, 'Tom, stop it! You're hurting me.'

'Don't hurt my mummy,' Sam commanded from the doorway, fixing them in a rigid tableau of violence. Slowly they both looked in horror towards the door where he was standing white-faced, his eyes fixed determinedly on Tom. 'Don't hurt Mummy,' he repeated. When Tom made a move towards him Sam flinched and backed away, so despite the searing pain Sharon went to him and took him gently towards the sofa. Sam allowed himself to be led but he kept his distance and his eyes averted from his father.

Wondering how to explain to a young child what he'd witnessed, Sharon began gently. 'It wasn't quite what you thought and Daddy wasn't hurting me.'

'But he was,' Sam insisted. 'I heard you crying and telling him to stop.'

Tom began to speak. 'No, you see, son...' but Sharon stopped him with a steely glare.

'I think you'd better go and do what you promised your mother, you've done enough damage here already.' He retreated into the other room and began to make some phone calls, willing someone to tell him it had all been a big mistake and Danny and Rick were already making their way home.

Sharon pulled Sam close and wrapped a rug round them both to keep warm; there was a chill in the air and she could feel him shivering. 'Do you remember when Daddy fell off that roof and had to go to hospital?' she asked, and he nodded vigorously. 'Well, I made him promise never to do anything dangerous again and I've found out today that he was planning to do just that. That's why I got angry with him and shouted and he grabbed hold of me right where my arm is sore. He was trying to stop me shouting, he didn't mean to hurt me. Do you understand?' He snuggled even closer to his mother.

'I think so,' he replied, 'but what was the dangerous thing he was going to do?'

'I don't know if you noticed but there were some people going fishing in Merebank today.'

'Of course I noticed, Mum,' he said indignantly. 'Anyway Dad was watching them when we went for our ice creams.'

Tom, cringing and gripping the phone, listened to his cover being blown. He was standing out of sight so this time there was no accompanying glare, but when he heard her say, 'Was he indeed?' the menace in her voice told him he was in for a rough ride. 'Well I'll have to speak to him about that,' he heard her say, 'but come on now, it's school tomorrow and way past your bedtime.'

When Sam was back in bed after enjoying the luxury of a hot chocolate and a biscuit, Sharon went back down and faced Tom. 'Is there any news?' she asked and he shook his head.

'You not only broke your word but I presume you must have lied to me when you said you were working on Danny's bike. We are going to have to talk about this because you've really hurt me, but I don't think this is the right time. I don't know if I'll ever be able to forgive you, I feel so angry.'

He stood abjectly trying to figure out a way to approach her. 'I'm so sorry,' he said, but she turned away.

'I don't want to talk to you, go away,' she told him bitterly. The phone rang again. 'You should answer that,' she said, sensing his hesitation.

It was the call he'd been dreading; the two missing men were almost certainly Danny and Rick. Arrangements were made for his mother and Danny's wife Amy and the children to come over to stay with Sharon while Tom made his way back to Merebank. A tearful Amy came on the phone and she spoke hurriedly to Tom to beg him to keep her up to date with any news he had about Danny. He gathered a few things together and as he was about to leave he heard Sam calling his name. Sharon nodded and urged him to go upstairs. 'We don't know how long you'll be gone and I don't want you to leave him like this.' Tom ran up the stairs two at a time and explained briefly what was happening, desperately trying not to alarm him as he knew he'd had enough upset for one day.

'Now I must go, look after your mum for me.'

'I will,' Sam murmured sleepily from under the duvet.

Despite her anger Sharon returned Tom's embrace. It lacked her usual display of affection but he was glad she wasn't forcing him to leave while they were still completely at loggerheads. He felt he was being punished enough for even considering such a stupid idea, so even though they would have to resolve their differences when all this was over, for now he had enough to contend with. Within minutes he was speeding away to return to the place they'd enjoyed so much such a short time ago, but he geared himself up for a very different experience this time around.

After Tom left, Sharon watched as the car disappeared from sight before putting the kettle on to wait for the arrival of her mother-in-law and Amy. With a feeling of pure dread she prepared herself for a long, watchful night, knowing she would have to be strong and support the two anxious women.

Chapter 9

The band had finished their first session and the mix of sixties music played by the fill-in DJ had drawn an enthusiastic and eclectic group of dancers onto the floor. The myriad coloured lights picked out the swirling skirts of the younger girls while the ultraviolet turned the pristine white of the men's shirts into ghoulish spectres. The more mature were throwing their inhibitions to the winds as they adapted their favourite rock and roll steps to accommodate their creaking bones and were leaving the more energetic and acrobatic steps to the youngsters.

Waistcoats and cummerbunds festooned the chairs and high-heeled shoes lay dotted around the floor while their owners wore the sparkling flip-flops provided by the thoughtful bride. Amelia had changed from the exquisite bead-encrusted wedding dress into a simpler but equally flattering shorter version, and was dancing enthusiastically with Piers and anyone else who grabbed her attention.

Marie's feet were tapping and her body was rocking in time to the music, and the call to get on the dance floor was strong. She knew it made sense to wait for the later, slower ballroom dances but she was tired of being sensible, and once again she railed against the confinements of having a bad back. If only she could speed up the start of the treatment it would be easier to tolerate, but at least the diagnosis had confirmed there was no serious injury. She'd been advised to be patient but that wasn't something she found easy to do. Under the beams of the strobe lights she was able to follow Bryony's progress as she made her way round the room performing her hostess duties and greeting as many guests as possible. The fleeting illumination added a dramatic effect to her exaggerated gestures making her appear like the heroine in a silent, flickering movie. Turning her attention back to the dance floor, Marie was caught up in the joyous mood and marvelled at the energy and vibrancy of young people. Even her own children were grown up now and here she was feeling like a teenager again, even if only inside her head. She was so engrossed it came as a surprise when Bryony dropped into the seat beside her and immediately began to massage her instep.

'Oh these shoes are killing me,' she exclaimed, 'but I daren't take them off because my feet are swollen and I'll never get the wretched things back on again.'

'Then don't,' Marie suggested. 'Do what the sensible ones have done and wear a pair of those lovely sandals.'

Bryony's fingers were probing the gap between her shoe and the instep of her foot. 'Do you know how much these cost me? No, don't ask, you really wouldn't want to know. Suffice it to say I can't justify the outlay if I can't manage one whole day out of them.' Inclining her head towards the empty chairs, she asked, 'Where are the others? Why are you sitting here on your own?'

'I'm perfectly content,' Marie replied. 'Celia and Russell are reliving their youth somewhere in the centre of the floor and Stuart is having a drink with Colin.'

Bryony grimaced. 'In that case you'll probably never see Stuart again for the remainder of the evening and he'll still be propping up the bar until it's time to leave.'

Marie shook her head. 'I don't think so, he doesn't share Colin's capacity for drink and anyway he's promised me a dance later when the mood slows down and the lights are dimmed.' They remained sitting together for a while without speaking but when Bryony saw Russell and Claire leaving the dance floor and advancing towards them, she jumped up. 'I'll just say hello to them and then I must carry on circulating,' she said. 'See you later.'

Watching her walk away, Marie marvelled at the easy way she moved, completely disguising the pain inflicted by her shoes. After briefly speaking to Russell and Claire she turned back to Marie and told her she would rescue Stuart from Colin's clutches as soon as she possibly could.

'Don't be so hard on him,' Marie replied, 'he's not that bad.'

'He's not that good either,' was Bryony's immediate response.

The couple sitting at the next table and now receiving Bryony's attention seemed vaguely familiar to Marie, but at first she couldn't place them. It took her a few moments before she recollected seeing them standing on the promenade when the photographs were being taken and she was sure it was Paul Sheridan and his wife. They hadn't looked happy then and they certainly didn't look any happier now. Claire and Russell returned, breathless and flushed from their exertions on the dance floor, but it didn't inhibit Claire's insatiable appetite for gossip. 'Who are the couple talking to Bryony?' she puffed.

Marie followed her gaze and played for time before replying. She would only succeed in arousing Claire's curiosity even more if she didn't tell her the truth, but there was no need for her to be given any personal details. 'I think he's Piers' boss,' she said.

'Wow,' Claire replied, 'isn't he the one...?'

Marie interrupted her. 'Be careful,' she said, 'Damian's coming over.'

'Hi Mum,' he said, 'do you mind if we join you for a while?'

Stuart was already arranging the chairs, helped by Claire, who was trying her best to manoeuvre everyone to make sure Louisa was sitting next to her, but Marie was one step ahead and guided the young woman to the empty seat by her side. Claire was frustrated by being trumped by Marie but she wasn't one to dwell for long on incidentals like that, and very soon she was putting all her energies into questioning Damian.

'What I can't understand,' she said as soon as they were all settled, 'is how you two haven't met before, as you are both friends of Amelia and you all attended the same university.'

Damian was in buoyant mood and not in the least put out at Claire's curiosity. 'Everyone seems to be interested in that,' he replied, 'but in a way there's a quite simple explanation. We were on different campuses doing different courses, and apparently on the few occasions I met up with Amelia's group, Louisa wasn't there for one reason or another.'

'I think our paths might have crossed at some time,' Louisa added, 'but we were both busy and involved in other things.'

'Oh, I see,' Claire said, 'and then you met here at Amelia's wedding. How exciting.'

Marie picked up a posy of roses from the centre of the table and handed them to Louisa. 'I brought this in here for you,' she said. 'I saw the staff clearing the other room and I thought they might get misplaced. I hope you don't mind.'

'Oh, thank you,' Louisa replied. 'I was beginning to wonder where it was I would have been sorry to lose it.'

'Did you catch the bouquet?' Claire exclaimed. 'This just gets better and better.'

'It's her own posy, she is a bridesmaid don't forget,' Marie said, throwing her a warning look, but neither of them seemed to be put out and Damian just grinned and shook his head at his mother. He'd grown up with Claire's tendency towards nosiness and it didn't usually bother him, but there had been times when he was younger when he'd been embarrassed by her interest in his love life.

'How were things when you got back here this morning? Did Bryony give you the third degree?' Marie asked them.

'No, not really, although fortunately we managed to sneak in without her seeing us so I suppose by the time she did miss us everything was back under control,' Damian said. He looked around to check Bryony wasn't in hearing distance, although he had waited until she'd left the Sheridan's table before bringing Louisa to sit with his mother. 'She seems to have been in a bit of a funny mood today though.'

Marie was aware Claire's antennae for picking up a juicy bit of gossip were working overtime, so she tried to head off any discussion about Bryony's behaviour, although she felt it was significant that people like Damian had noticed something wrong. 'It's just the stress of the day I suppose,' she said, 'it all kicked off this morning with the cockle pickers and a few things went wrong after that but I'm sure she's alright now.'

Damian gently slipped his hand into Louisa's. 'Mmm, the cockle pickers, I wonder what's happening out there now. There's a rumour one of them has gone missing.'

'Oh, what a shame,' Claire said. 'Does that mean you might get called out?'

'Possibly,' he replied, and Marie could tell he knew more than he was letting on. Louisa looked alarmed but Damian did his best to reassure her. As an experienced and regular member of the crew Damian was regularly called on to take part in rescue operations, but for Marie it never got any easier. If Louisa was serious about this blossoming relationship she'd have to learn to cope with all the worry and stress involved, because to Damian it was a way of life he wouldn't want to change. She exchanged a worried look with Stuart before encouraging the couple to re-join their friends. If there was a chance Damian would have to leave, they needed to make the most of the evening that was left to them.

'They look really happy together,' Claire commented as she watched them walk away.

'Yes they do,' Marie agreed. 'Let's hope it stays that way, they're both due a little happiness.'

Claire nodded and the two men exchanged knowing glances; it was nothing new for their wives to be engaged in romantic discussions involving the younger generation.

'Here comes another happy couple,' Claire announced, and Marie turned to see Amelia and Greg approaching their table.

'She's like a whirling dervish,' Greg panted. 'I don't know where on earth she gets all her energy from.'

Amelia hooked her arm round his neck. 'You know what,' she said, 'I'm as high as a kite.'

Greg's expression changed to one of utter disbelief. 'Please don't tell me...' he began, and Amelia pealed with laughter.

'Oh, you are so easy to wind up,' she told him. 'I'm high on happiness, pure and simple happiness.'

'You little minx,' he replied, looking at Marie and grinning with relief.

'Hi guys,' Amelia said. 'Are you all enjoying yourselves?' Everyone assured her it was the best wedding they'd ever been to, but her eyes kept flicking over to where the Sheridans were sitting. 'I wish Katy could enjoy herself,' she said wistfully. 'Uncle Greg, will you do me a favour?' Her lips formed a little moue and Greg looked at her with apprehension. 'Oh dear,' he said, 'the only time you call me Uncle nowadays is when you want something, so I'm now feeling very nervous.'

Amelia patted his arm reassuringly. 'Oh it's nothing really, but you've met Piers' boss and his wife haven't you?'

Greg hesitated. 'Yes,' he replied, obviously wondering what was coming next. 'I've been introduced but I wouldn't say I know them. I am aware there is a problem of some sort and I do hope you're not getting me involved in any kind of domestic dispute.'

'No, it's nothing like that,' she told him. 'All I'm asking is, will you please go over and ask Katy to dance? Just one dance, that's all you need to do.'

Marie could see he was weakening. 'Put like that it sounds a fairly simple request,' he replied, 'but she's with her husband, who in case you haven't noticed has got a face like thunder and he may very well take exception to some stranger coming up to waltz his wife away.'

Amelia was good at being persuasive and persistent. 'But that's just the point you see, he won't care what Katy does. All he's concerned about is trying to talk to Louisa and understandably she doesn't want to speak to him.' Her face clouded over. 'You see the truth is, when Louisa was seeing him, apart from us telling her the usual things like she was stupid and he was the proverbial philanderer, we didn't consider his wife's feelings at all. When it seemed like there might be a future for Louisa and Paul we simply believed the marriage must have been on the rocks long before Louisa appeared on the scene.'

'I don't see how,' he said, looking towards the couple, 'asking her to dance makes any difference to all that.'

Amelia nodded thoughtfully. 'Well I don't suppose it will really,' she conceded, 'and I don't know her very well but she looks so unhappy and to be honest I feel guilty.'

Greg shrugged. 'I don't think you need to blame yourself for anything, it was his and to be fair Louisa's choice to behave like they did, but if it makes you feel any better I'll try to pluck up courage and ask her to take to the floor with me. What happens if she refuses?'

'At least you'll have tried.'

'And walk away feeling a real idiot.'

Amelia hugged him. 'So you'll do it? Bless you, Uncle Greg. If you like we could casually walk over in their direction and have a chat to open up an opportunity for you to ask her.'

'That sounds like a good idea except for the fact that I am already exhausted. I don't think I'm physically capable of doing any more dancing before I've had a break.'

Tugging his arm, she began to pull him away. 'Don't talk nonsense,' she exclaimed, 'there's a lot more energy left in you.'

Marie watched as Amelia grasped his hand to navigate him towards the table where the unhappy couple were sitting. Amelia successfully involved Katy and Greg in conversation while Paul Sheridan remained morosely staring across the room. As Greg led Katy to the dance floor, Amelia tripped lightly back to her friends, giving a triumphant thumbs up to Marie as she passed. Marie had no idea what Amelia was hoping to achieve but she was confident Bryony wouldn't share her elation if she saw Greg and Katy dancing together. An exchange she'd overheard on the downs concerning Katy had revealed a vulnerable side to Bryony's feelings about Greg which she hadn't shown to Marie that morning.

Chapter 10

Bryony glimpsed Greg and Katy dancing. They were comfortable in each other's arms as they moved effortlessly around the floor, and as she watched them a rising sense of panic enveloped her. The sooner she and Greg sealed their future together the better it would be. Suddenly Katy pulled away and began dodging between the other dancers to hurry towards the door leading out of the ballroom into the residents' area. It was impossible to make out Greg's expression but when he rushed after her she decided to follow.

The crippling shoes slowed her down and at first she could see no sign of them, but she hurried along the corridor towards the residents' cloakrooms. There was no reason for Katy Sheridan to be familiar with this part of the hotel and she was just about to turn round when she heard the sound of voices. Carrying on round the corner she almost bumped into Greg and she was shocked to see him holding Katy in his arms. He gestured to her to remain still and quiet and the reason why soon became obvious when she became aware of raised voices in an exchange which was quickly descending into a heated altercation.

When the woman's voice became clearer she was almost certain it belonged to Louisa, which must mean the person she was arguing with was Paul Sheridan. She slowly moved towards them. 'What's going on?' she asked, but Greg shook his head and held his hand up to silence her, but she held her ground, after all this was her hotel and her daughter's wedding. If there was any possibility of something wrong she had a right to know. 'What's going on?' she asked again, but then the answer became glaringly obvious as they all clearly heard Paul Sheridan imploring Louisa to renew their relationship. Before Louisa had time to finish her unmistakable rejection Katy pulled away from Greg to round the corner and confront them.

Bryony and Greg followed but she placed a hand on his arm to stop him going to Katy, who appeared to be in control. 'Don't worry,' Katy said, 'I'm not going to make a scene.' She stood quite still apart from a slight turn of her head as she looked intently at her husband. 'It comes as no surprise to learn you've been having an affair,' she said to him, and when Louisa tried to speak Katy stopped her. 'No, don't say anything Louisa, it is not the first time this has happened but as far as I'm concerned it will certainly be the last, because our marriage is over. Feel free to carry on.'

Bryony was surprised when Paul Sheridan made no effort to explain or console his wife but Louisa was distraught. 'I'm sorry, really sorry,' she said to Katy, 'but it's all over and it has been for months.'

'I know,' Katy replied. She stood looking at her abject husband. 'It's not a very edifying position to be in hearing your husband begging his ex-lover to take him back, but at least it has given me the determination to do what I should have done long ago.'

She turned to Greg, who led her away and Bryony walked beside them. 'She's probably in shock,' she said under her breath. 'We'll take her somewhere quiet where she won't be disturbed.'

Greg shook his head and she inwardly recoiled at the coldness in his voice. 'I'll deal with it,' he said. 'You get back to your duties, people will be wondering where you are.'

'But I want to help,' she insisted. 'I'm not trying to interfere.' She could hear the pleading in her own voice and she hated it, after all she'd done nothing wrong.

'You can help by leaving us alone for now. I'll find you when this is sorted out, I need to speak to you anyway but now isn't the right time.'

They'd reached the conservatory and Greg stopped outside the door. Katy was trembling and leaning heavily on Greg. For a moment Bryony sympathised with him but she was smarting from his rejection and after all, she was far more important to him than Katy. 'We do need to talk,' she said to him. 'I've got something important to tell you.'

His eyes were cold. 'So I believe,' he replied.

She turned away without speaking, there was obviously nothing to be gained by forcing the issue now and it was impossible to broach the subject in front of Katy Sheridan. All her earlier optimism had somehow drained away but she was determined to get something out of the evening's entertainment, so she returned to the ballroom in search of one of the few interesting, available men to lead her onto the dance floor.

Her prayer was answered when she caught sight of Amelia talking to a man Bryony recognised as Piers' uncle, but whose name she couldn't remember. After the introductions were completed and Amelia had reminded her that his name was Ethan Denning, it was only a matter of moments before he was expertly whisking her round the floor.

Enjoying a drink together afterwards, she was fascinated to learn about the chalet he owned in France, and for a few seconds her heart skipped a beat when he invited her and Colin to join him on a forthcoming skiing trip with a group of friends. Coming quickly back to reality, she admitted it was inconceivable to contemplate such a thing with Colin, but the possibility of a future trip with Greg filled her with excitement and longing. If only he would catch sight of her in the company of such an attractive man, she was positive it would push all thoughts of Katy Sheridan from his mind, but although she kept looking there was no sign of him. When Ethan offered her another cocktail she gracefully accepted, after all the night was still young.

Chapter 11

The pain relievers and water she'd consumed for the last hour had worked their wonders in easing her headache and bouts of dizziness, but in its wake had followed an even worse sensation. She'd successfully blotted out the feelings of panic when she considered the possible repercussions following her phone call earlier, but once again they came back into focus with a blinding reality of knowing she'd acted too hastily. What made it even worse, she had no idea how to retrieve the situation, and all she could do was sit it out and hope that Debbie had the good sense to ignore what her mother had told her. She mostly did that anyway so maybe it wasn't too much of a vain hope.

It might help if she had someone to talk to but Bryony was busy being the perfect hostess and she couldn't burden Stuart with it even if she wanted to, which at the moment she didn't, as she felt too ashamed. Claire wasn't an option as her thirst for gossip always got in the way of rational consideration. She did vaguely and briefly consider telling Greg but he seemed to be in a funny mood, and most unlike him, he'd seemed unwilling to talk when she'd tried chatting with him earlier. The welcome arrival of

Damian and Louisa pushed it temporarily from her mind and she turned to them in anticipation of sharing some happy conversation.

'Are you alright, Mum?' Damian asked. 'You were very deep in thought just then.'

'I'm fine,' she replied, 'just going over some of the events of the day. It's been lovely and I've really enjoyed it.' She looked at the two beaming faces. 'How about you two, are you enjoying yourselves?'

'Yes, it's fantastic,' Damian replied. 'Bryony and Stuart have done Amelia proud.'

'They certainly have,' she said, and watched with interest as the best man approached and asked for Damian's permission to steal Louisa away for a spell on the dance floor. They were already being treated as a couple by their friends and when Damian readily agreed but followed it up with a joking request to keep it short, he was obviously thinking along the same lines.

'My, you are smitten,' she said when he turned back to the table and he grinned and nodded.

'You could say that.'

'Well you seem very happy with each other, but try not to rush things, you've only just met after all.'

'Mum, stop worrying,' Damian replied. 'I'm not a little boy anymore.'

'I know,' she persisted, 'but I've heard she was involved with Paul Sheridan and I don't want you to get hurt again. I'm not interfering but...'

'Actually there was a bit of an incident earlier,' he said, 'but it's confidential.' His eyes flicked swiftly in Claire's direction and Marie nodded her understanding.

'Paul Sheridan followed Louisa when she went to the cloakroom and accosted her in the corridor. As if that wasn't bad enough his wife followed them and heard him begging Louisa to take him back. Apparently Louisa was just telling him to get lost in no uncertain terms when Katy interrupted and announced she was leaving him.'

'Oh dear,' Marie said, looking round the room for evidence of trouble, but everyone seemed to be enjoying themselves, oblivious to the situation. 'What's happening now?'

'From what I can gather he's already left and Greg is taking care of Katy. Apparently the marriage has been virtually over for ages but understandably she's feeling upset that this has happened here. Louisa, as you can see, is fine. Well, she was a bit shaken up too, but she recovered quickly.'

Marie was thoughtful. 'I suppose that means Paul Sheridan is now free to do whatever he wants.'

'Like get back with Louisa?' Damian asked with a broad smile. 'I don't think there's any danger of that happening.'

Marie returned the smile. 'I'm sure you're right,' she replied, 'but I don't understand; why is Greg taking care of Katy?'

'Oh sorry, I missed that bit out. Greg was with Katy when she witnessed everything.'

'Was he indeed?' Marie said. She had no idea why Greg and Katy were in the corridor together but she decided not to ask and simply hoped for everyone's sake that Bryony didn't find out.

'It's not looking too good in the bay,' Damian told her. 'I went out and had a chat with Geoff and it seems two men are thought to be missing and a search is still going on. As it's been a long and busy day for the lads there is a good chance I will have to join them later, so I'm determined to make the most of the time I have left here.'

His eyes were smiling and Marie was reminded of the cheeky little boy who was able to win her over with just one look. 'Louisa's on her way back,' she told him, 'so go and enjoy yourselves while you can, and don't worry if you have to dash off, I'll see she's taken care of.'

'Thanks Mum,' he replied, 'you're a star.'

Chapter 12

Bryony accepted the glass being thrust into her hand and expertly and delicately took a tiny sip. If she'd only consumed a fraction of the drinks bought for her during the course of the evening she'd probably be lying on her bed nursing a headache by now. Looking round the room, she wondered who was benefiting from other peoples' generosity, because she was certain the waiters weren't clearing her full glasses from the tables.

She tapped her foot impatiently; she was desperate to see Greg and tell him her news but the opportunity simply wasn't presenting itself. On the rare occasions when she found a chance to disappear for a short time Greg was nowhere to be seen, and when he was available she couldn't leave for one reason or another. At this rate she would end up telling no-one.

The incident between Louisa and the Sheridan couple had the makings of becoming a juicy bit of gossip, but she couldn't help feeling sorry for Damian if he was being used as a pawn by Louisa to regain her ex-lover's interest. What she couldn't understand was Greg's involvement in it all, but she decided against asking him as for some reason he'd been very reluctant to tell her anything.

The image of him with his arms around Katy Sheridan kept imprinting itself on her eyes no matter how many times she tried to convince herself it held no significance, but what on earth was he doing getting himself involved in other people's affairs? He hardly knew them and Louisa didn't appear to be in any way distressed. He'd been very interested in the couple when he spotted them outside and he'd seemed particularly concerned about Katy Sheridan, but whatever was bugging him was a mystery as far as she was concerned. She resented the fact that he seemed to be taking it out on her when she'd done nothing wrong. All this made it more important to talk with him and she resolved to do it soon whether it was convenient or not. 'It's beginning to resemble a farce,' she muttered under her breath.

'Oh Bryony, there you are, we've been looking for you for ages,' shrilled a voice from one of the groups nearby. 'Can you possibly have another word with the DJ? The music, well if you can call it music, is much too loud.' Patting her chest dramatically, she added, 'I can even feel it throbbing in here.'

Bryony felt like telling her to enjoy the feeling while she had the chance but with superhuman effort she managed to control herself, and with a tight smile told her she would try to get Colin to do something about it. 'There are other places to sit, of course,' she added with a touch of sarcasm, but she turned round quickly when she heard Greg say her name. Smiling apologetically at the bemused guests, he led her away.

'Bryony,' he said when they had walked a few steps, 'we need to talk.'

'You are dead right,' she said, 'but I've had the distinct feeling you've been trying to avoid me.'

'That's not true,' he said, 'but is there something wrong?'

'I don't know, you tell me.'

Pulling her into the seclusion of a corner behind a pillar, he said quietly, 'I had a little chat with Marie earlier.'

She waited for him to elaborate but he said nothing and so for a few moments neither of them spoke. 'Is that supposed to convey something to me?' she asked impatiently.

'I thought it may do,' he replied, 'but obviously it doesn't so I'll refresh your memory. Marie told me what you're planning to do.'

'I still have no idea what you're talking about,' she replied, playing for time while she tried to remember the conversation earlier in the day, but a lot had happened since then and her memory was hazy. She was fairly certain she hadn't mentioned Greg by name but Marie had probably guessed anyway, it wouldn't have been difficult for her to work it out. Her heart was pounding with dread; surely Marie hadn't broken her promise after all these years. 'What exactly has Marie told you?' she asked.

'Simply that you're intending to tell Colin and Ralph that you are leaving Colin to be with me. Why? Is there something else she could have told me?'

'Of course not,' she replied with relief, 'but why is that such a surprise? You knew I was going to do it sometime, but I can't believe she told you. Why would Marie do that?'

'Don't blame Marie,' he replied, 'she was totally oblivious to the fact that I wasn't in on your secretive plan, and who can blame her? It is hardly credible, after all.'

'Oh God,' she exclaimed, 'I remember now. I meant to tell her it was going to be a surprise and I don't think I did.' She lifted her face to him. 'I'm so sorry Greg, I'm really sorry.'

'Were you really going to break it to Colin and Ralph this weekend?' he asked in disbelief. 'Before you'd even told me?'

'I was going to tell you first,' she explained, 'but I just wanted it to be a surprise.'

'Well we can safely say you've achieved that,' he replied. He turned to leave but she stretched out her hand and laid it on his arm to hold him back.

'Greg, please listen to me. I know you're upset but this doesn't change anything. Of course I won't do anything this weekend if you don't want me to, but I am leaving Colin no matter what happens.'

'You must do as you wish,' he said, 'you usually do anyway.'

His reaction shocked her and she challenged him in anger. 'I suppose you're hurrying back to console Katy Sheridan.'

His face blazed with fury. 'What is that supposed to mean?' he demanded.

'Well if you don't know I can't tell you,' she retorted.

'I think we'd better leave it there, before one of us says something we don't mean. I'll see you later, perhaps by then we'll be in a better frame of mind to talk. I can only suppose that you have been affected by all the stress of the wedding.'

She grabbed the lifeline. 'I'm sorry Greg, you're right of course. I haven't been thinking straight. Can't we go the conservatory and talk? There will be less chance of us being disturbed there.'

'Let's leave it for now and decide later, I think I'll go out for a walk to clear my mind.'

She remained where he left her until he was lost from sight, and she knew she had to find a way to convince him that nothing had really changed. The only thing she was guilty of was making a decision without consulting him first, which wasn't exactly an unforgivable crime. She was annoyed with Marie for telling Greg, but in fairness it was probably better that he'd found out before she'd actually made a complete fool of herself in his eyes.

Chapter 13

Tom drove as fast as he could without exceeding the speed limit; he didn't want to add to his problems by being stopped by the police and delay his journey back to Merebank. His thoughts flew rapidly between the family he'd left behind and his brother and friend who he was desperate to see safe and sound. He was clinging on to the hope that it would all turn out to be a mistake and he'd find them celebrating their success with money stacked away in their pockets. Deep down he didn't really believe it would happen but the alternative didn't bear thinking about and he pushed it from his mind.

When he'd first heard about the opportunity to fish in Merebank Bay it had seemed like a golden opportunity to make some much needed money. He already owned a dinghy so he'd believed it wouldn't prove too difficult to arrange, but after a quick inspection he'd decided it needed some repairs. The cost of taking it into the workshop at the boatyard was now beyond him, so he'd decided to carry the repairs out himself. Once the decision was made he'd confided in Danny and Rick and between them they decided on a day for working on the dinghy, so they would be ready when the cockle beds in Merebank

Bay were opened.

The worst thing proved to be lying to Sharon, who he knew would forbid him to go if she found out what he was planning. Lying didn't come easily to him and especially to her, but desperation drove him on and once he'd mentioned it to Danny and Rick there was no going back. When the weather forecaster promised an unseasonably warm weekend, Sharon started to make plans for a family trip to the seaside, allowing him the opportunity to concentrate on the proposed fishing trip. Surreptitiously, he tried to check the whereabouts of the things they would need to keep themselves safe. Now he was wishing he'd never heard of cockles and most of all that he'd ever mentioned it to Danny and Rick. Danny was headstrong and he could just imagine him putting pressure on Rick to ignore Tom's warnings and decision to call off the trip. He would have to be prepared to face Amy and Rick's wife Beth when he returned home whatever the outcome. How he would look his mother in the eyes was not worth contemplating, but he hoped and prayed his brother and best friend would be with him.

When he arrived he quickly found somewhere to park before half walking and running towards the seafront, where he could see a lot of activity around the jetty he'd visited earlier in the day. The light was falling but the horizon was visible and he looked with fear beating in his chest at the thought of what might be out there. What he couldn't understand was why neither of them had made any contact with their family or the emergency services; it didn't make sense when they both had mobiles. Surely it couldn't be something simple like a failure to get a signal, but even then they'd be surrounded by other fishermen who could help them out.

He walked towards the group of official-looking men but as he got near them he lost his nerve and stopped abruptly, before turning to walk back in the direction he'd come from. His head was spinning and he didn't know what to do. He knew he should phone Sharon to tell her he'd arrived but she would demand news which he hadn't got, but then if he waited until he'd found out something it may not be what she wanted to hear. Full of indecision, he strode backwards and forwards, vacillating between the options open to him, but still he struggled to know what to do. He was aware that someone would be waiting to speak to a relative of the missing men but at the same time he couldn't rid himself of the picture of the three women anxiously waiting his call.

He groaned when he heard the ringtone coming from his pocket telling him the decision had already been taken away from him. Apprehensively, he took the call, and with a mixture of dread and relief he heard the familiar sound of her voice.

'Tom?' she said, her voice was quivering with trepidation. 'Is there any news?'

'No,' he replied, 'but I've only just arrived. I'm just going down to see what I can find out, but it isn't easy to know who to ask. How are things there?'

'As you would expect,' she told him, 'we're all frantic with worry. Amy's crying all the time and your mum's making endless cups of tea. I'm awash with tea already, I don't know what I'll be like by morning.'

Morning seemed like a lifetime away and he couldn't picture how he would pass the time and survive it if something didn't happen before then. 'Let's hope it doesn't last that long,' he said.

'What's it like there?' she asked.

He considered how to describe the scene without adding to her fear. 'It's a bit unreal, very different from when we were here today. The place is full of the people involved with the search and there are lots of spectators, including some from that wedding party you saw this afternoon.'

'Oh gosh, that seems ages ago now,' she whispered, and ruefully he agreed.

'I must say they look a bit out of place in their wedding finery to say the least.'

He could hear voices in the background and guessed it was either Amy or his mother, and he was in no mood to speak to either of them, so when Sharon told him he'd better go and find out was happening because Amy kept asking her what he was saying, he readily agreed. Despite that, he was reluctant to cut off his connection to the only person he could talk to and once again he tried to explain. 'Sharon, I'm really sorry...' he began, but she stopped him.

'I know,' she said, in a tone which made clear she was still angry with him. She wasn't ready to forgive, he had a long way to go before he achieved that.

He picked out a man who seemed to be in charge and began to walk towards him, but he hung back and waited when he saw another man walk over to talk to him. He couldn't help overhearing as they raised their voices above the noise of all the activity around them, and when he realised they were discussing the rescue he moved closer and stopped to listen.

'What's the latest news, Geoff?' the man asked,

and for some reason Tom thought he sounded vaguely familiar, but he didn't know why.

'Not a lot unfortunately, Greg,' the other man replied. 'It would appear that two men might be missing but we can't be sure. One of the local fishermen said he'd seen two novices struggling to pull their dinghy free from a sand bank but they'd refused his offer of help, and then not long ago another local returned and told a similar story. My fear is that they aren't aware of quick sands out there and getting out of the dinghy could put them in real danger.' Tom lost the drift of the conversation when a helicopter hovered nearby, but when it moved away he heard the official telling his friend, 'It's a worst-case scenario in some ways. We've got to employ all the emergency services but it could all turn out to be a false alarm. The two men could be safe at home with their wives counting the money they've earned.'

'I suppose we've got to hope so,' the man called Greg replied, 'even if it does cost a fortune for no good purpose.'

'You are so right,' the official replied, 'but if they are out there I wish one of their families would get in touch, we need all the information we can get. Anyway Greg, aren't you supposed to be at the wedding?'

Tom realised where he remembered the man from, he'd helped to catch Rusty when he'd interrupted the wedding group having their photos taken. 'I certainly am,' he heard him reply. 'I just came out for a breath of fresh air but I suppose I'd better be getting back. Hope it all has a successful conclusion. See you later.'

Tom knew he was wasting time and he had to do

something, so summoning up all his strength he approached the man who'd been talking. 'Can you tell me what's going on?' he asked.

The man turned to face him, 'In what way?' he asked brusquely, his patience with idle sightseers already wearing thin, 'other than two men are missing.'

'I know,' Tom muttered. Something in his voice made the man look more closely at him. 'One of them is my brother,' Tom added gloomily and the man's demeanour changed instantly.

'Come with me,' he said, and looking round, added, 'are you on your own?'

Tom nodded and followed him. It was a long time since he'd been unable to keep up with anyone but he found himself struggling to keep pace with the man's steps as he strode quickly along the prom. At first Tom had no idea where they were going until they approached the lifeboat station and he was led into a room at the side where the man went immediately to fill a kettle and switch it on.

'Fancy a coffee?' he asked. 'I'm having one so it's no trouble.'

Tom was impatient to find out what was happening but he could see the man would be ready in his own good time and not before, so he nodded. 'Yes please, milk and one sugar if you've got it.'

'You'd be surprised what we've got here, everything except alcohol. That goes without saying obviously.' He handed Tom a mug of coffee and indicated for him to sit on one of the chairs while he walked round to sit facing Tom across a small table. Tom took two big gulps.

'Thanks,' he said, 'I didn't realise how thirsty I was

but I suppose I haven't had a drink for ages.'

The man picked up a pen and placed a sheet of paper in front of him on the table. 'First things first, what's your name?'

'Tom, Tom Lester.'

'Geoff Hayes.' He held out his hand and took Tom's in a firm handshake which left him thinking he would be lucky if he found all his fingers in one piece afterwards. 'Okay. Do you live locally?' he asked, and Tom shook his head. 'I think before we go any further,' Geoff said, 'there are a few things I'd like to clarify about the state of the vessel they were in and how much experience of this kind of fishing they've got. Do you think you can help with that?'

Tom nodded. 'I'll try.'

'Right, first things first, who owns the boat?'

'I do,' Tom replied.

Geoff's eyebrows lifted with surprise. 'Well at least that means you'll be able to tell me what condition it was in,' he said.

'We checked it over yesterday and it seemed alright when we'd finished,' he said thoughtfully, remembering the rush job they'd made of it. At the time he'd been reasonably happy it was safe to use but that was before he'd found out about the complications of collecting cockles. They'd probably spent too much time shortening the handles of garden rakes to use to scrape the sand, which he'd heard somewhere would make good substitutes for the real tools used by experienced fishermen. 'It hasn't really been used a lot this last few years,' he added lamely.

'I see. What condition was the engine in? If it

hadn't been used for a long time it was probably in need of a thorough service.'

'Well it has been checked out from time to time because a mate has borrowed it occasionally and he's a mechanic, so he's serviced it for me.'

Geoff was making notes which he scribbled on a scrap of paper. 'You said your brother is one of the men out there, is the second man related to you?'

'No, he's my best friend.'

'Am I right in thinking they don't have much sailing experience, especially at sea?'

'They have no experience of sailing at sea.'

Geoff raised his head and looked straight into his eyes. Tom shuffled uncomfortably, the man obviously thought he was idiot and he couldn't argue with that.

'The sea is a very unpredictable element of nature,' Geoff said, 'and it requires treating with respect. It can also be very dangerous and every eventuality should be addressed before setting sail on her. But still,' he said, resting his chin on his hand, 'I realise you are very worried so I will get this over as quickly as possible.' He sat back in his seat and looked at Tom. 'I need to establish some facts but I'm not here to judge you or criticise the actions which got your brother and friend into this situation. Our sole purpose is to help and rescue people in danger or difficult situations, and that I can assure you is what we're trying to do.'

Tom nodded gratefully but the more questions Geoff asked the more nervous he felt. This man obviously put his life in danger trying to rescue people and he must think Tom was an absolute idiot, despite what he said.

'Right, let's make a start with a quick run through of the basic essentials. Is the boat equipped with flares, whistles, a radio, telephone, and life jackets? Do they have high-visibility jackets and warm clothing to wear and do they have a contingency plan in place if something goes wrong?'

Tom's head was reeling. 'I think the emergency stuff like flares and things are all there, and the life jackets, well there's at least one. No, I'm sure there are two. I have no idea what they are wearing and I'm pretty sure they have no contingency plan.' He slumped and the rickety chair almost gave way. He guessed they had no plan at all, never mind a contingency one, whatever that may consist of.

'We've nearly finished,' Geoff said, but there is just one last question. 'Do they have a permit to fish the cockle beds?'

'No,' Tom said. 'It was a last-minute decision, it was my idea originally, but I saw it on the news and realised it would be too dangerous so I called it off. They must have decided to go ahead without me. I've been here all day with my family and I had no idea Danny and Rick were out there.'

'Where are you family now?'

'At home worrying and cursing me, I expect.'

'I see,' Geoff said at last. 'Perhaps you can explain something. There are other men out there who've got into difficulties but they've signalled for help and we've managed to bring them in safely. The thing that's puzzling us is why your brother and his mate haven't contacted anyone. I presume they both have mobiles.'

Tom nodded. 'I know, that's what I can't understand. They never go anywhere without their phones. Please,' he begged, 'please can you tell me what's going on? I've heard nothing except a little snippet I heard on the news before I left home.'

Geoff adjusted his position on the small chair. His large body, made even bulkier by the waterproof clothing he was wearing, left him very little room for comfort. 'I'll tell you all we know, which actually isn't very much. One of our local experienced fishermen told us he'd come across a light dinghy with two men aboard who seemed to be stuck in the mud-bank. Worried in case they didn't get out before the tide turned he offered to help, but they turned him down, saying they had got it all under control. Later another fisherman told a similar story but by the time he saw them the situation was getting more serious and he offered to get help to pull them out. This time they accepted but when he told them they'd have to throw some of their catch overboard to lighten the boat they again refused.'

Tom's eyes were wide, his expression incredulous. 'Why would they do that?' he gasped.

'Money,' Geoff replied, plain and simple money. 'They said they couldn't throw the equivalent of two or three hundred pounds away and were determined to get themselves out.'

'Had they only earned that amount of money for a full day's work?' Tom asked, remembering the astronomical figures talked about on the television.

'Oh no,' Geoff replied, 'they will have been handing over their catch to the big boys who take large containers out to collect from all the individual small boats. They say it's to allow the fishermen to collect more without having to keep coming back to shore and also to move the cockles on to be refrigerated while they are still fresh. The fact that some of them use it to their own advantage to avoid declaring how much money they are raking in is neither here nor there to them.' He stood up. 'I'm sorry I can't tell you much more but as you've probably seen already, we are doing all we can to find them.'

Tom pushed himself up wearily. 'How serious is it?' he asked fearfully. 'Just how much danger are they in?'

'With a bit of luck, if they didn't manage to free the boat the tide will have done it for them. In that case they will probably try to head for shore if the engine is functioning, or if not or the tide's too strong they might be drifting out to sea. Either way we should spot them and pick them up before very long.'

It sounded horrific and Tom shuddered at the thought of his brother drifting in God knows which direction. He wasn't even a good swimmer, not that that would make much difference out there. 'What's the worst-case scenario?' he asked, bracing himself.

'We don't consider that around here,' Geoff told him, 'we believe in keeping positive.'

'But what if...?'

'Don't start what-iffing. Now let's get out there and see if there's any news.' Geoff was locking the cabin door behind them when they heard the sound of Tom's phone ringing. 'You'd better answer that, son,' Geoff said, and Tom pulled it from his pocket.

'It's my wife Sharon,' he said.

'Well be quick and see what she has to say. With a bit of luck they might have arrived home.'

Tom put it on loudspeaker and Sharon's voice split the air. 'Tom!' she shrieked. 'Tom, something's happened.'

Tom's heart hammered in his chest. 'What's happened?' he asked.

'Amy went back home for some of the things she needed for the children and she heard a beeping...' Her voice broke and Tom waited impatiently for her to continue, his eyes on Geoff who was listening intently.

'Sharon,' Tom shouted, 'tell me what's happened!'

'She found where the noise was coming from and it was Danny's phone. He'd left it on charge where he thought she wouldn't see it last night but he must have forgotten it.'

Tom's shoulders slumped with relief; this wasn't as bad as he'd expected and would at least answer one question, but his relief was short-lived when Sharon continued, 'but that's not all, his inhalers were with it.' Her voice rose even higher. 'Tom, he's lost out there without his inhalers.'

Tom gasped. 'Oh Jesus,' he whispered. 'Is Amy sure he hasn't got any others with him?'

'Well he isn't likely to have left his phone behind deliberately so those must be the ones he intended to take. Oh Tom, I'm so frightened, I don't know what to do. I've got to go, one of the children is crying and he'll wake the others up. Amy's not coping, I wish you were here but I know you can't be. Have you heard anything, is there any news?'

'No, but I'm with the man in charge and he's very optimistic they'll find them soon.'

'Let's hope so,' she called.

Tom whispered, 'I love you Sharon,' but she'd already gone.

'How important are those inhalers?' Geoff asked.

'Very,' Tom replied, tears running down his face. 'He can't go without them for this length of time even on an ordinary day.'

Geoff's face was resolute as he walked away from the hut; an emergency had turned into an even more desperate situation with this latest turn of events. He would have to double check if there was anything more they could do to step up the search.

Tom followed him out and went to lean on the railings. He cursed his own stupidity which had set this chain of events in motion. Geoff had promised to contact him if there was any news so he decided to get away from the constant reminder of what was happening and walk inland. Pubs were catering for the swell of customers who were invading the town to witness the drama which was unfolding, and his stomach groaned with hunger. The smell of food reminded him he hadn't eaten since the picnic on the downs and he'd hardly drunk any liquid.

He fingered the money in his pocket but he resisted the urge to buy food. Sinking onto a bench, he folded his arms across his griping belly and bent over, doubling his body and taking solace in the pain. He refused to eat as long as Danny and Rick were lost out there and he groaned with despair at the thought of the fear they must be feeling. Knowing them they'd probably only taken enough food and drink to last them for as long as they were expecting to be fishing. He guessed they were planning to be back before dark so they could get home at a reasonable time. Either they'd got into difficulties from the start or they'd got carried away with their success and then something had gone wrong.

From what Geoff had heard it sounded like the latter, which would surely mean they couldn't be too far away. He shivered in the light clothes he was wearing but he didn't want to be comfortable, he believed that by being cold and miserable he would be able to share their suffering and maybe by doing so he could somehow make things better for them. He lost track of time but when he stood up his body was stiff and cold, and rubbing his arms to generate some feeling, he began to walk slowly back to the jetty. As he approached he saw the lifeboat returning and oblivious to his aching bones, he started to run to the lifeboat landing station. Panting for breath, he grabbed the first person he came to. 'Have they found them?' he demanded. 'Are they safe?'

Hearing the urgency in his voice the man sensed this was more than a simple enquiry and told him what he'd heard. 'I don't know any specific details but I think they've escorted a boat in.' Reluctantly, aware that he would be dashing the young man's hopes, he added, 'I'm not sure but I don't think it's the one that's missing.'

Tom looked around, desperately trying to catch sight of Geoff, but in the falling light he found it difficult to differentiate one man from another. He approached an official-looking man who showed no patience with his enquiry until Tom blurted out, 'It's my brother and best mate you're searching for, have you found them?'

'Sorry mate,' the man said, 'this isn't them. We know the crew of the boat we've escorted in and it definitely isn't them. We've been helping to get them back to shore for a while. Geoff is over there, go and have a word with him.'

'Thanks,' Tom said as he wearily made his way across to where Geoff was standing talking.

'Hi,' Geoff said when he caught sight of Tom. 'The crew are changing over and then going out to make another search helped by the coastguard helicopter. The tide is quite strong now so they may have drifted further out.' He caught a close sight of Tom's fear-stricken face. 'Have you had anything to eat or drink?'

Tom shook his head. 'I don't want anything,' he said under his breath.

'Why?' asked Geoff. 'You won't help them by not having a drink, and don't forget we need you to be on the ball when we bring them in. Go and get yourself something so you can be of some use to your brother and your mate when they're safely back on shore.'

Tom couldn't feign optimism. 'If they come back safely,' he said.

'Don't you forget what I told you earlier,' Geoff insisted. 'Now do as I say and go and get something to eat and drink.'

Tom had lost all appetite for anything and when Geoff asked him if he had any money he nodded and walked disconsolately away. He desperately wanted to hear Sharon's reassuring voice but he couldn't face the inevitable questions, so he stroked the instrument in his pocket and willed her to know how much he loved and needed her.

Chapter 14

Energy and excitement flowed through the building; it was like a charge of electricity slowly fizzing in preparation for the time when it would fire up the magnificent grand finale of the firework display. Bryony was determined to enjoy herself and a delicious sense of achievement alleviated the niggling worm of apprehension following the confrontation with Greg earlier. Having the whole hotel at their disposal gave everyone the choice to take part in the dancing, have a quiet drink in the wine bar, or sit chatting in the lounge while still feeling part of the proceedings. It had turned out to be even more successful than she'd envisaged and she silently thanked Ralph once again for his fantastic foresight.

Now when everything was running smoothly without her direction, she'd finally allowed herself to enjoy several of the delicious cocktails put at her disposal, and gradually the potential fallout from her actions didn't seem so scary. As she'd so rightly pointed out to Greg, no harm had been done and so there was no reason why anyone would get hurt. She supposed his pride had taken a knock because it was she who'd made the move, but they had been planning this, or at least a version of what she'd had in mind, for months. The biggest hurdle was achieving everything before the deadline for their departure to embark on the cruise. She harboured no doubts of her ability to win him over when he heard about her decision to join him, but it would need a certain amount of finesse to keep his tightly guarded self-esteem intact.

Needing to do something more satisfying than drifting from group to group or maintaining a constant and futile check on Colin's consumption of alcohol, she made her way to the kitchen. The staff had voluntarily taken part in drawing lots to determine which shifts they would work during the course of the day and evening, but Luke, the head chef, had remained adamant that he would remain on duty for the whole time. Only under her direct orders had he taken regular breaks since coming on duty and she was determined to remunerate him generously to show her appreciation. There only remained the task of providing the bacon sandwiches after the fireworks and then he could have a well-earned rest.

Initially she'd been unable to understand the necessity for providing more food, but she'd been persuaded of the benefits of a tempting hot sandwich for the guests who ventured outside to watch the firework display. Wanting to persuade as many people as possible to witness the display had been instrumental in helping her to make a final decision, and she'd consoled herself that offering this simple incentive was a small price to pay. Privately she'd recognised a wonderful opportunity to showcase the innovative and flexible choices available to prospective wedding customers, but she agreed to the proposal without pointing that out.

Both Luke and Justin looked suitably discomforted when she walked into the kitchen and found them talking, but Ralph, who was also taking part in the discussion, returned her gaze with his usual equanimity. 'What's going on?' she asked. 'Is there something I should know about?'

Ralph was the first to reply. 'There's nothing going on and nothing for you to worry about.' Turning to include the other two men who'd recovered slightly from being caught out by their boss, they were still reluctant to incur her anger, so Ralph decided to explain the situation himself. 'We were just discussing what to do about the supper,' he said. 'I made the suggestion that it wouldn't be appropriate to have the firework display at all if the men haven't been rescued, but that we could still provide the sandwiches.' Before she had time to interrupt and point out it was her decision to make, Ralph held up his hand. 'As it turns out we are left with no choice as Geoff has just informed me there can be no fireworks while the rescue operation is underway. There are the helicopters to consider and the rescuers are still hoping to see a flare from the missing boat.' He shrugged with resignation and sympathy for her obvious disappointment. 'We have no option but to comply,' he said, 'but it would be a nice gesture if we could include the onshore crew and all the other helpers by offering them some food.'

Bryony tensed but although she kept her eyes averted she knew Luke and Justin were waiting for her anger to explode, and she wasn't going to give them that satisfaction, especially in front of Ralph. Fury was burning inside but her response was measured and controlled. 'Unfortunately we haven't got enough bacon or bread rolls to include all and sundry,' she said sweetly.

'That's not quite how I would describe them, Bryony,' Ralph replied with mildly implied criticism. 'They are our friends and very brave men, to say nothing of the fact that they've been working voluntarily all day. Personally I think the least we can do is offer them a bacon sandwich.' He waited for Bryony to comment but she was struggling to contain her anger, which was directed towards all of them for discussing this without her knowledge. Never before had this happened and it was a bitter pill to swallow. Ralph was waiting but when she made no reply he went on. 'The food issue has already been resolved by Luke who's going to supplement it with the bacon and sausages put aside for breakfast.' Bryony began to protest but was forestalled by Ralph, who continued, 'And he's already taken the emergency store from the freezer so it will be ready for tomorrow morning.' With a satisfied smile, he added, 'So you see, everything is under control and you really have nothing to worry about.'

Luke and Justin could barely look her in the eye but still they'd gone along with all this subterfuge and she would find it hard to forgive. The hardest thing to understand was her father-in-law's attitude; it was a break from his normal behaviour and she didn't quite know how to respond without appearing rude.

'I suppose you've already had a word with the men and cancelled the fireworks,' she said, with a hint of sarcasm in her voice.

'Of course not,' Ralph replied, 'that would be too presumptuous of us.'

Fixing her eyes on Justin, leaving him in no doubt who she was holding responsible for the situation he found himself in, she said coldly, 'I don't understand why no-one consulted me about these rather important changes to my plans.'

Justin faced her. 'I did try, Mrs Portland,' he said, 'but you were busy so I didn't want to disturb you.'

'I'm sure I would have preferred to be disturbed than have matters taken out of my hands. I can't think of anything I was doing that would be deemed more important than this.'

'I sent Justin to find you,' Ralph told her, 'twice actually, but you apparently waved him away both times. He told me you were in a discussion with Greg and obviously didn't want to be disturbed.'

His voice was steady and no-one noticed any change in his manner, but Bryony caught a sign of something curious in his eyes as they held her gaze for a few seconds longer than normal. Could it be he was already suspicious of her and Greg? If so, it was becoming even more imperative for them to finalise their plans so she could tell Ralph in a calm and reasonable manner, but before that could be done she had to deal with the current situation. By the use of a little ingenuity she could turn this episode to her advantage by giving Justin the opportunity of demonstrating his managerial skills to Ralph.

The smile was well rehearsed and perfectly formed, ready for any situation, but it was no less appealing for that. 'Well, I must say I'm very grateful to you. I confess I was so taken up with enjoying myself I lost touch with what was happening and of course you're right, Ralph, it would be very thoughtless to go ahead with those two poor men missing.' Turning to Luke, she asked with genuine concern in her voice, 'Will you be able to manage? You've already put it in far too many hours.'

'No problem,' he replied, 'don't forget I've already got all my staff here on the premises.'

Her beaming response left him in no doubt that she considered him a gift from heaven, and then she turned her attention to Justin, but not before slipping her arm through Ralph's in a gesture of affectionate possession.

'I'm sorry Justin, but I'm going to insist my father-in-law accompanies me back to the dance floor. He's spent far too much time away from his guests already, and especially his granddaughter.' Now the full blaze of her attention was turned onto Ralph. 'You really should be enjoying yourself instead of worrying about details like this, I have full confidence in Luke to provide the food and absolutely no qualms concerning Justin's ability to organise things, so come along, let's go and dance.'

Ralph allowed himself to be drawn away but his expression showed he believed he'd somehow been outmanoeuvred by Bryony, who after just one dance excused herself on the pretext of remembering something pressing she had to do.

When Justin tentatively approached her sometime later he was surprised to find her in a relaxed and approachable mood. 'I'm sorry Mrs P.,' he said, 'I didn't want to go behind your back but it was hard with Mr Portland asking us to do it.'

'Don't worry,' she was quick to assure him, 'it's quite alright, and you did the right thing. I meant what I said, you know. I really do have confidence in you and I'm quite sure you and Ellie are destined for great things.'

Justin was almost overcome with relief and surprise. 'Thanks,' he said gratefully.

'It's a pleasure,' Bryony told him. For a few seconds after he'd turned away to go and pass on the good news to Ellie, she stood and wondered if he was ready to take over her position. He looked so young and frightened of being on the receiving end of a dressing down she began to doubt whether he had it in him to be the one giving the orders and reprimands, but it was too late for that now. Hurrying after him, she called him back. 'A little word of advice,' she said quietly, 'don't cancel the fireworks just yet, those men might well be brought back safely and then there'll be cause for a double celebration. You don't want to be found to have acted too soon.'

'Oh, thanks for the advice, Mrs P.,' he replied, and Bryony simply smiled and watched him hurry back to Ellie to tell her they had the best boss in the world despite her unpredictable nature.

The slow trickle of people leaving the hotel hadn't registered until she was confronted by the sight of Damian rushing through the reception area, oblivious to anyone who happened to be in his path. Louisa, who was witnessing for the first time a member of the lifeboat crew answering his call to duty, was standing wide-eyed and fearful, and Marie had draped her arm around the girl in a comforting gesture. As Louisa was significantly taller than Marie, Bryony thought they made a comical sight but she went over to find out the latest news as they would surely be aware of what was happening.

She directed her questions to Marie, who she felt would be able to provide a more rational response to her enquiries because although she would be full of concern for her son, she was well used to the part he played in the rescue operations. 'Are there any further developments?' she asked. 'I haven't heard anything for a while.'

Marie shook her head and slipped her arm back to her side. 'No,' she said, 'there's nothing to report, I'm afraid.' She shook her head. 'I only wish there was.'

Bryony was puzzled. 'But hasn't Damian gone rushing off? I thought he was only on emergency callout.'

'Well yes he is, but this is an emergency and some of the crew have been on duty for hours. They've called in the standby crew to take over the search.'

Bryony nodded. 'I see.' She turned to Louisa who was listening intently. 'It's a shame for you but don't let it ruin your night, you are a bridesmaid after all and I'm sure Damian will soon be back safe and sound.'

'He will be,' reiterated Marie, 'and hopefully with the lost fishermen safe and well.'

'Amen to that,' Bryony replied. She waited until Louisa had drifted away with her friends before challenging Marie. 'Why did you tell Greg what I was planning to do?' she asked.

Marie looked thoughtful. 'I'm not sure I know what you mean, I don't think I've told him anything.'

'Oh come on,' Bryony said impatiently, 'you told him I was leaving Colin. I must say I never expected you to break a confidence.'

Marie waited until the people milling around had passed but Bryony was almost past caring and couldn't stop herself making little tutting noises. 'I did mention,' Marie said at last, 'that you were intending to leave Colin soon, but I didn't tell him anything he didn't know already, although I must say he seemed to be surprised that you were planning to do it this weekend. Anyway,' she added, 'how could I have *told him*, as you say, when you'd planned it together?'

'But you see we hadn't, it was all meant to be a surprise and now he's cross with me.' She saw the incredulity on Marie's face. 'Oh for goodness sake don't look so shocked, we've always intended to be together but we just hadn't worked out the details. I thought it would be a nice surprise but unfortunately Greg didn't see it that way.'

'At least you've confirmed what I suspected; it is Greg you are leaving Colin for. Tell me something, I remember now that you said it all had to be sorted before you go on holiday. Are you both going on the cruise?'

Bryony nodded. 'Please don't say anything about this before we've had a chance to discuss it, I have a suspicion now that he will be far from happy when he learns about it but I know I can win him round.'

Marie stared at her. 'You're not going on the cruise without telling him first. Please tell me you're not.'

Bryony was losing her patience and responded sharply. 'You sound as if he wouldn't want me there.'

'Oh Bryony,' she said quietly, 'I have no idea of Greg's feelings but you said he's annoyed at your plan to break the news to Colin this weekend. How do you think he'll react to hearing this? I can't believe you intended to spring it on him this weekend of all times.'

'Well it seemed a good idea at the time, but I must admit I'm having second thoughts, so stop worrying about it. Now I must go and carry on circulating, I thought I'd spoken to just about everyone but someone new keeps popping up. I'm not sure they've all been invited but I expect Colin has been throwing out invitations to all his cohorts.' Clasping Marie's hands in hers, she tried to shake off her own apprehensions and reassure Marie. 'I think you need a drink, why don't you go back into the ballroom and take your mind off things?' Her eyes were drawn to a group of men walking past them to go outside and she audibly sighed. 'I do hope everyone doesn't decide it's more interesting out there, I can't imagine what they expect to see anyway.'

'I suppose it seems exciting to people who've never witnessed anything like it before,' Marie said, 'but to family of the crew it's a worrying time. Oh look, here come Stuart and Russell.'

'Oh don't tell me they're leaving too,' Bryony exclaimed as the men approached. 'There's going to be no-one left soon.'

'We're not going anywhere,' Stuart assured her, 'I was just coming to find Marie, and Russell joined me to help carry some drinks from the bar. We'd better be quick because we've left Claire on her own waiting for a gin and tonic.' He looked at Marie with concern. 'Are you alright?' he asked, and she nodded.

'I'm fine. I need a sit down and a drink, that's all.'

'Well that's easily remedied,' Stuart said. 'Has our Damian gone already?'

'Yes, much to the disappointment of his new girlfriend.'

Bryony listened with interest and wondered how Louisa had become so intensely involved with Damian in such a short time. Young people these days seemed to throw themselves into relationships without the steady build up to intimacy. She couldn't help feeling the girls were missing some of the most enjoyable aspects of being pursued by the man. It was a long time since she'd experienced it but the memories never left her. She went in search of Greg, who she hadn't seen around for a while.

Chapter 15

Sick with worry and faint with hunger and thirst, Tom lay curled up on a bench seat set into an ornate shelter on the promenade. At first the sound of laughter and cheerful voices spilling out from the hotel had tapped at his already taught nerves, but gradually it had turned into a comforting background noise. It still didn't seem right for people to be celebrating and happy, oblivious to the drama of life and death being played out close to them, but in a peculiar way the normality of it all gave him a sense of being cocooned in a small space of time which would end with the safe arrival of Danny and Rick.

He'd rung Sharon a few times just to hear her voice, but when she told him it was upsetting his mother and Amy he forced himself to leave his phone unused in his pocket. She'd told him they were keeping up with the news on the local radio but every time the phone rang it raised their hopes, only to end in floods of tears when he had nothing to tell them. He could envisage the scene at home but he tried to blot it out of his mind, he had enough to deal with here and he knew he would have to face them later.

The shelter provided some protection from the

cold breeze blowing in from the sea, but his joints were beginning to stiffen up so he unfolded his limbs and stretched out before pulling himself into a standing position. The sea was dotted with points of glimmering lights and the sky was filled with the noise of helicopters as they flew further and further out to sea, searching for a tiny vessel lost, for the moment, without trace.

The interview with Geoff had illustrated how totally inexperienced and unprepared Danny and Rick were, and no matter how hard he tried he couldn't tell him with any certainty just what they had in the way of emergency equipment. If he'd been going he would have searched the garage for the flares and life-jackets, but he couldn't be sure they would have taken the time to do that. He'd been tempted to ask Sharon to go and check if the equipment was still there or not, but he'd been afraid of the answer, knowing it could add not only to his concern but their worry as well. He wanted to be near Geoff to get any news as soon as it came in but he wanted to avoid any more questions, which he was certain would come, and then he'd have no choice but to ring home. Geoff hadn't been critical but he didn't need to say anything to make him feel guilty, he couldn't feel worse than he already did.

Leaning on the rails, he tried to close his ears to the talk going on around him. It seemed as if everyone had opinions on the likelihood of the men being found, and one man was being vociferous on the subject of them getting no more than they deserved, citing the dangerous situation it was putting the lifeboat men in. It made him so angry he felt like turning round and punching the man, but he had neither the strength nor the will.

'Tom?' he heard someone saying, and he turned round to see a vaguely familiar face peering at him. 'It is you, I wasn't sure when I first saw you. We met earlier today when we were trying to catch your dog.' He held his hand out and Tom reluctantly shook it. 'Greg Robson.'

Tom impatiently pulled his hand away and muttered, 'Tom Lester.'

Greg examined Tom's face closely, forcing him to turn away. 'Are you alright?' he asked.

'Sort of,' Tom replied. He wished Greg Robson would go away. He had no idea why he was here but neither did he wish to know. He could just imagine his response if he found out about Danny and Rick. Well he certainly wasn't going to find out from him. He turned away and fixed his eyes on what he presumed to be the horizon, but try as he might he couldn't make out where the sea and the sky met.

'It's a bad situation,' Greg said, nodding vaguely in the direction of the water. 'I wouldn't like to be lost out there, it must be very cold and miserable I should imagine.'

'I wish it was me out there,' Tom replied gruffly.

'I can't imagine why,' Greg replied, 'they're in a pretty dangerous position. I can't help wondering what makes men with no experience go out in a dinghy with practically no equipment to collect cockles of all things.'

Tom's patience snapped and his throat felt as though it was gripped in a vice, stopping the words from leaving his body. 'I'll tell you what makes them do it,' he croaked, 'it's desperation, sheer desperation. Now why don't you go away and leave me alone?'

The last thing he needed was a well-to-do stranger passing his unwelcome superior opinions on the situation but Greg Robson was persistent and seemed determined to find out why Tom was here. Tom had had enough of his interference and when he was asked again if he was alright, he growled angrily, 'I would be if you'd go away and leave me alone.'

Greg shrugged his shoulders and after a few moments he walked away, and Tom turned and watched him saunter back in the direction of the hotel where the wedding celebrations were still taking place. He saw him stop and talk with a woman who was sitting on a bench at the side of the entrance, and after a few minutes they entered the hotel together. Wearily, Tom turned back and slung his arms over the top of the railing for support; his body slumped against it like a lifeless, wilting scarecrow.

He closed his eyes and behind his lids he visualised a young Danny playing on the beach in the sun while Tom raced to the sea, jumping the waves, all the time urging his brother to join him. Reluctant at first, Danny plucked up courage and ran up to Tom, who held out his arms to him but instead of stopping he carried on past, going deeper and deeper into the sea until he disappeared into the distance. Tom tried to follow him but the water turned into treacle, gripping his legs and preventing him from moving. He tried with all his might but he couldn't make any headway. Gasping for breath, he screamed his brother's name but helplessly he watched him bobbing out to sea in a tiny dingy. He could hear his brother's frightened voice desperately shouting his name. 'Tom!' he screamed. 'Tom, help me!' But Tom couldn't help him.

Chapter 16

Louisa had joined them at the table. She seemed eager to talk about Damian and Marie was happy to oblige. Although she'd grown accustomed to him taking part in rescue operations, the fear never left her, but recognising the depth of Louisa's distress she did her best to convince her that on this occasion there was no need to be too concerned. 'Don't forget, my dear,' she said, 'they are not in any real danger tonight as far as I'm aware.'

'How can that be?' Louisa asked. 'Surely any callout for a lifeboat spells danger.'

Marie explained how different situations affected the danger levels involved in the rescue operations and Louisa listened intently. 'In one respect the weather conditions play a very important part, but the reason for the callout is important too. Fortunately the sea is fairly calm at the moment and they are trying to locate a dinghy and bring it back to shore. There is a big difference between that and going out in treacherous conditions to rescue people in great danger.' Louisa nodded thoughtfully and smiled gratefully.

Inevitably it wasn't long before Stuart and Russell were discussing many aspects of the cockling industry, and despite having little knowledge of the subject they both held strong views which diverged on several points. When they became locked in a disagreement about the laws regulating the requisite size a cockle had to reach before it could be legitimately caught, Louisa's eyes began to glaze over with boredom and Marie suggested it was probably a good time to re-join her friends to have some fun. Louisa glanced over to where some of her crowd were light-heartedly fooling around and trying to appear indifferent, she agreed maybe she would. Marie, sensing her hesitation and guessing the reason for it, quickly reassured her that no-one would be offended if she left them.

Marie watched Greg and Katy enter the hotel together and she couldn't help worrying about his involvement with her, but she was surprised to see them walking over to where she was sitting. 'Do you mind if we join you?' he asked, and everyone shuffled round until they could make sufficient room. 'How is Bryony?' she asked pointedly, but Greg's expression never slipped.

'She was fine the last time I saw her,' he replied casually, 'but she's got a lot to keep her busy so I haven't seen her for a while.' He gave Marie a look which she thought was intended to convey something meaningful. 'It's turning out to be a day of surprises,' he said.

'It is indeed,' she agreed, 'some of them intentional and some not.'

'You can say that again,' he replied with feeling.

As soon as the opportunity arose for Marie to speak without being overheard by Claire, she told Katy she'd heard about the fracas involving her husband and Louisa. 'I feel a little uncomfortable about it all because it is my son who now seems to be getting involved with Louisa,' she said, but Katy was quick to try and reassure her.

'Please don't concern yourself,' she said. 'It has no bearing on what happened between us. I suppose in different circumstances I would be grateful to Louisa for making their break final, but as it stands it makes no difference because our relationship is now at an end.'

Greg had been listening with interest. 'I couldn't help noticing you leaving the room for a short time, with your husband,' he said, 'and I know it's none of my business but I was a little concerned.'

Katy shrugged. 'Unfortunately you became entangled in my domestic problems whether you wanted to or not and I'm sorry about that, but you mustn't worry about me. I'm fine. It was I who suggested we went somewhere more private to talk.'

Greg relaxed. 'Did you resolve anything?' he asked.

'I told him that I meant what I said, it's over,' she said simply. 'I'm leaving him.'

'Oh,' Greg said. 'How did he take it?'

'His initial reaction was annoyance but mainly with disbelief, I think. He doesn't believe I'll go through with it and thinks I'm making empty threats simply because of his behaviour today.'

'I think he's already left,' Marie said. 'I presume that leaves you with the logistical problem of getting home. If there is any way we can help please let us know.'

Katy smiled. 'Thank you. I appreciate your offer

but I'm sure I'll be alright. I've already left a message with a friend of mine who I'm sure will pick me up tomorrow. She's been advising me to leave Paul for a long time so this will come as no surprise to her. In fact she will probably be very pleased.'

'That just leaves the problem of where you're going to stay tonight,' Greg said.

'Thankfully that isn't a problem either,' Katy told them with a smile. 'Although Paul left me with no means of getting home we were already checked in at the hotel where we were planning to stay, so I'll be fine.'

Marie relaxed. 'So now that everything is sorted out we can all start enjoying ourselves again,' she said. She was a little concerned about Greg becoming too involved in Katy's welfare and couldn't help feeling it was somehow tied up with his reaction to Bryony's impulsive behaviour. It wouldn't help anyone if he became entangled in all this messy business, but he was very level-headed and she was fairly certain he was simply offering support. Greg stood up and asked Katy to dance.

'You are quite right, Marie,' he said. 'It is time we all started enjoying ourselves again.' As they started to walk away Marie was perturbed to hear him offer to drive Katy home the next morning if she failed to make contact with her friend.

On the pretext of going to the bathroom she sought out a quiet corner to try and make contact with Debbie, and once again was unsuccessful. Standing in the bay of the conservatory windows, she had a panoramic view over the bay where the sun was slipping out of sight, washing the surface of the water with a reddish tint. In stark contrast the sand-beds in the estuary were already in darkness.

Most of the day trippers had already left but a few stragglers who'd hung on to their day at the seaside were finally beginning the journey home. There was obviously a chill in the air following the sun's disappearance, but with a hardiness common to visitors, most disdained the comfort of sweaters and cardigans. The local dog walkers were taking the place of the homeward-bound visitors, and while they were enjoying the camaraderie of friendly greetings the dogs took advantage of their long-awaited freedom.

Seagulls were soaring and gliding on the residual heat of the thermals but their calls were less strident than earlier in the day. A young couple with three children walked past but they were making very slow progress. The man, who was slightly ahead of his wife, carried a small child on his shoulders and held the hand of another slightly older boy, who was dragging his feet. The mother was manipulating a buggy laden with all the accoutrements of a day at the seaside as well as the baby in the main body of the pram. Their weariness was evident but when the man turned to give his wife an encouraging smile she beamed back at him.

Marie's heart gave a thudding jolt. Supposing the couple she'd heard were just like that family and she'd made a monumental mistake. The enormity of what she'd done was becoming more obvious the longer it went on and she desperately wanted to find some way out. If only she could talk with someone, maybe they'd try to convince her she'd done nothing wrong, but she couldn't tell Stuart or Claire, and Bryony neither had the time nor would she have the inclination; she was too tied up in her own problems. Greg wasn't in any frame of mind to help, so she would just have to leave it for the moment and hope it would sort itself out. It felt heartless to hope she would be proved right when she thought of the implications that would mean. She wished with all her heart they'd never gone to the Sands café today, or at least that their visit had been at the earlier time they'd originally planned. If only Stuart hadn't forgotten to meet her there this would never have happened.

To prevent the possibility of Stuart coming to find her she reluctantly put her phone away, and after checking there was no-one around to wonder what she was doing, she quietly left the conservatory. Catching sight of Greg and seeing he was alone, she went over and managed to waylay him. 'I'm sorry, Greg. I had no idea Bryony hadn't told you what she was planning to do, otherwise I wouldn't have said anything. You must think I was interfering.'

Greg shrugged. 'Don't be silly, we've known each other too long for that. As a matter of fact you did me a favour letting me know, because whatever Bryony and I decide to do, it will definitely not be during the weekend of Amelia's wedding. It wouldn't be fair on her and Piers to have their day remembered as the one when her mum walked out on her dad.' He bit his lip. 'That is never going to happen.'

'That's why I was so surprised when Bryony told me, not so much that she'd cooked up the plan but that you'd agreed to it.'

'Well now you know I didn't.'

'Yes and I'm glad. Are you coming to the lunch planned for tomorrow?'

'I certainly am, it'll be nice meeting Piers' family informally where we can talk and get to know each other better. Then we'll be waving the happy couple off on their honeymoon.'

'Yes we will, now I really must hurry back before they send a search party out looking for me.'

Chapter 17

'Tom. Tom.' The voice was insistent. 'Sorry to intrude again, but you were calling out.'

Tom shook off the nightmare but he came back to a reality that was even worse and the pestering man was back again. 'What do you want now?' he grumbled. 'I've told you already I don't want you around.'

'Sorry to intrude again but you were calling out. I'll leave you alone but just tell me one thing before I do. Where is your wife?'

'What's it to you?' Tom replied. 'But if you must know she's at home with the children. Where else would she be?'

'Did you take her home before coming back here?'

Tom swung round, his face creased with anger and fear. 'What is this, an inquisition?' he demanded. 'And just why are you so interested in my affairs?'

Greg didn't respond to the intimidating threat in Tom's voice and pressed on with his questions. 'Is your being here something to do with this emergency?'

The directness of the question took Tom by surprise and he finally buckled. 'It's my brother and my best mate they're searching for out there.'

'Oh God. Tom, I'm sorry. I had no idea and here I was waffling on about the right and wrongs of it. Have you told anyone you're here?' he asked.

'Yes, there's a man called Geoff who's got my number.'

'Has he been able to give you any information? I mean, are there any more developments in the search?'

'No, they are none the wiser.'

'I'm really sorry, this must be a nightmare for you.'

'You could say that.'

'You're shivering a bit, haven't you got a sweater or anything else to put on? I know it's been hot today but it is September and the temperature will drop quite dramatically soon.'

Tom rubbed his arms; it was true he was feeling cold but until the man had pointed it out he hadn't even noticed. 'I've got a sweater in the car but I can't go and get it. I'll have to stay around here in case something happens.'

'You told me Geoff has your number, so he'll ring you anyway.'

'I know but my battery is running out of charge so I don't know whether to keep it on in case they want to contact me or switch it off to save the energy.' He lifted his head and his eyes scanned the darkness again, watching the bobbing silhouettes and flickering lights, hoping against hope that Danny and Rick would be amongst them soon. 'I still keep thinking they will ring me but as they haven't made contact with anyone that's not very likely.'

'I tell you what,' Greg said, 'I'll go and find Geoff. He's a friend of mine anyway and I'll give him my number, and then that way you can save your battery for later.' Without waiting for an answer he walked off and called over his shoulder, 'I won't be long so don't go away.'

'As if,' Tom said to himself. 'Where would I go?' Despite that, he was tempted to move away to escape Greg's interference, but he lacked the energy to make a decision and anyway he had to admit it was a useful answer to the problem of his phone.

'That's sorted,' Greg declared when he returned a few minutes later, 'but Geoff told me he didn't think you'd eaten for a while.' Tom didn't reply but Greg persisted. 'When did you last eat, Tom?'

He shrugged dismissively. 'We had a picnic at lunch-time. Oh, and then we had a coffee and cake at that café on the beach. That was a disaster, it was supposed to be a treat from my mum but it all went wrong.' He gave a weak smile as he remembered. 'I suppose I can smile about it now but at the time it didn't seem funny.'

'What happened?'

'Rusty ran into the waitress and the food went everywhere. Unfortunately I was on a short fuse because I was worried that Danny and Rick might have taken the dinghy and I couldn't do anything about it, especially as Sharon didn't have a clue what we'd been planning to do.' Just thinking about it brought back the feeling of doom, but when Greg joked that Rusty was a little scruffy bundle of mischief he couldn't help smiling. 'Don't let my kids, or Sharon for that matter, hear you call him scruffy, but you're right, he is a pest at times. As it happens we did get our treat despite him; the owner came across and offered to replace everything free of charge. I was all ready for leaving but Sharon wanted to stay and I knew she'd be disappointed if we left. I must say it was a pretty good scone.'

'He's a generous man Billy; I'm not surprised he did that.'

'Yeah, he didn't have to do that, but he certainly saved the day.'

'But that doesn't alter the fact that you've gone too long without food.' He prised one of Tom's arms off the rail and keeping a tight hold of it, he said, 'Come on Tom, we're going to get something to eat.' Tom's strength was matched by Greg's determination and although he gripped the rail as tight as he possibly could, he was surprised to feel himself being pulled away. He lacked the inclination to put up a struggle so he gave in and ambled by the side of Greg, away from the seafront towards the tempting smell of food.

The square was lit by Victorian-style lamps on the walls of the buildings, and the candles on the tables flickered in the breeze which lifted the edges of the cloths between the clips holding them in place. There was muted laughter and the background music lent a continental feel as everyone enjoyed the unexpected luxury of al fresco dining on a late September evening. It was very inviting but Tom turned and started to walk back the way they'd come. 'No, I can't,' he said, and started moving away.

Greg hurried to catch him up. 'You need to eat.'

'Would you want to eat if it was your brother out there?'

'Probably not,' conceded Greg, 'but then I think I would realise it was probably the most sensible thing to do. I'm no use to man or mouse if I'm hungry so I believe I would force myself if necessary.'

Tom's steps slowed but he carried on walking away. 'I can't go back there,' he said.

'No, I understand that, but I'll tell what we can do. There's a very good fish and chip shop not far from here, you can probably smell it. Let's go there.'

Tom unwillingly allowed himself to be led the short way to where the fish shop was doing a roaring trade, but they saw a table in the corner of the tiny dining room which they just managed to squeeze into. Neither of them spoke while they demolished the delicious portions of fish and chips and drank the large mugs of tea placed in front of them by a pretty waitress. Greg stabbed his last chip. 'Do you want another of those?' he asked, indicating Tom's empty mug.

'I wouldn't mind actually,' Tom replied. 'I hadn't realised how hungry and thirsty I was.'

'What I can't believe,' Greg said, 'is how I've managed to eat all that food; I had a good meal at the wedding earlier. Mind you,' he added ruefully, 'a lot has happened since then.'

'You can say that again but how come you're here anyway?' Tom asked. Despite everything he did feel a bit better from having had something to eat and drink. 'I thought you'd still be enjoying yourself at the wedding. It was still going on as far as I could see.'

Greg nodded. 'Yes it is, but to be honest I had a bit of a disagreement with someone and I wanted to get away for a while, so don't worry, you're not keeping me from enjoying myself, I'm quite happy to be here.' He saw Tom's face darken. 'I'm sorry, that was an idiotic thing to say, what I meant was...'

'I know what you meant, don't worry about it,' Tom mumbled. He was getting restless but he dreaded going back, so he drank the hot tea brought by the same young girl. Something had been puzzling him ever since Greg had approached him and he was interested to find out the answer. 'How did you know my name?' he asked. 'When you came to me the first time you called me by my name.'

'Oh that's easy to explain,' he replied. 'Remember when Rusty gate crashed the photo-call?' Tom nodded and Greg continued. 'Your wife left me in no doubt that your name is Tom when she was trying to get your attention.'

Tom agreed. 'I should think everyone in Merebank reached the same conclusion.'

'I've been wondering,' Greg said, 'am I right in presuming you've got somewhere sorted out to sleep tonight if you need it? I presume your brother and friend will be taken to hospital for observation when they return.'

Weariness swept over him. 'No,' he replied, 'you are not right in presuming anything of the sort.'

'I'm sorry,' Greg replied, 'I was only trying to help but if you...'

Tom stood up and turned to go, but the room was so crowded he found his way blocked and he struggled to keep the scorn from his voice. 'You have no idea about anything, the only place I can afford to stay is in a shelter on the promenade.' Rummaging in his pocket, he pulled out a note and some change. 'I've got barely enough to pay for this, never mind somewhere to sleep.' Pushing himself up, he gathered the money together and wound his way between the tables, but before he had time to pay he saw Greg thrust enough to cover the cost of both their meals into the waitress's hand.

'There was no need to do that,' he told him. 'I don't need charity.'

'I never suggested you did,' Greg snapped back, 'but surely you're not above a simple gesture of friendship when you're in trouble.'

Tom's head and shoulders slumped as he walked disconsolately along the narrow cobbled street, and despite being oblivious to the cold air which had descended, his body gave an involuntary shiver. He knew he'd been unreasonable when all Greg was doing was trying to help him, but the stress of everything was getting to him and he just didn't have a clue what to do next. When Greg offered to lend him a jacket which he'd left in his car, he was just about to refuse when he was caught by a cold gust of wind which prompted him to reluctantly accept the offer. The car was parked in a side street and when Greg handed him the coat he shrugged it on and admitted it did make him feel warmer. 'It's probably the poshest one I've ever worn,' he said, 'and I'll probably ruin it in the shelter tonight.'

'Let's hope it doesn't come to that,' Greg said, 'but don't worry about the coat, it's nothing special.'

Tom strode away, impatient now to get back to find out if there was any news. What would it look like if they'd brought Danny and Rick back to shore and he wasn't there because he was so busy filling himself up with fish and chips? Greg had trouble catching him up and when he did he was breathless.

'What's the hurry?' he panted. Tom didn't slow down.

'I need to know what's happening,' he replied.

Speeding up his steps, Greg tried to keep up with him but he was showing signs of getting out of breath. Despite everything else Tom's physical fitness was superior to Greg's, something which he would have been proud of in different circumstances.

'I've been checking my phone,' Greg puffed, 'as you've probably noticed, and there's still no news.'

The scene on the prom hadn't changed much since they were last there. Onlookers were constantly changing as people stood around for a while before drifting off when they realised there was very little to see, but they were quickly replaced by ever more interested observers. After seeking Geoff out to make certain there had been no developments they were unaware of, they went to sit in the shelter where Tom had rested earlier.

'I've got to ask,' Greg said, 'so don't bite my head off...'

'Go on,' Tom replied.

'When I commented earlier about the dangers the inexperienced men were putting themselves in, you said it was due to desperation. What exactly did you mean?'

Tom battled with his customary instincts to keep his problems to himself, but he had to admit he owed something to the man who'd gone out of his way to help him, especially as he could have been enjoying himself at the wedding. Despite that, it didn't come easy to him and he kept his voice low.

'You wouldn't understand,' he said, 'but it's the feeling you have when you suddenly lose your job and can't provide for your wife and family.' He dropped his head into his hands. 'I'd never had a day off since I started work and now this happens.'

'What is your job and what's happened?'

'I'm a bricklayer; I went to college but a fat lot of good that's doing me now. There's no work for craftsmen or labourers when the building work stops.'

'Are Danny and your mate in the same position as you?' Greg asked.

Tom's head jerked up. 'Practically everybody's in the same position. There's no work, building or otherwise, full stop. If people have no money to spend the shops close down and that means more people out of work. The only jobs are in pubs and the landlords are giving them to the women so they can keep the wages down. Sharon's got a really bad cut on her arm and it's getting infected. She did it doing a crappy job just to keep us afloat. The landlord at the pub where she's working made her carry a heavy crate of drinks up from the cellar and she stumbled and scraped her arm on a rough wall.' He turned to look to see what effect his words were having but Greg just sat there listening, making no comments, so he carried on. 'We used to give loads of things to the charity shops, now we are dressing our own kids with things from the same places.' He snorted. 'Last week Sharon came back with a tee-shirt she thought Sam would be well pleased with and he refused to wear it because he said it had belonged to the school geek. Have you any idea how that makes me feel?'

'No, but I'm beginning to get the drift,' Greg replied.

'It isn't a drift that's happened to us,' Tom replied bitterly, 'it's a bloody avalanche.'

'I'm sorry Tom,' Greg replied, 'I don't know what to say.'

'There's nothing you can say,' Tom said wearily. 'There's nothing anyone can say to make a difference, but maybe at least you can now understand why the opportunity to make some money seemed too good to miss.'

'Yes, I think I can,' Greg conceded miserably.

When his phone rang they both jumped with the unexpectedness of it, and Greg answered it immediately. 'It's Geoff for you,' he said, handing it to Tom.

Geoff wasted no time. 'They've located a dinghy,' he said.

Tom jumped up. 'Thank God!' he shouted, and tried to peer through the darkness as if he would see them. 'Are they safe? Is Danny alright?'

'Tom, don't get too excited,' Geoff urged. 'I said they'd located a dinghy, I didn't say they'd found them. The men in the boat we escorted back earlier told us they'd been trying to help two other men before getting into difficulty themselves. We think it might be your dinghy but we don't know if there is anyone in it yet. I'll get back to you as soon as I learn anything. Now I must go and Tom...'

Tom slumped wearily back onto the bench again. 'Yes?'

'Keep positive.'

'I'm trying but it's not easy.'

'I know.'

'Come on,' Greg said, 'let's have a walk. There's nothing we can do here and Geoff will contact us as soon as there's any news.' Reluctantly Tom pushed himself upright, and with his hands thrust deep in his pockets he walked morosely in step with Greg.

'You know, it's funny,' Greg said as they approached the jetty, 'but this reminds me of a picture I've got at home. All these shadowy figures, boats, and tractors and things, and yet in a way it's nothing like it. It's by an artist called Lowry.' He turned his head and looked at Tom in surprise when he heard him voice his agreement.

'I think I know what you mean,' he said, 'it is a bit like his pictures in a funny sort of way.'

'Do you know Lowry?' Greg asked incredulously.

'Well not personally,' Tom said with a flash of humour, 'but don't sound so surprised.'

He heard Greg curse himself under his breath. 'I'm not,' he began, but Tom's laughter cut him short. 'I don't know the first bloody thing about art and I can't tell one painting from another, never mind the bloke who painted them.'

'Then how...?'

'How did I know about Lowry? Ages ago before we were married, we used go to Manchester for the day and sometimes Sharon dragged me into an art gallery. She loved his pictures so I bought her one for her birthday and we had it framed. She kept it until we bought our own house and it's had pride of place on our living room wall ever since. Other than that I wouldn't have had a clue what you were talking about.'

'Well I must say your Sharon has good taste.'

'Of course she has, she married me.'

'You're quite the comedian aren't you?'

'Given half a chance, mate, given half a chance.'

The mention of Sharon brought everything rushing back, and he knew she wouldn't be thinking he was the best thing since sliced bread at the moment.

Chapter 18

It was very satisfying, basking in the admiration and praise of guests who were well acquainted with the finer things in life, especially Piers' family and friends who she'd desperately hoped to impress. She guessed even they were unaccustomed to attending weddings which included an overnight stay with free hospitality and use of all the amenities of a luxury hotel, and some were so taken with it they were already planning a return visit. She'd persuaded the photographer to send some internal shots to the main editor of the local newspaper, overriding the actions of the paper's own reporter, and she was convinced these would prove very flattering to her and the hotel, and of course Amelia.

Justin and Ellie had carried themselves with the professional ease she'd come to expect of them and Ralph had circulated with a mixture of pride and satisfaction at the sight of so many people enjoying themselves. If he was carrying a shadow of concern at what was happening over in the bay, no-one was made aware of it unless they themselves brought the subject to the fore. Despite the shaky start, it was turning out to be a very successful day and she was feeling very pleased with herself.

The only thing which still remained to be done to turn it into a perfect day was something she contemplated with almost unbearable anticipation. She was so close to fulfilling her dream she sometimes found it hard to breathe, and she was counting down the minutes. She'd persuaded Greg to meet in her bedroom and she was confident she would be able to persuade him that everything could still be achieved before he was due to go on holiday. The small matter of her intention to accompany him could be left until later, it was essential to smooth things over before breaking that to him. She accepted that maybe her original intention to tell Colin today had been a little thoughtless, but once Amelia and Piers were safely out of Merebank there would be no reason for delay. The local people would find out soon enough anyway so there was nothing she could do about that, whenever it happened.

Making absolutely sure no-one was looking for her, she slipped away to her room where she carefully poured two drinks, checked her appearance in the mirror, and sat down to wait. She made allowances for the first anxious few minutes when Greg didn't arrive, it was possible he'd been side-tracked by someone he couldn't avoid, but when he still didn't come she began to feel concerned and then angry. Undecided what to do, she paced the room, finished both drinks and cursed him with all her might. Surely he couldn't have forgotten? She'd impressed on him the importance of what she had to say and although he'd shown some reluctance he had agreed to the arrangement.

She intended asking him where he'd kept disappearing to during the evening. She'd felt a chill of apprehension at the sight of him entering the hotel with Katy Sheridan, and felt thoroughly aggrieved when they were dancing together afterwards. It was highly improbable that they were forming a romantic attachment but feelings of apprehension kept pressing their way through her mind, making it even more important to settle their future together. When the phone rang she snatched it up and before he could speak she demanded to know where he was. Her throat was choked with emotion but she paced the floor in frustration when she heard Justin speaking instead of Greg. She was determined to cut him off in order to clear the line but something in the tone of his voice caught her attention.

'Mrs P.,' he said urgently.

'Yes,' she replied, 'what do want? It had better be important.'

'I'm sorry to disturb you but it is rather urgent. It's Mr P. He's collapsed in the office, can you come quickly?

'I'll be there right away,' she told him. 'Does anyone else know about this?'

'No, there's only me and Ellie here.'

'Keep it that way,' directed Bryony.

She replaced the phone and ran from the room, it was imperative for her to take charge of the situation before it ran out of control. It wasn't the first time she'd had to retrieve Colin from making a fool of himself in public, but she was determined it must not happen today. It would only take one person to see him in a drunken state and the news would spread rapidly amongst the guests, and the thought that an incident like this could mar the perfection of the day filled her with rage. As the lift doors opened she took a deep breath and walked slowly towards the office where she ushered Justin and Ellie away before pulling the door behind her.

He was slouched on a seat with his legs splayed and arms hanging loosely by his side. His face was puffy and his features seemed to have folded in on themselves, and the eyes trying to focus on her were vacant and confused. Her first reaction was to ask herself how he had become this way despite her constant checks and the dire warnings she'd given him throughout the day and into the evening. She'd been prepared for the eventuality of him drinking too much but she'd tried to moderate him and placed nibbles of food within his reach to counter the effects of the alcohol. Obviously she'd underestimated the number of people plying him with drinks and she silently cursed their generosity.

She glared at him with revulsion. 'Look at you,' she said, 'you're a disgrace. You couldn't remain in control of yourself for one single day. You turn my stomach.'

His voice was slurred and self-pitying. 'What's the matter, Bryony? Is it wrong for a man to enjoy his daughter's wedding day? The trouble with you is you can't relax.' He reached for his glass and tilted it dangerously close to his chin. 'Come on, and join me in a toast to our lovely daughter Amelia.'

Frustration and tension was boiling up inside her and she could barely stop herself from physically lashing out at him. Even now he was threatening to ruin Amelia's wedding day and she hated him with a passion that had built up over the years, making her want to hurt him. 'You're a fool,' she said, 'look at the state of you.'

'What you mean is, I'm enjoying myself celebrating my daughter's wedding day, and what's wrong with that? Why don't you relax and join me having a bit of fun, or have you forgotten how?'

Something inside her snapped and before she knew what she was doing the words were out and she was saying the one thing that would hurt him above anything else in the world. 'She's not your daughter. Any man with an iota of sense would have guessed it years ago, but you're a fool, you never saw what was right under your nose.' For a few seconds there was complete silence while Colin strenuously shook his head as if he was trying to clear it to make sense of what she'd said.

'What do you mean she's not my daughter? Of course she's my daughter, she's Amelia.' Pointing his finger at her, he gave a knowing smile. 'I know what you're doing, you're trying to hurt me because I'm enjoying myself and you're not. Anyway it doesn't matter what you say, I'm still going to enjoy myself.'

'It will matter very soon,' she told him, 'because I'm leaving you.'

'You'll never leave me,' he slurred, 'because if you leave me you lose all this.' His arms were waving ineffectually in the air.

'That's just where you're wrong, I am leaving all this.' Her eyes remained fixed on his face, willing him to be shocked. 'I've trained Justin to take over and I'm leaving you and the hotel.'

'Am I right in guessing you'll be leaving with the man who just happens to be my best friend?'

'You're deluded,' she replied. 'He isn't your best friend, but yes I'm going with Greg, Amelia's biological father actually. It's something I should have done years ago.'

Ralph's voice, level and commanding, filled the room. 'Bryony stop, that's enough.'

Twisting round, she saw Ralph and Greg standing together, their faces frozen with shock at what they'd witnessed, and her heart was banging against her ribs as she tried to guess how much they may have heard. In her haste she'd pulled the door to when she arrived but hadn't closed it, and in the heat of the argument she'd been oblivious to everyone except Colin. Greg's expression cut through her and she wanted to run into his arms. 'Greg,' she cried, reaching out to him, 'I was going...' but he gave her one searing look before turning on his heels and walking away. She made to run after him but Ralph blocked her way.

'No, Bryony,' he said firmly. 'It wouldn't be very seemly for you to be seen chasing through the hotel after a man. We have to deal with this situation with as little fuss as possible and try and keep it away from public view. You can manage your affairs later.' Turning to his son, he asked him if he could stand.

Colin tried unsuccessfully to pull himself upright so Ralph went out and asked Justin to come in and assist them. Once they'd reached the door he enlisted Ellie's help in checking if they would be able to reach the lift unseen. 'It's clear at the moment,' she told them, 'should I lead the way? I was just thinking the more there are of us the better. We can hide...' Her voice tailed off.

Ralph, his face grey and expressionless, answered

her, 'Yes please, Ellie. That's a good idea.' The tone of his voice changed when he spoke to Bryony and told her to take Colin's arm. 'Try to look casual,' he said coldly, 'we'll discuss everything else later.' He turned to Justin, who was trying to keep Colin upright. 'When you get him to his room will you help Mrs Portland to deal with her husband? If possible I'd like him to be sobered up in time to continue with the evening's entertainment, we don't want people thinking the worst.'

'Don't you worry about it, sir,' Justin replied. 'We'll have him ship-shape in no time.'

They made a strange tableau as they tried to maintain a semblance of normality while waiting for the lift but fortunately most people were too involved in their own pursuits to notice anything amiss. Ralph waited until they were safely inside the lift and avoiding her eyes, smiled gratefully in the direction of Justin and thanked him. Bryony knew that what he'd heard had shocked him, but it was the unseemly way it had been disclosed which he would find unforgivable. Now he would be concentrating on how to limit the damage to the business, but especially the family he loved.

They reached Colin's bedroom without drawing unwelcome attention, but every nerve in her body was on fire as she and Justin frantically tried to sober him up. It was imperative that he recovered sufficiently to be able to function as normally as possible. She forced him to drink soda water which she knew he hated, and after he'd thrown it all back up again along with what seemed like gallons of spirits, they practically poured coffee down his throat.

With his face splashed and wearing a clean shirt,

he appeared almost back to normal and they escorted him back downstairs. 'You are going to sit with Marie and Stuart,' she instructed him, 'so they can keep their eye on you. You will not,' she told him, staring him in the eyes, 'are you listening to me? You will not drink any more alcohol.'

Looking suitably chastised, he nodded, but before they reached the table she guessed he would already be trying to figure out how he could add or substitute a shot of vodka or gin to the lemonade being placed in front of him. Knowing there was no way he could spend the rest of the night stone cold sober and having lost any interest in trying to keep him under control, she decided the only solution lay in trying to make sure he was kept occupied. The best person she could think of to do that was Stuart. Then she could try to find Greg and attempt to put things right.

As casually as possible she accompanied him to where Marie and Stuart were sitting and pushed him onto an empty seat. 'I'm sorry to burden you with him,' she said apologetically, 'but would you mind if I leave him here for a little while?' She threw Stuart a knowing look. 'I'll just go and get him a drink, a non-alcoholic drink, and then I'll relieve you of him as soon as I possibly can.' Stuart raised his eyebrows at Marie, who shrugged her shoulders but she looked as baffled as he was and there was no time to explain.

She found Greg in the wine bar with several empty glasses in front of him and a full whisky tumbler in his hand. Sliding onto the empty stool by his side, she ordered one for herself before attempting to speak to him. He made no movement apart from raising the glass to his lips, but his reflection in the mirror behind the bar was cold and unresponsive. Fearful of pushing him away, she searched for a way to break the silence but he gave no indication of acknowledging her presence so she whispered hesitantly, 'I know you must hate me at the moment, but can we at least go somewhere more private so I can explain.'

The eruption of anger which she'd anticipated was strangely absent and his voice when he spoke was empty, devoid of emotion. 'Where do you suggest we go?'

She shook her head. 'I don't really know, maybe the conservatory or my bedroom?'

'Do you think that's wise under the circumstances?'

'I don't know what's wise and what isn't anymore, but does it matter?'

At last he turned to her, but she quailed when she saw the look on his face. 'Oh yes, it matters,' he said coldly. 'It matters very much.'

She rubbed her forehead to ease the pressure of the pain which sometimes spelled the beginning of a migraine attack. 'Why are you twisting my words? You know exactly what I mean; you're just trying to complicate matters even more than they are already.'

He shook his head in bewilderment. 'Bryony, I just can't imagine how you believe I can possibly make things any more complicated than they are.' Glancing round, he dropped his voice, they were beginning to attract attention by their serious stance and muted conversation. 'Tell me how it will be possible for us to reach your room without drawing attention to ourselves.'

Desperation drove her. 'I'll go in the lift and you go up the back staircase. There will be no reason for anyone to notice if you head towards the gents' cloakroom.'

'Fine,' he said, 'I'll see you in a few minutes.'

He never moved when she slid off the stool and left him and her hands were shaking when she reached her room and anxiously hid the champagne flutes in the mini bar. The time for celebration had passed and a terrible panic gripped her stomach as she re-lived the unexpected events of the last hour. She dabbed her wrists with fragrance but the headiness of the perfume increased her nausea, so she ran them under the tap and applied a touch of refreshing cologne to her temples instead. The face reflected in the mirror was pale under her make-up but she didn't want Greg to think she was unaffected by what had happened so a slight touch of lipstick was all she allowed herself.

It was the first time he'd ever visited her room but he made no comment when he entered and she was shocked to see him looking strained, his face etched with shock and concern. She longed to reach out and reassure him that everything would be alright but why should he believe her when there was no way she could be sure how it would turn out? He seemed reluctant to move into the room and when offered a seat he refused with a shake of his head. Lost for the right words to say to him she mutely appealed for his help, but it was obvious he had no intention of making it easier for her and he was waiting for her to speak. 'I don't know what to say except I'm sorry. Can you forgive me?'

'I don't think forgiving you is the highest on my list of priorities just now,' he replied.

'I'm so sorry, Greg,' she repeated. 'I never meant it

to turn out like this.'

Slowly he began to walk round the room, one hand touching each piece of furniture as he passed while the fingers of the other were distractedly combing through his hair. 'During the course of one day I've found out that you were planning, without my knowledge, to tell Colin that you are leaving him for me, and then in the most hurtful way imaginable I discover that Amelia is my daughter.' He swung round to face her. 'And then you have the gall to worry about whether or not I'll find it in me to forgive you.'

'I told you, it was never meant to happen like that! I just got so carried away when Colin collapsed. I'm sorry, what else do you want me to say?'

His stricken eyes locked into hers. 'Sorry doesn't even come near, but you know what is even more incomprehensible is your apparent inability to understand what you've done wrong.' He took a deep intake of breath. 'I'm finding it hard to believe anything you say but tell me truthfully, is Amelia my daughter?'

'Yes,' she told him, 'she is your daughter.'

'Why,' he cried, 'have you kept the truth from me all this time? Why did you never tell me?'

'I couldn't, not at the beginning. You know what it was like at that time, it would have brought everything crashing down. Later on I didn't know how you'd take it so as time went on it just never seemed appropriate.'

'Appropriate? Didn't you think I had a right to know?' His voice was rising and for the first time she realised the magnitude of what she'd done. 'You asked if I will forgive you,' he said, 'and the answer is no, I'll never be able to forgive you.'

Crushed and frightened, she moved towards him but he held his arms out, his hands outstretched to hold her at a distance. 'I thought it would complicate your life,' she said, 'I did it for your sake as much as mine, believe me.'

'How can you possibly say that? You didn't know how I'd feel or how I would have reacted. Even I can't say for sure what I would have done, but at least you could have given me the opportunity to find out.'

'Greg, try to understand. You couldn't have acknowledged her as your daughter so it wouldn't have made any difference, and you've always played a big part in her life.' Rejected and desperate, she slumped onto her chair, frightened to ask the question uppermost in her mind. His expression when she turned to him was softer and sadder. 'What are you going to do?' she asked.

'It's more a question of what we're going to do. How are we going to tell Amelia?'

Whatever else she was dreading to hear, nothing had prepared her for this, and she couldn't let it happen, it would ruin everything; not just for herself but everyone else as well.

'You can't mean that!' she cried. 'We can't say anything to Amelia, it's too late to tell her anything now.'

'Bryony, there is no way we can just leave this. Apart from the fact that I wish to acknowledge my own daughter there are too many people who know the truth, not least of all Colin, who is hardly likely to keep this to himself. I don't want her wedding day to be overshadowed but I need time to think.' She watched him moving towards the door and fought back the impulse to try to make him stay. The room was silent for a few seconds and she dared to hope he would change his mind but he merely turned to face her, shaking his head. 'Despite all my instincts to protect Amelia from being hurt on her wedding day, my gut instinct is to tell her before someone else does but at the moment I have no idea how to do it.'

Their hopes of a future together were slipping away; he didn't need to spell it out, she could read it in his face but she wasn't about to give up yet. 'Greg, I need to know. Where does this leave us?'

'I think there are more important things for us to worry about than what the future holds for us,' he replied, before turning to walk out of the room.

Chapter 19

Greg and Tom were sitting in the shelter, deep in thought. Tom was thinking he'd rather be dead than have to tell his mother that Danny had not survived. He'd no idea why Greg kept coming out to keep him company and although at first he'd been loath to admit it, it did help having him around. He couldn't imagine how he was managing to get away with disappearing all the time because he knew Sharon would be onto him like a ton of bricks if he behaved like that when they were supposed to be at a wedding. He'd nearly mentioned it a couple of times but Greg was in a funny mood and didn't seem to want to talk, which actually suited him fine. He kept looking over to where he could make out the men standing round the jetty, but there was no sign of much happening and he felt himself plunging into another cloud of despair.

Sitting around doing nothing was driving him mad so he stood up and walked to the edge of the path before bending beneath the rails to drop down on the beach below. He felt his knee jar on the unevenness of the pebbles below, but after giving it a brisk rub and a brief glance back to the jetty, he set of at a brisk pace in the opposite direction. Pushing his hands deep into the pockets of Greg's coat, he kept his eyes on the shifting surface underneath his feet and tried to empty his mind of everything around him. When he reached the end of the curve in the bay he turned round and slowly made his way back and as he pulled himself up he was surprised to see Greg still sitting where he'd left him. Neither of them spoke and Greg apparently had no interest in what had prompted his impulsive decision to walk away, and he had no desire to try to explain his actions. It was, he decided, just as well because he couldn't explain it to himself. For some reason Greg seemed to be as fed up as he was and after a while he couldn't resist commenting on the amount of time Greg was spending away from the wedding celebrations. 'Anyone would think you weren't enjoying yourself, but won't they be wondering where you are?'

'I don't think anybody will notice, but anyway I'm not concerned if they do. I need some time to think.'

'You and me both,' Tom replied, 'I've been in some scrapes but nothing as bad as this. It's like a bloody nightmare.'

'That's strange,' Greg said. 'I feel exactly the same.'

'Do you want to talk about it? It's okay if you don't.'

Greg shrugged. 'I suppose it might help to get my head round it because at the minute I'm struggling to take it all in.'

'It would help if I knew what *"it"* was,' Tom said.

'The fact that I've got a daughter I didn't know about.'

Tom took a few moments while he tried to digest this information before he said anything stupid, this was obviously not a time for a flippant comment and he struggled to put himself in the man's shoes and failed miserably. Obviously someone had turned up at the wedding and dropped the news into the conversation, which must have come as quite a surprise, but he couldn't help thinking that Greg must have had some idea it was a possibility. Trying to think of something positive, he said, 'Looking on the bright side, there are loads of older parents these days. I see them on the school run all the time, sometimes you can't tell if they are the kid's parents or the grandparents.' Greg's puzzled expression made him wonder if he'd heard it all wrong but suddenly he heard a sort of muffled snort as Greg realised the implications of what Tom had said. 'That, I could accept,' Greg said, 'it's finding out I've been a father for twenty-five years I can't get my head around.'

Tom lifted his head, pulled his chin in and muttered in disbelief. 'Jesus wept. You're kidding me.'

'I wish I was. No! I don't mean that. Oh God, I don't know what I mean. I suppose what I'm trying to say is that I'm thrilled she's my daughter but I wish I hadn't just discovered it, especially the way I found out.'

Tom whistled through his teeth. 'You've had a daughter for twenty-five years and you had no idea. That's crazy.'

Greg pulled his shoulders up into his neck. 'That's the understatement of the year,' he said. 'I had a faint suspicion when she was born but when her mother didn't say anything I thought I must be wrong.' They both sat in silence, Greg staring into space and Tom shaking his head from side to side.

'Blimey,' he said at last.

'It's a funny thing you know,' Greg said, 'but I've always said she felt like a daughter to me, and now I've discovered she really is.'

Tom felt he was danger of losing the plot, but he felt he owed it to Greg to try and keep up even though he was struggling. 'Who is she?' he asked. 'And does she know?'

Greg relaxed his body and turned and looked at him. 'Oh, didn't I say? It's Amelia, the bride. And no, she doesn't know. In fact that's what I've come out to think about. How do we tell her without spoiling her wedding day?'

'Now you've lost me completely,' Tom said, shaking his head again. 'You'd better tell me everything,' he said firmly, 'before I begin to think I'm going crazy.'

He listened as Greg briefly told him how it had all come about and shook his head in disbelief when he heard about Bryony's outburst at her own daughter's wedding. He couldn't help thinking her timing could have been better.

'There you have it in a nutshell,' Greg said.

'What are you going to do?'

'I haven't a clue,' Greg replied, 'but talking about it helps a bit.'

When the phone rang in Greg's pocket they both went rigid. Greg scrabbled in his pocket and listened intently to the voice on the other end before handing it to Tom. 'I get the feeling something's happened,' he warned him, 'you'd better prepare yourself.'

Reluctantly Tom took the phone from Greg and held it to his ear; his hand was shaking uncontrollably.

The familiar voice of Geoff came over the line and Greg leaned over to catch the words.

Geoff was blunt and to the point. 'We've picked up one of them,' he said, 'unfortunately that's all I know. You'd better get yourself off to the hospital, Tom, you'll find out more there.'

Tom clutched the phone to his ear, hardly daring to breathe. 'How can it be only one of them?' he asked. 'They would never separate.'

'I'm sorry mate, I can't tell you any more. Obviously the search is still ongoing so if I hear anything I'll be in touch.'

'Geoff, is the one at the hospital OK?'

'Apparently he was unconscious, but he was airlifted so I don't have any information at this stage.'

Tom was paralysed with shock. He'd tried to prepare himself for the worst but his mind was unable to take in the significance of Geoff's words and he remained seated, his body shaking from head to foot. After a few moments Greg began shaking him, rousing him from his stupor. 'Come on Tom, you heard what Geoff said, you've got to get yourself to the hospital. Maybe by the time you get there they'll have picked up the second man, you'll only find out when you get there.'

Tom couldn't move, something didn't seem to make sense. 'It can't be one of them,' he said, 'they would never have split up.'

'You don't know what happened; they may have had no choice.' Greg tried to hoist him up but Tom was suddenly spurred into action and abruptly pushed him away.

'I've got to get going, I need to know what's happening!' he shouted as he ran erratically along the promenade, but Greg sprinted after him and grabbing his arm he swung Tom round.

'Where the hell are you going?' he demanded.

'Get off me,' Tom growled. 'I'm going to the car like you told me to. I've got to get to the hospital to find out for myself what the hell is happening.' They were tussling like kids in a playground and Greg could feel himself losing ground, but he held on, gasping for breath.

'Not like this you're not, you're in no fit state to drive a car.' With one last surge of energy he held Tom fast. 'Look at yourself, you're shaking from head to foot. Think about your wife and kids at home if you go and kill yourself on top of everything else.'

He didn't want to think about Sharon and the kids but Greg's words pierced the fog in his brain and he gave up the struggle. 'What else can I do?'

'I'd drive you there but there is far too much alcohol in my blood so I'll do the next best thing. Here's the money for a taxi.' Tom started to object but Greg thrust the money into his hand. 'Look Tom, we're wasting valuable time here. Stop thinking about your precious pride for once and take it, otherwise I'll have to force you into a cab and come with you. I'd do that anyway but I've got a few things I need to sort out over there first. Now are you going or not?' Tom nodded and Greg walked with him to the taxi rank, where he instructed the driver to take Tom to the Accident and Emergency Department at the local hospital.

Chapter 20

Bryony called Marie from the safety of the store room adjoining the kitchen. She was in no fit state either mentally or physically to be seen by any of the guests, the time for acceptable tears shed by the mother of the bride had long passed and she was in no mood to explain her appearance to anyone. Marie, already puzzled by the deposit of a seemingly sober Colin at their table, wondered what Bryony could want from her now. Deliberately avoiding Claire's questioning look she excused herself from the table and went to the store room. She had no idea what to expect but the sight of Bryony cowering in a corner crying more tears than her lacy handkerchief could cope with took her by surprise.

'Whatever's happened?' she asked in alarm as Bryony launched herself at her and collapsed into her arms sobbing.

Marie held her for as long as she was able but eventually she eased herself away and tore open a pack of kitchen roll. 'Here,' she said, 'wipe your eyes and pull yourself together, I can't help you if I don't know what's happened.'

I didn't take long for Marie, despite Bryony's

garbled, incoherent explanation, to understand that the gist of the matter was Greg's response to her plan to tell Colin she was leaving him. 'You were right,' she muttered, 'he didn't agree with me doing it this weekend and now he's really angry with me. I don't know what to do.'

'He'll come round,' Marie said, 'he's obviously surprised and angry but it isn't the end of the world, he'll get over it soon enough.' She guessed it was probably not as bad as Bryony was describing. She'd always been prone to exaggeration, especially when her own wishes were in danger of being thwarted.

'It's not as simple as that, I've never seen him like this before.' She lifted her mascara-streaked face to Marie. 'Will you help me?'

'And do what exactly?' Marie protested. 'It's a private matter between the two of you and Greg certainly won't thank me for poking my nose in.'

'He respects you and I'm sure he'll listen to you. All you have to do is persuade him I made a mistake and I'm really sorry.'

Greg's supposed strong reaction seemed out of character and Marie suspected there was more to the situation than Bryony was telling her. She had no idea how she could help and she was reluctant to put her lifelong friendship with him in jeopardy by her interference. 'Have you told me everything?' she asked. 'You promise you're not being a little bit economical with the truth?'

Bryony was getting edgier and she made no attempt to control her irritation. 'For goodness' sake Marie, I'm not asking you to do much, just have a word to calm him down. I've told you everything there is to tell.'

Marie still wasn't convinced she was in possession of all the facts and she was beginning to feel irritated by Bryony's attitude, which wasn't exactly conducive to an appeal for help. 'I'm not promising anything but if the opportunity arises I'll try and find out how he's feeling. I'm sure Greg will already have forgiven you, he doesn't usually hold a grudge for long.'

'I know but he was this time he is really furious with me.'

Marie had no idea how she could help, especially as her sympathies were all with Greg, but once again she gave in to Bryony's cries for help; there was nothing to be gained by pointing out that this was the inevitable outcome of Bryony's own actions. 'It's you he's cross with so it should be you who explains and apologises,' she said, but when Bryony started to protest Marie held her hands up in resignation. 'Don't worry, I've already said I'll do my best. Now come along, you've already been out here too long.'

'I can't be seen like this,' Bryony wailed. 'I must look an absolute wreck.'

'I wouldn't say that exactly, but you are in need of a few repairs. I suppose it goes without saying that you have some make-up in your bag.' Bryony was already taking out a compact from her tiny clutch bag but she groaned when she saw her reflection in the mirror.

'I'll never get this mascara off, it's everywhere.'

'Here,' said Marie, 'I may not have as much make-up as you but I do have wipes. These claim to wipe away even waterproof mascara so they should do the trick.' In much less time than it usually took her to put on her public face, Bryony took a last satisfied look at her reflection before leaving the room and locking the door behind them.

Still holding a distinct feeling that Bryony was hiding something, Marie went back to the table. There were different vibes in the air as rumours were circulating about a successful outcome to the rescue operation, but there was no sign yet of Damian having returned. Marie knew it would probably be some time before he was able to leave his colleagues to come back to join his friends but Amelia went out of her way to waylay Marie and give her a hug.

'It's such good news,' she said excitedly, 'and I'm so pleased for everyone involved.' Pulling an apologetic downturn of her mouth, she whispered, 'I hate to say it but I can't help feeling a bit relieved that it's over, because apart from everything else, it was definitely casting a shadow over the celebrations.'

'There is nothing to be ashamed of in wanting your wedding day to be happy. Now go along and enjoy the rest of it.'

Amelia pealed with laughter. 'Thanks Marie,' she said. 'Oh look, there's Louisa; she's hopping with excitement at the thought of Damian coming back. I think you may have a rival for your affections, I hope you don't mind.'

Amelia's enthusiasm was infectious and she couldn't help smiling back. 'It's very early days,' she replied, 'but I couldn't be happier and she's a lovely girl. You know what they say, if she's a friend of yours that's the best recommendation there is. Now off you go, I can see Piers on his way over.'

Claire was consumed with curiosity but Marie

successfully deflected the inevitable questions about her absence, but seeing Stuart's worried frown she did her best to reassure him there was nothing to worry about. She was desperate to get the latest news about the rescue operation which was the topic of conversation on everyone's lips, but Colin had tired of the topic already and was looking disconsolately into his glass of lemonade.

'I guess you've been with her,' he said, 'I suppose she told you what happened in the office.' Marie threw him a warning look but he was obviously past caring and completely ignored her.

'She never mentioned the office,' she replied brusquely, in the hope it would deflect him from further conversation, but he doggedly carried on.

'Oh well, if she didn't tell you I may as well. She told me she was leaving me.' He looked round the table to gauge their reaction and seemed pleased when Claire's, as usual, didn't disappoint.

Looking at him in disbelief, she exclaimed excitedly, 'Leaving you? Are you sure?'

'As sure as I'm sitting here,' he replied, 'going away with Greg. Would you believe it? After all these years she's leaving with my best friend.'

His words stunned everyone into silence and while they stared in disbelief Marie tried her best to prevent Colin from going into details, but nothing was going to stop him now. Indignantly he pushed her hand away from where she placed it over his. 'Oh, I know you are on her side, I suppose you've always known about it,' he said with bitterness in his voice. 'Interestingly,' he continued, giving Marie no time to protest, 'that wasn't all she told me.'

He paused to look slowly from one to the other of the group who were following his words with interest and fascination. He was enjoying the attention and the opportunity to get back at Bryony. After keeping them in suspense for a few seconds, he took a deep breath. 'She finally came clean and told me what I suppose I should have already suspected.' He paused once again for effect, and dreading what he was going to say, Marie tried her best to make him stop, but it was no use and she waited with a feeling of dread.

'She told me,' he said, 'that Amelia isn't my daughter. So not only is he taking my wife but he's stealing my daughter as well.'

Apart from the sudden intake of breath there was a deathly silence round the table. Marie turned swiftly to check if there were any bystanders who may have overheard but hopefully the music was drowning out his voice to anyone except those close to him. Suddenly he leaned his head backwards, opened his mouth wide and his bellicose laughter burst out and reached upwards towards the rafters.

Marie looked at Stuart for help but he was sitting completely nonplussed and helpless. It was obvious now that Colin's behaviour had grabbed the attention of several people but she was relieved to see most of them discreetly turn away. The hope that Colin was finished with his revelations was swiftly dashed.

Grimacing as he took a sip of his drink, he looked around at his bewildered audience. 'You haven't heard the best bit yet,' he said. 'What she didn't know was that my father and Greg heard the lot. They'd arrived without her knowing and they heard every bit of her grubby outburst.'

Marie was appalled. It threw a whole new light on the situation and one which confirmed her earlier suspicions. Bryony had very cleverly concealed the truth from her while at the same time begging her to help. She was the first to break the shocked silence. 'Let me get this right, Colin. You're telling us that Bryony told you all this in front of Ralph and Greg?'

'Got it in one, Marie,' he said. 'Oh, and not to forget Justin and Ellie who weren't in the room but I'm pretty sure they would have heard. Not that they'll be very sorry as she said she'd trained them up to take charge of the hotel.'

'Did Greg and Ralph hear that as well?'

'They sure did.'

'Why were you there in the office having this discussion?' Stuart asked. 'It seems a funny time and place to do it, especially today and when there are so many people around.'

'Ah well, I can explain that. You see I was in the office when I fell. I think I was a bit drunk and Justin sent for Bryony to come and help. She was hopping mad and she just couldn't contain herself.' He shook his head. 'It all came out in one outburst. One thing I can't understand is how Greg took it all. He seemed shocked and walked away and wouldn't speak to Bryony.' His face contorted with bewilderment and Marie felt a rush of sympathy for him. He'd learned about Bryony's affair and the outcome of it in full view of other people and she couldn't imagine how he must feel. No matter what kind of failure as a husband Bryony thought him to be, he didn't deserve this kind of treatment.

Despite that, she hoped he'd finished, but there

was obviously something puzzling him because although he carried on speaking it was almost as though he was talking to himself. 'What I couldn't understand, Greg seemed as shocked as me. He wouldn't speak to Bryony and he left in a huff.' His head moved from side to side as they all waited anxiously for him to continue.

'He must have known she was going to tell me otherwise she wouldn't have said it.' He looked blearily around the table, his adrenalin rush already depleted. 'They did a good job of sobering me up, not very pleasant actually but then I suppose I am still considered to be the father of the bride and it's important to keep up standards.' He turned his bloated eyes onto Marie. 'She thought you'd be the one to keep me out of trouble but surely I'm allowed one little drink now if I promise to behave myself?'

'You're a grown man, Colin. You can do what you like as far as I'm concerned,' she said angrily. She was livid with Bryony for deliberately lying and misleading her and she shuddered at the thought of what a fool she'd have made of herself if she'd spoken to Greg on Bryony's behalf. 'Come on love,' she said to Stuart, 'let's go and find out what's happening out there.'

Stuart had seen the effect Colin's words had had on Marie and it didn't take much understanding to guess that as it had sometimes happened in the past, it was Bryony who was the cause of it.

'We'll all come,' Claire said, and they all followed the crowd heading for the door.

'It looks as if she's burned all her bridges in one go,' Stuart whispered to Marie.

Marie agreed. 'Yes it does,' she replied, 'but this

time I'm not getting involved. From now on I refuse to be manipulated by her.'

'You've said that before,' Stuart reminded her, 'several times.'

'I know but this time I mean it. Unfortunately that isn't the most important thing at the moment and I'm worried sick.'

'Come on love, you've just said you're not getting involved, what on earth are you worried about now?'

'We're already involved,' she replied. 'It's Amelia, how on earth do we prevent Colin, or anyone else for that matter, talking about it to Amelia?'

'Oh my god, I never even gave that a thought.'

'No, and unfortunately I doubt if anyone else has. I must try and have a word with Greg. Things are bad enough now but that would be a complete disaster.'

Stuart put a restraining hand on her arm. 'It's a very delicate situation, are you sure you want to get more caught up in it?' Gently she pulled away.

'Unfortunately I already am.' Scanning the room, she walked to the reception area where she caught a glimpse of Greg entering the revolving door, and despite hurrying as fast as she was able he'd disappeared before she was able to catch up with him.

Chapter 21

Bryony was trembling. Despite Greg's firm stance she refused to believe he wouldn't come to his senses, but she couldn't afford to take any chances, it was imperative to secure her position at the hotel. Ralph had reluctantly agreed to meet her but persuading him her words had been spoken in the heat of the moment was proving much harder than she'd anticipated. He was a fair and reasonable man and she'd fully expected him to be receptive to her state of mind, but although he readily accepted her nerves were probably stretched by all the planning and work leading up to the wedding, he was less willing to believe it made any difference to what she'd threatened to do.

If only she hadn't extolled the virtues of Justin and Ellie quite so effectively he might have been more apprehensive about the future success of the business, but he seemed very confident of his nephew's abilities. He was in fact, showing more confidence in Justin's abilities than she was feeling. Despite that, he was looking weary and in her love for him she felt a sudden and genuine regret for inflicting this on him, today of all days.

She seemed to have spent the day apologising to

various people but this time it was said with conviction. 'I'm sorry,' she whispered, and he nodded sadly despite his reservations.

'I'm afraid I'm finding it difficult to understand, but how and why you did it today is incomprehensible. I suppose at least you have the excuse of acting on the spur of the moment. What is very obvious from your previous actions is the fact you've obviously been planning this for a long time, and that signifies a marked decline of your interest in the business whatever you say to the contrary.'

The ground seemed to be slipping from beneath her feet, why did no-one believe a word she was saying? 'No!' she cried. 'You know that isn't true and you have no cause to say it. I had no intention or desire to give up my involvement in the hotel, what I said about Justin was in the heat of the moment and we both know Colin is incapable of taking over.'

'Sadly that's true, but maybe things could change,' he said. 'Maude had a theory that a strong woman would help Colin to mature and settle down and she never wavered from that view. I tended to agree and we both envisaged you as that person. Of course we were aware of your involvement with Greg but we naively believed you'd broken off your engagement because you'd fallen in love with our son.' His face clouded with memories. 'Unfortunately it soon became clear it was the business which had been the attraction and your affections remained elsewhere.'

Although he was speaking the truth about her loving Greg she must make him see it had had no impact on her commitment to the hotel, she'd devoted her life to it and been instrumental in maintaining and even building on its success. Somehow she had to remind him of that if there was to be any chance of her further involvement in the business. 'Tell me, have you ever had reason to complain in all the years we've been married?' she asked.

Ralph shook his head. 'No,' he replied with a faint smile, 'that is the sad part; you've been a good wife to our son and an excellent mother to our grandchildren in all but two respects.'

Bryony waited, her heart was banging with apprehension and her hands were clammy with fear; this wasn't going as she expected and she'd rarely seen Ralph looking so stern. Desperately she tried to think of a way to win him over but he continued, giving her little chance to intervene.

'You didn't love Colin and should never have married him. I believe Maude was right, he could have been a better man if he hadn't been forced to live with the knowledge that he was a poor second best to his friend. Despite that, he would probably have developed his skills with a little support and encouragement from you.'

Shocked and hurt, she recognised the truth behind his words but she would never be prepared to accept the suggestion that she'd been the cause of Colin's failures. 'So I'm to be blamed for all Colin's shortcomings,' she protested vehemently. 'Well I'm sorry Ralph but that is grossly unfair.'

'No Bryony, I'm not suggesting that; Colin has no-one to blame for his behaviour but himself. All I'm saying is I believe things could have been better if you'd refrained from constantly making it so clear how inferior you thought he was.'

Torn between walking out and trying to secure her future, she stood her ground. 'What do you intend to do? Am I to be thrown on the scrap heap after all the years I've dedicated to the business?'

Ralph looked jaded and wearily shook his head. 'Oh Bryony,' he sighed, 'how has it come to this? Of course I'm not forcing you out, you've done that yourself.' His compassionate eyes expressed the affection he'd felt all the years she'd been a part of his family, but she knew he would find it was impossible to ignore what he'd witnessed earlier. 'I'm impressed with Justin and Ellie,' he told her. 'You've done an excellent job of training them up to take over the running of the hotel and I appreciate that. Hopefully they have the passion and ideas needed to take it forward.'

Bryony stood helplessly as Ralph extolled the virtues of the couple she'd presented so successfully as her successors. 'They could work together under me,' she protested, 'we make a good team.' Never had she felt so out of control of a situation and there was so much riding on the outcome it scared her. The chair Colin had slid off earlier remained on its side on the floor, a reminder of the unpleasant episode which had pre-empted this conversation.

'When we put you in charge of the running the business I don't think you'd have taken kindly to having to answer to someone in a position of seniority, and I believe we have to accord the same principle to the current situation. If Justin is deemed to be worthy of the position, and you have convinced me he is, then we must show confidence in him.'

Bryony didn't know whether to laugh or cry. 'What is to happen to me?' she asked. 'Do I figure anywhere in your future plans?'

Ralph was thoughtful for a few moments, deliberating on the unexpected events of the day. 'You have given a lot of your time to the business and the benefit has been immense, I won't forget that,' Ralph said, 'but I also have to think of my son and I believe the only chance he has, is to be allowed or even forced, into taking on some responsibility.' Moving towards the door, indicating the conversation was coming to an end, he added, 'You have made your intentions and priorities very clear and they obviously don't include Colin, so I wish you good luck, my dear.'

Bryony couldn't believe what was happening and she began to panic. 'I will take no part in the business then, despite all the years I've given to it. Is that all the thanks I get?' she demanded.

Ralph looked genuinely bemused. 'Bryony, I honestly don't know what you want me to say. You will of course receive more than adequate remuneration, commensurate with your contribution to the company.'

The tears she'd been trying to contain welled up and ran down her cheeks and she struggled to speak, but there was something she needed to know. 'Wait!' she cried. Ralph stood patiently waiting for her to continue. 'You told me,' she said at last, 'there were two reasons for being disappointed in me. My treatment of Colin, what was the other?'

Ralph's face saddened. 'When we guessed that Amelia was not our biological grandchild.'

Her body slumped as his words confirmed her worst fears; during all the years since Amelia's birth, the one thing she'd hoped for above all else was that Maude and Ralph would never know. 'I'm sorry,' she whispered, but even she knew how trite the words sounded in these circumstances.

'It never made any difference to our love for her,' he replied. 'She is and always will be ours.'

'Will that stay the same now?' she asked.

'Of course, she will always be our granddaughter whatever happens.'

Bryony nodded. 'I must go now.' Their shared look of affection almost broke them both but she whispered, 'I never meant to hurt you,' and slipped out of the room.

She left the room, ineffectually wiping her face but she was past caring about the streaks of mascara once again running down her face. She'd struggled to produce the traditional tears during the ceremony but ever since then she felt as if she'd done nothing but cry. Keeping her face averted, she walked quickly and wordlessly past Justin and Ellie.

Ralph's reaction and determination to exclude her from the business was shocking and painful. She couldn't believe he'd suspected the truth about her and Greg but most especially she was shaken to learn that Maude had also known. She understood how traumatised she must have been and a great sense of sadness overwhelmed her. It was even more important than ever to persuade Greg that tonight hadn't changed anything, but her confidence was draining away.

Maybe she could turn his newly found fatherhood

to her advantage. Even she recognised how calculated her actions would appear to Greg if he became aware of what she was doing, but she knew he loved both of them and it was a desperate situation needing serious action. It was a risk she was prepared to take.

Finding him deep in conversation with Katy didn't help to improve her mood but by now she was indifferent to what anyone thought, and when she asked for a few words in private Greg immediately agreed. Katy merely smiled obligingly but in Bryony's opinion he was too quick in assuring her he would return as soon as possible, and she struggled to hide her impatience.

In a matter of moments they were walking away and she could feel the tension in his body. 'You don't look well, are you alright?' he asked. When she nodded he added, 'Was that really necessary then?'

'Yes it was actually, it's the small matter of my...' she quickly corrected herself, '*our* daughter and how we are we going to deal with the situation.'

'It's a bit late in the day to involve me,' he pointed out. 'Twenty-five years too late to be precise.'

'Oh, why are you being so obtuse?' she cried. 'You know very well what I mean, I've agreed we need to talk to her but we must be careful to pick the best time to do it.'

'You know my feelings on the subject already,' he said. 'I want her to know as soon as possible, especially now it's practically been made public.'

She was beginning to feel distraught, nothing was going to plan and there was nowhere to turn. 'It will ruin her wedding day, Greg. Surely one day won't make any difference,' she pleaded.

'It will do if someone else tells her first.'

'But no-one would be so cruel, they would have to be deliberately setting out to hurt her and there isn't one person here who would want to do that.' She could sense him weakening; she knew the last thing he wanted was for Amelia to be hurt.

'I don't know,' he said, 'suppose someone lets it just slip out by mistake.'

'It would have to be a monumental mistake. Trust me, after the honeymoon would be kinder.'

'Trusting in you doesn't give me much confidence,' he told her, 'but very well. I'll go along with your suggestion if you really believe it's for the best.'

Sagging with relief, she said, 'I do, I really do. Now how about the dance you promised me earlier.'

'No thanks. I promised to go back to Katy and then I have to go out for a while, there's someone I want to see.'

His curt dismissal stunned her and having no desire to see him meeting up with Katy again, she turned away from him and walked away.

Chapter 22

The taxi pulled up outside the brightly lit entrance. An ambulance with blue flashing lights pulled up in the cordoned-off area and green-uniformed paramedics jumped out and swiftly pushed a stretcher through the door. Tom couldn't see the patient being wheeled in and he was tempted to run after them to see if it was Danny or Rick, but he was fumbling in his pocket trying to find the money Greg had pushed into his hand. When he handed the crumpled note to the driver, he waved it away. 'This is on me,' he said, 'call it my little contribution to the rescue operation. My cousin's one of the crew,' he explained as Tom tried to force the money on him. Muttering his thanks, Tom turned and hurried towards the entrance, but the driver left his cab and followed him.

A long queue was winding towards the glass-fronted reception desks but the driver made his way to an enquiry kiosk and following a few explanations, they were guided towards a row of seats at the side of the room. It was explained to Tom that he would be called as soon as he could be taken to the room where the rescued man was being evaluated. 'They are aware who you are here for and have promised you'll be dealt with as soon as possible,' the driver told Tom.

'Good luck mate, hope you get good news.'

Tom nodded and thanked him. There was no point trying to explain that whatever news he got it wouldn't be all good. No matter what he was told about the man lying there, it still left one missing and that was something that didn't bear thinking about. He seemed to be surrounded by a waiting room full of men with self-inflicted injuries, mainly picked up on football fields or in alcohol-fuelled fights, judging by the look of them, and he was filled with anger at them all. They were no better than Danny or Rick in his opinion, having conveniently forgotten the numerous times he and his mates had been in exactly the same position. He fidgeted nervously until a young nurse approached and instructed him to follow her.

When she led him to a small room and told him to wait he had to fight off the urge to flee. Having no idea who'd he'd find in the hospital bed made him panic. Would it be his brother or his best friend? How could he possibly wish for one above the other? They were both husbands and fathers and whatever happened he would have to pass on the unbelievably bad news. He would be blamed and so he should be, but he shuddered at the thought. What a bloody idiot he'd been and what bloody idiots they'd been, but still none of them deserved this. He tried to tell himself this over and over again until his head was spinning.

The nurse returned and gently beckoned him to follow. 'He isn't unconscious,' she explained, 'but we're keeping him sedated for the time being to allow his body to recover. Don't be too concerned about the tubes and things; it looks far worse than it is.'

Tom nodded but hung back before going in the

room. At the sight of the man on the bed he slumped onto the chair placed just within reach and dropped his head in his hands. The nurse tried to reassure him, explaining the routine procedures they'd put in place but which some people found alarming. He couldn't bring himself to tell her his reaction had nothing to do with all the equipment but was due to his shock at seeing Rick lying there instead of his brother. What kind of a man did that make him?

When she was satisfied he'd recovered sufficiently to be left alone she left the room, telling him she was going to bring him a cup of tea. When she'd gone he stood up and after a few seconds he tentatively approached the bed.

'I'm glad you're still alive, mate. I really am,' he told the sleeping figure, 'but I just wish it was both of you.' His body shuddered with silent sobs and when the nurse returned he allowed her to lead him back to the chair.

'You really mustn't upset yourself,' she said gently. 'I'm sure your friend is going to be alright, but the doctor will be along shortly and he'll be able to explain things better than I can.' She handed him the mug and he took a deep drink before turning his tearstained face towards her.

'You don't understand,' he gulped, 'he was with my brother who's still missing.'

For a few seconds she looked at him, trying to make sense of his words, and then her face flushed with sympathy. 'Oh, I'm sorry. I didn't know there were two men missing.'

'Yes, they both went out in the bay together but only Rick has been rescued. I think they've found the dinghy but there's no sign of my brother.' He massaged his scalp in agitation. 'I don't know how I'm going to tell our mum and Amy, that's his wife; I just don't know.'

Her manner changed to brisk efficiency. 'Now come on, I think you're jumping to conclusions much too quickly,' she replied, 'it's far too soon to give up hope yet. I know what those lifeboat crews are like and they certainly won't have given up searching, and they won't do until there is absolutely no hope left. You've got to stay positive. Now drink that tea and I'll be back soon with the doctor.'

Tom nodded disconsolately but did as he was told.

His head was lolling on his chest when he became aware of someone speaking in the room. Jerking it upwards, he looked towards the bed but Rick was still lying unaware of his surroundings, and he slowly recognised the voice of the young nurse. 'Tom, the doctor's here to speak to you.'

Heavy with exhaustion, he pulled himself up to a standing position and apologised. 'I must have fallen asleep,' he explained unnecessarily, rubbing the back of his neck which was aching from the uncomfortable position he'd been slumped in. The doctor smiled in sympathy. 'I know just how you feel,' he said. 'I think I would fall asleep on a clothes line if I was given half a chance.' He was wasting no time as he checked Rick's pulse and moved a stethoscope across his chest while he was speaking. 'Everything seems to be going according to plan,' he said as he drew up a seat and indicated for Tom to sit down again. 'The patient is a friend of yours, I believe.' Tom nodded and the doctor flicked through the papers in a file and said slowly, 'We're a bit short on details concerning your friend; I'm hoping you can fill in the gaps.'

Tom was impatient to find out how serious Rick's condition was and what had happened to him, in the hope it might give an inkling as to how he'd become separated from Danny, but as tired as he was he knew that he'd find out nothing until he'd co-operated with them. He knew Rick as well as if he was his own brother so it didn't take long to give them the information they were asking for. All he could tell them of his medical history was that he never seemed to ail anything, but they smiled and said that kind of data was available to them now they had his name and address and the details of his GP's practice.

'What's the matter with him?' Tom asked wearily. 'Why is he in such a bad way?'

'He was picked up from the sea,' the doctor explained, 'and he'd swallowed a considerable amount of water, some of which had entered his lungs. He was also suffering from hypothermia.'

'But it was a really hot day!' Tom exclaimed. 'Lots of people were in the sea.'

'During the day maybe, but not at night if they've got any sense, and don't forget it is much colder away from the shore. Unfortunately people don't realise how cold it gets further out and it gets even worse when the sun goes down.'

Tom realised how stupid he must have sounded but he seemed incapable of thinking straight and his body gave an involuntary shiver at the thought of Rick and Danny struggling in the freezing water. He still didn't understand how they came to be in the sea and he wondered if anyone knew how it had happened. The possibility of finding out the condition of the dingy was to blame scared him, but he had to know, and fixing his eyes on Rick he asked, 'Why were they were in the water? Had the dinghy capsized?' The doctor shook his head, apparently unable to cast any light on the matter.

'I'm afraid we have no details of what happened, your friend was in no state to answer questions when he was brought in.'

'So we have no idea if my brother may still be in the water.'

'Were your friend and your brother together when they set out?'

Tom nodded and the doctor laid a hand on his shoulder. 'I'm sorry I can't help you,' he said as he left the room.

He was asked if he wanted to make any phone calls but like a coward he shook his head and refused, telling himself that Sharon wouldn't be expecting to hear from him. He would have to face the music later when she'd question why the hospital hadn't offered the use of a phone, but for now he was hiding behind the excuse of a phone out of charge. He only hoped the news of Rick's rescue hadn't been reported on the news, but the last time they'd spoken she'd told him they were all going to try and catch a few hours' sleep before the children woke up. She'd extracted a promise from him to let her know as soon as there were any developments but he couldn't bring himself to tell her Rick was safe before he had some news of Danny.

He had no idea what time it was or how long he'd been dozing when he felt a hand on his shoulder, pulling him back from his nightmares. It took a few seconds for him to realise it was neither a nurse nor a doctor but Greg who was responsible for his rude awakening. Roughly rubbing his eyes, he blinked under the subdued night lighting and asked him gruffly what he was doing there. Greg smiled. 'Well I've had more enthusiastic welcomes but I'll let you off under the circumstances. How are things?'

'How do you think?' Tom replied. 'Sorry,' he muttered, 'but nothing's changed.' He ran his fingers through his hair. 'Oh, I forgot you don't know. It was Rick who'd been rescued, but he's sedated so I still don't know what happened. I think they are letting him wake up in the morning so maybe at least I'll find out something. Not that it'll make any difference; Danny will still be missing.' His chin dropped. 'Have they called off the search?'

'They hadn't when I left but they might do soon.' Tom's groan was heart wrenching but Greg didn't give up. 'I don't want to give you false hope, Tom, but what's your surname?'

Tom turned to him in disbelief. 'Are you playing some kind of game with me? What difference does it make what my name is?'

'Just tell me.'

'It's Lester, if you must know. Now are you satisfied?'

'Yes, very, as a matter of fact. Tom, I can't be certain but I think your brother is safe.' Tom's body froze but his thoughts whirled, hardly daring to believe what he'd heard. Slowly he turned to face Greg. 'You're not having me on, please tell me you're not having me on.'

'I wouldn't do that,' Greg said, 'but all I know is that there is a man called Danny Lester who is in a bed just down the corridor.'

Tom leaped up and was already at the door. 'Where is he?' he demanded, but Greg held him back.

'I know how you must feel,' he said, 'but the doctor is on his way to see you. He'll be here any minute now.'

Tom was pulling away. 'I must go to him, I need to see him.'

'You don't know where he is and if you leave now you'll miss the doctor. Just hang on for a few minutes,' Greg said.

No sooner had he finished speaking than a doctor Tom hadn't seen before entered the room. 'Mr Lester?' he asked. Tom was twitching nervously.

'Where's my brother?' he asked breathlessly. 'Is it true? Is he alright?'

To Tom's frustration the doctor sat down and looked at the notes in his hand. 'We just need to clear up a few points, and then we'll take you to see him.' After a few brief questions about whether Tom's brother had been in the bay collecting cockles, who he was with and what kind of boat he was in, the doctor smiled and told them he was satisfied the man they'd admitted that night was in fact Tom's brother. 'If you'd like to follow me I'll take you to him,' he said with a smile. Tom wanted to race down the corridors but he recognised he wouldn't have any idea which way to go so he stayed between the two men who, understanding his impatience, moved at a brisk pace. He hardly dared look in the direction of the bed when they at last entered a room but the unmistakable voice of Danny broke the silence.

Moving the nebuliser mask from his face he said sheepishly, 'Hi Tommy, I'm sorry about this.'

Tom sank with relief onto the chair close to the bed. A rush of all the emotions he'd experienced in the last few hours flooded his body, but the overriding one was thankfulness that both men were still alive.

'Well I don't think there's any doubt we've got the right man,' the doctor said, 'so I'll leave you to it.'

'I'll do the same,' Greg said, but Tom stopped him. 'No! You stay, you've been with me all through this.'

'Are you going to introduce us?' Danny said, but Tom shook his head.

'Not until you've told us what the hell has been going on,' he replied. 'You've got a lot of explaining to do.'

'Where do you want me to start?' Danny asked.

'Well first of all I'd like to know how you two got separated.'

Danny nodded. 'That's the easy bit. When we were having difficulty with the dinghy some fishermen offered to tow us in. At first we agreed but when they said we'd have to throw some of our catch overboard we told them we would manage on our own. The dinghy was stuck in a sandbank and the engine wouldn't start. Rick said he knew what to do but I don't think he did because it never did get going again.'

'Hang on a minute,' Tom interrupted, 'are you saying he tried to start it when it was out of the water?'

'Yes, I told you we were stuck in a sandbank.'

'You're bigger idiots than I took you for,' Tom said in despair, 'you don't know the first thing about outboard engines. Anyway, go on.'

'Later when my breathing was getting worse and some other fishermen offered to help and take us with them, I accepted. Rick still refused; he kept saying there was no way he was going to throw hundreds of pounds overboard into the sea. I was running out of my inhaler so I knew I needed to get back. I kept thinking of the time it would take to get home and I could feel an attack coming on and I panicked.' His face crumpled with apology. 'I'm sorry Tommy, I know we should have stayed together but I knew I'd be in trouble if I didn't get back quickly. How is Rick? The doctor just told me he's going to be alright.'

'Yes I think he is, but he's been dead lucky. Don't forget he's the one who was in the wrong, he should have done what you did and left the bloody cockles where they were. Oh, I know...' he said when Danny tried to interrupt, 'it's money, but what's the point of that if you lose your life saving a few hundred pounds?'

A nurse came in and told them that in the interest of the patient's welfare she would have to ask them to leave. 'I suggest,' she said, looking pointedly at Tom, 'that you go and get some sleep and come back in the morning. There is nothing you can do here tonight, your brother needs peace and quiet and I intend to see he gets it.'

For the first time since he'd learned that Danny and Rick were missing, Tom allowed himself to smile. He recognised when it was useless to argue, he'd seen that look on Sharon's face many times. He gave Danny a fierce hug before tearing himself away; he didn't want to lose sight of him so soon after finding him again but he was left with no choice, and after promising to be back later he joined Greg, who was already striding down the corridor towards the exit. 'What I don't understand,' he said, getting into the taxi, 'is how you found out that Danny was there.'

'It was quite bizarre,' Greg told him. 'When I came back to the hospital to find you, I asked a doctor if he knew where the man rescued from the bay was. By a sheer fluke he'd been there when Danny was admitted and so he took me to him. I asked a member of staff what his name was and although I didn't know your surname it seemed too coincidental when they told me he was called Danny. It was only when I tried to locate you that we realised there were two survivors and you were with the other one. I don't know any more than you how your friend was admitted without the connection between them being made, but I suppose we'll have to wait until tomorrow before we can ask any more questions.'

'You're right there,' Tom agreed, 'I certainly wouldn't like to cross that last nurse we saw. That reminds me,' he said, laughing, 'I must ring Sharon ASAP.'

Chapter 23

The atmosphere was charged as news of the rescue spread round the building. Marie watched Amelia and her friends throw themselves into the dancing with an abandonment which had been missing since Damian had been called to his post as a crewman. It had touched her to see their concern translated into such a genuine reaction and she was glad for everyone's sake that it was having a happy ending. She thought about the men who'd been rescued and the terrible distress their families would have suffered while they waited for news.

She could just make out Ralph and Greg on the far side of the room and by their body language they seemed to be deeply engaged in conversation. It was impossible from this distance to determine whether it was a casual conversation or one which involved the tricky subject of Amelia. Both men's lives would be changed irrevocably by what they had learned but she was relieved to see they didn't appear to be engaged in any kind of disagreement. She felt a wave of sympathy for both of them; Ralph, who'd learned his granddaughter was not strictly of his bloodline, and Greg, who'd discovered he had a daughter. Whatever reasons had prompted Bryony's decision to hide the truth about Amelia's parentage, it was now having a profound effect on the people most closely linked to her.

She'd tried to make contact with Greg but for some reason he'd been missing for quite a while and now he seemed to be avoiding her, but whether he liked it or not she was determined to speak to him. She had to know what decisions had been made concerning Amelia and how they were going to avoid the possibility of her finding out the truth. She could understand his wish to acknowledge her, but today wasn't the right time and it would be disastrous if Amelia inadvertently overheard something. Whatever else happened, that had to be avoided at all costs.

Despite the need to speak to them both, she was reluctant to interrupt their conversation, so for a little light relief she turned her attention back to the dance floor where Louisa was dancing with a group of her friends. Marie was amused to see her eyes constantly flicking towards the door and when she suddenly stopped dancing and darted towards it Marie knew instinctively that Damian had returned. When they walked arm in arm towards her, she welcomed them warmly. 'I didn't expect you back so soon,' she said, whispering into his ear as he dropped a kiss on her cheek.

'It was practically sewn up as I arrived,' he told her, and she nodded without replying. Knowing from experience Damian's reluctance to discuss rescue operations immediately following the event, she steered the conversation away when Claire looked ready to jump in and question him.

Stuart's pride in his son was obvious to everyone

but he contented himself with laying his hand on his son's shoulder as he stood up and asked him what he'd like to drink. Due to the possibility of being called out Damian hadn't touched a drop of alcohol all day but he declared his intention to make up for lost time now. From first thing in the morning when it became obvious there might be a need for extra volunteers, he'd made his position clear to Geoff that despite the wedding he was on emergency callout and would be ready if he was needed.

Stuart was full of admiration for all the crew and he was determined to ensure Damian enjoyed what was left of the evening. After establishing that Louisa would also love another cocktail, he left them and went to take his place amongst the crowd of people jostling round the bar. The news of the rescue had increased sales of alcohol as most people wanted to toast its success, but instantaneously the crowd moved aside, making a space for Stuart in a solid gesture of appreciation for the part his son had played, and his pocket was no lighter when he made his way back with a tray full of drinks paid for by them.

Numerous toasts were drunk. 'To the rescued, the rescuers, and the happy couple.'

'Which happy couple is that?' one of Damian's friends asked. 'The newlyweds or you two?'

Louisa blushed but Marie saw the look she exchanged with Damian, and she raised her own glass happily when an amended toast was suggested. 'Let's propose a toast to all our happy couples.' Catching sight of Stuart looking in her direction, she smiled as she leaned over to clink her glass to his.

'What time are the fireworks?' someone asked.

'Oh of course!' a delighted Louisa exclaimed. 'The display will be back on again now.'

'Now it can be a double celebration!' Marie exclaimed. 'One for Amelia and Piers and the other for everybody being back safe and sound.'

'Sounds good to me,' agreed Damian, 'but is it going to be before or after the bacon butties? I'm starving.'

'There are plenty of nibbles around the place,' Stuart told him, but Damian laughed off the suggestion. 'Nibbles are definitely not going to hit the spot,' he said. 'I might just go to the kitchen and beg something to keep me going.' As she watched them walk away Marie spotted Greg walking over to the bar, so she made a garbled excuse and walked over to where he was standing apart from everyone.

'Can we talk?' she asked, but when he didn't immediately reply, she added, 'I think that's the first time in our lives that I've had to ask permission to speak to you and I don't know what I've done to deserve it.' He shrugged his shoulders dismissively. 'I think I've somehow upset you, Greg, and if I have I'm sorry, but this isn't just about us. Amelia should be our first concern.' Greg's face momentarily softened but he gave Marie no encouragement to carry on speaking, and although he seemed implacable she wasn't prepared to let the problem lie, there was too much at stake. 'We'll have to sort our differences out later but this can't wait, surely you can see that. For goodness' sake, Greg, at least say something.'

'All I am sure of,' he said, 'is that I've been told the most important thing of my life and I just don't know how to handle it.' Turning round to look at her, his voice heavy with emotion, he said, 'I presume you've always known, but you never thought to tell me. I must say, Marie, I'm disappointed. I thought we were good friends.'

'So this is what it's about. Well you're right, I did know the truth about Amelia, but think about what you're saying. I couldn't break Bryony's confidence, but I begged her to tell you at the time and as strange as it may seem we never discussed it again. I never really knew if she'd taken my advice and even though I suspected she hadn't it makes me cross to think she's kept this from you all these years.'

She willed him to believe her, he was after all a very dear friend and she didn't want to lose him because of something she'd never wanted to do.

'I have tried to understand her motives,' he said, 'with little success, but I sought some consolation in her explanation that she was waiting for the right time, and that the time was when we could be together. Now, I believe she never had any intention of telling me the truth.'

Marie nodded. 'Who knows what she was planning to do? But to be honest Greg, I'm getting more than a little bit fed up of being involved in your complicated lives. One thing I do know, the most important person in all this as far as I'm concerned is Amelia.' All at once her dander was up and she no longer cared about other people's touchiness or resentments. 'You are feeling sorry for yourself and Bryony is wallowing in self-pity and all the time the volcano, by the name of Colin, is bubbling up ready to erupt.' She faced him down. 'It's your daughter's wedding day,

Greg. Do you want it completely ruined?'

His surprised expression at her outburst almost made her laugh, and Greg looked at her with a rueful smile. 'You are so right, as usual,' he said. 'I'm sorry Marie, we have no right to drag you into our miserable affairs.' He smiled again but this time it reached his eyes. 'Sorry about the pun, but I shouldn't have taken my frustration out on you.' Suddenly his expression changed as his mind registered the enormity of what she'd said. 'You don't really think Colin will say anything do you?' he asked.

'He already has,' she replied, 'that's what I've been trying to tell you.'

Chapter 24

The men were busy trying to make up for lost time, setting up the elaborate firework display. Ralph had pulled a few strings to obtain permission for it to be held on the beach directly opposite the hotel, but this in itself posed a few problems. Although the platform had been sectioned off from the rest of the beach and a team of men had taken it in turns to guard it throughout the day, the stringent health and safety regulations prevented most of the largest fireworks being in position until the start of the display was imminent. On what had turned out to be one of the hottest days of the year this precaution was even more important. All the usual stipulations and conditions had been adhered to but the doubt about whether it would even be held at all had added to the problem. With the successful outcome of the rescue operation, the need to work at top speed to get everything into place soon had the men rushing up and down the structure and fixing the enormous fireworks securely into place.

Bryony was determined the spectacular show should not be compromised in any way by the events of the day or even the shortage of time left for setting it up, so she went to speak to the man in charge to make her instructions clear. Unknown to Ralph she'd paid a considerable amount of money in addition to his arranged fee, to make sure it was a display to outdo all the others for miles around, including the resort further down the coast, whose boast was always to hold the most spectacular annual display in the north of England. Until now this had gone unchallenged but it was Bryony's intention to break their hold on the title for this year at least. If the organisers of the event suspected her motives they kept their thoughts well hidden, but she was not fooled by their compliance, which she guessed was fuelled by the opportunity to wring even more money out of her generous cache of funds. As a businesswoman herself she had no problem with that; as long as both sides got what they wanted it simply meant a sensible deal had been struck.

The small crowd of people who'd hung around watching the unfolding drama surrounding the rescue operation, had been joined by the groups of diners who'd been taking advantage of the late al fresco experience in the square. Together with the wedding guests the celebrations had turned into a public display, and Amelia dragged her parents outside despite both their protestations. 'Don't be such a pair of old fogies; everyone else is going so you two have to be there,' she insisted. 'I know you're tired Mum, but it's not like you to miss the fun.'

Bryony gave up trying to catch Marie's attention and allowed herself to be carried along with the exuberant flow of people. She'd have to wait to find out if Marie had spoken to Greg. Every time she'd managed to catch her eye she pointedly looked away, but Louisa and Damian were with her so she was probably too wrapped up in the budding romance of her son and his new girlfriend to worry about her oldest friend. Amelia and Piers pulled his parents over to join them, forcing Bryony and Colin to make some effort to present themselves as the proud parents of the bride, although both of them were preoccupied with their own thoughts.

The grand finale took everyone's breath away when the sky was lit up by the intertwining names of the bride and groom surrounded by a shower of red hearts. Bryony was bereft of any sensations of pleasure or satisfaction at what should have marked the culmination of all her hard work and planning.

Amelia threw her arms round her mother's shoulders. 'Oh Mum, thank you,' she said. 'You've given us the best wedding we could have ever dreamed of.'

'Well it hasn't turned out quite as planned,' Bryony sighed, 'but as long as you've enjoyed it that's all that matters I suppose.'

'Enjoyed it doesn't come near,' Piers said with a grin. 'It has been an unforgettable experience. Am I allowed to give my new mother-in-law a kiss to say thank you?' Without waiting for a reply he threw his arms round her before turning to shake Colin's hand. 'Thank you both,' he said, 'and of course not forgetting you two,' and he repeated the exchange with his own parents. Bryony forced a smile when Piers' mother and father congratulated her effusively on organising not only the perfect wedding but the whole happy experience of the weekend.

Bryony felt Amelia tug her hand and surreptitiously point a finger towards a couple silhouetted against the sky. 'You know what's making it even more special?' she said. 'Just look over there at Uncle Greg, he looks so happy. I have a premonition that my wedding is going to prove to be the starting point of more than just one romance.' Bryony looked over to where Greg and Katy were standing and her heart sank; she didn't like the way he had a protecting arm around her shoulders and she definitely hated seeing Katy's head resting against him.

'Won't it be fantastic if they fall in love?' Amelia said.

'Don't be so silly, Amelia,' Bryony snapped. 'They've only just met, and don't forget she is still a married woman.'

Amelia, bursting with happiness and wanting everyone else to be a part of it, was oblivious to Bryony's annoyance. 'I know,' she replied, 'but wouldn't it be lovely if they've clicked? It's about time he settled down with someone.' She gave a deep, satisfied sigh. 'Maybe my plan worked after all.'

'What plan?' Bryony asked impatiently. 'What do you mean?'

'I persuaded him to ask Katy to dance,' Amelia said, 'on the pretext it was to make her feel better because I was feeling a bit guilty. He was a bit reluctant at first but I'm sure he's glad now.'

'I really don't think Greg needs you to assist him sort out his love life, you should have left well alone,' Bryony snapped, but Amelia snorted good-naturedly.

'I don't think you can say that, Mum, otherwise he wouldn't be still single when he's nearing his half century.'

Bryony stopped herself from replying; she was

sailing very close to the wind and if she carried on there was a danger of revealing her true feelings. She was saved from thinking of a suitable reply by the sound of Colin's voice rising above the noise. 'Come on you two,' he called, 'I'm sure I can smell bacon butties.'

'Oh shut up,' Bryony said under her breath. 'Sandwiches, Colin,' she corrected him. 'Bacon sandwiches.'

'Whatever you say,' he responded with a laugh, 'but no matter what you call them they still taste as good.'

Bryony was sure she saw a snigger pass between the faces of Piers' parents, but for once she didn't give a damn what they thought.

Chapter 25

Tom lolled on the easy chair and stretched his legs out until his feet rested on the coffee table in front of him. Almost as soon as they touched the polished surface he snatched them back as the image of Sharon's disapproving face planted itself on his retinas. Swinging his body round, he slung his legs over the arm of the chair; another action guaranteed to incur her wrath but not considered a crime as heinous as using the table as a stool. Setting an example to the children was the mantra Sharon lived by and many was the time he'd been held to account on their behalf.

He looked around the room and saw it through her eyes, the luxury and what she would call the tastefulness of it. She was big on things being tastefully thought out and he knew how much she would love this place. Even if they could afford to stay in a hotel it wouldn't be anything as grand as this, and there was no way they'd be able to let the kids loose. Maybe sometime in the future he'd be able to treat Sharon for just one night, but until he got work even that was out of the question. The crackling splutter of the rockets before they exploded their colours into the night sky drew his attention for a short time, but the horror of what might have happened in the dark waters of the bay made him draw the curtains against the images thrown up by the flashes of light. Some of the vehicles and tractors were standing idle by the jetty but there was no sign of the lifeboat which he presumed was back in its housing, being prepared for its next outing. He thought of Geoff and made his mind up to make contact with him as soon as possible.

His mind was in overdrive and as tired as he was, he knew he wouldn't be able to sleep so instead he decided to have a bath. He'd been shown all the amenities by a young girl who'd told him her name was Tracy, and before she left she'd demonstrated how to work the bath. His amusement at the thought of guests needing help to run their own bath water had quickly changed and he'd practically gawped when she'd shown him what it could do. He still didn't understand how he came to be staying in this place, all he could remember through the fog of his confusion when they'd left the hospital, was Greg making a call before telling him there was a room waiting for him at The Portland Arms. His first reaction had been to refuse but without any alternative available to him he'd allowed himself to be brought here. At the thought of all the posh wedding guests he'd nearly turned tail and made his escape, but Greg led him to a back entrance and along a secluded corridor which led to the back stairs where Tracy was waiting.

With his clothes in a heap on the floor he stepped into the biggest tub he'd ever seen. Bubbles enveloped him and testing some of the knobs placed strategically handy, he found himself massaged by vibrations and jets of water similar to the Jacuzzi's he'd seen installed in some of the big houses he'd built. Moving his hand over a sensor caused the room to change through a spectrum of rainbow colours, and he grinned at the sight of his body turning into what Sharon would call "girly pink". What fun they'd have together in this contraption. Pressing an exploratory finger on a remote control transformed the wall mirror into a television, but he switched it off again and lay back and closed his eyes. When he woke up he had no idea how long he'd been dozing but the water was still warm so he thought it must have been only minutes, and then he remembered Tracy telling him there was an inbuilt thermometer to gauge and maintain the temperature at a chosen heat until the bath was emptied.

The bathrobe was thick and white and reminded him of the towel Sharon used for Lily. She was very careful about making sure that everything coming into contact with a baby's skin had to be soft and fluffy. Although it was only hours since he'd come back to Merebank, it seemed like years and he couldn't wait to see them again. He'd rung Sharon as soon as he got here and she'd told him that although they'd heard on the radio that both men were believed to be safely on land again, she couldn't dare believe it until it had come from Tom himself. When he'd told her all he knew he explained how he came to be staying in The Portland Arms and how Greg had arranged it. 'He's been great and I don't know how I'd have got on without him,' he said truthfully. So much had happened in a short time he'd forgotten Sharon hadn't even met him and she was puzzled. 'Why is he being so nice to you?' she asked, and Tom couldn't give any explanation other than he just seemed a decent bloke.

Sharon laughed. 'I told you he was nice,' she reminded him. 'Maybe Rusty did you a favour when he ran into the wedding group, because if he hadn't, Greg would have had no reason to remember you.'

'Remind me to buy Rusty a bone when I get home,' Tom chuckled. 'Now I must go, I'm using the hotel phone.'

'Oh, that reminds me,' Sharon said, 'your mum and Amy asked if you found out why Rick didn't use his mobile to call for help and how Danny managed without his inhalers?'

'Oh, sod it! I forgot. I'll ask tomorrow, well technically it's today,' he said, noticing the clock on the wall. There was a few seconds' silence before Sharon spoke, and when she did her voice was low, all animation gone.

'Tom, I'm still angry with you for what you were planning to do.'

'I know. I'm sorry and I promise...'

'No. Don't say anything now, we need to talk when you come home.'

'OK.' He wished he'd been a bit more with it at the hospital and found out more information to tell her, then she might have been more likely to forgive him, but the memory of the nurse ushering them out reminded him why he hadn't. Tentatively, he told Sharon about her. 'There was a nurse there tonight who reminded me of you.'

'Oh. Was she pretty?'

'Not as pretty as you, but she was...' he hesitated and Sharon stepped in.

'A bit stroppy?'

'Yeees, you could say that.'

Sharon laughed. 'So that's why you didn't ask enough questions. You are a coward, Tom Lester.'

'It's just that I've learned when to hold my tongue.' His throat suddenly constricted with emotion but he needed to tell her so he forced the words out. 'I love you, Sharon.'

'I love you too,' she replied. 'Take care of yourself.'

'I will,' he said, but he decided not to tell her yet just how well he was taking care of himself. There would be plenty of time for them to talk about that later.

He made himself a cup of tea and turned on the television. Flicking through the channels, he was amazed to see the variety of programmes there were available through the night, and he wondered about the people who watched them. The knock on the door sent him flying back into the bathroom to grab his boxers and try to pull them on as quickly as he could. There were no fastenings on the dressing gown and he had no intention of answering the door to Tracy with his full frontal on display. Hopping around on one leg with the robe flapping round his legs, he called out, 'Be with you in a second,' and was surprised to hear Greg burst out laughing on the other side. When he finally got his legs in the right places he hurried to open the door and Greg marched straight in, carrying a tray which he put on the small table.

'What was all that about?' he grinned. 'Were you afraid the lovely Tracy would find you in a state of dishabille?' Tom didn't have a clue what he meant, but guessed it probably just about covered what he'd been worrying about and he tied the belt firmly round his waist. 'I guessed you'd probably be hungry so I've brought some bacon sandwiches up,' Greg said, walking over to open a cupboard containing glasses of all shapes and sizes. Tom was secretly impressed by Greg's confidence in everything he did, but quickly brushed it aside; it was easy to be sure of yourself when everything was handed to you on a plate. Even so, Greg didn't have to do all this and he decided to make the most of it while it lasted. Greg handed him a pint glass and a bottle. 'I've brought some beers up,' he said, 'they go better with bacon I think, and if it's alright with you I'll take the liberty of joining you.'

'You're more than welcome,' Tom told him, 'but shouldn't you be downstairs at the wedding?'

'I suppose I ought to be but I don't think I'll be missed, not by anyone that matters anyway.' He took a large bite out of the bread roll. 'Ah, that tastes good. It seems a long time since we were eating fish and chips.'

Tom nodded. 'A lot's happened since then and I definitely wouldn't like to go through it all again.' His voice dropped with embarrassment. 'Thanks for all your help, by the way.'

'Don't mention it. I suppose you've spoken to your wife, has she forgiven you yet?'

'No,' Tom replied ruefully, 'but she will in time.'

Greg looked doubtful. 'How can you be so sure? Mightn't she use it against you in the future?'

'No,' he replied emphatically, 'Sharon's not like that. Anyway, what's the point? Life's too short to hold grudges. Mmm. These are good.' He remembered to use the napkin to wipe his lips. 'What did you decide to do about your news, your daughter I mean?'

'Against my better judgement I've gone along with

her mother's decision to leave it until after the honeymoon. I'm just scared she finds out from someone else before then but Bryony assures me that won't happen.' He stood up and piled the dirty plates and glasses on the tray. 'We've only got to get through what's left of the night and negotiate the lunch with a few members of the families and friends tomorrow before they set off on their honeymoon. Then and only then I will be able to relax.'

'How are you feeling about it?' Tom asked.

'I'm more concerned with how she will feel,' Greg said. 'Now I suppose I must go and make an appearance, but you try and get some sleep. You'll be served breakfast in your room in a few hours but stay put because there's something I want to discuss with you.' He picked up the tray and walked to the door. 'See you tomorrow.'

'See you,' Tom replied, and when he slipped into bed he had no problem whatsoever falling fast asleep.

Chapter 26

'Come on Debbie, please pick up,' Marie desperately urged her daughter. She was becoming more and more concerned that she'd acted too hastily when she'd reported the behaviour of the young couple in the café. To make matters worse Debbie was still away at the conference and she remembered her being quite put out at the restrictions placed on mobile phone use for the duration of the weekend. Apart from emergency situations there were limited windows of opportunity for the group to make contact with family and friends. When Debbie had first told her mother of the restrictions Marie had been unable to see why it was considered such a big deal, surely anyone could survive a weekend without being constantly available at the end of a phone, but now she was rapidly changing her opinion.

'What harm could a simple phone call do?' she muttered to herself from the safety of the ladies' toilets. Being cloistered in a remote conference centre was supposed to centre the mind, but her own mind was well and truly becoming more and more centred with each passing minute, and that was in the middle of noise and activity bordering on chaos.

Toying with the idea of contacting Debbie's husband to check if he'd arranged a call to her, she hesitated. He would inevitably imagine it presaged some emergency situation and probe for details. Standing by the washbasins, the hand-dryer had started up several times in response to her dithering so she finally gave up and went out to try and locate Stuart. She would have to tell him what she'd done but for the time being she preferred to keep it to herself.

People were drifting back in from the firework display and queues were forming at the long table in the dining room where the bacon and sausage sandwiches were piled up on huge platters. Amelia and Piers were standing together helping to serve them, much to the amusement of their friends, who teased Piers mercilessly about having been turned into a model of domestication so early in their marriage.

Catching sight of Greg trying to balance some bottled beers on a tray with a plateful of sandwiches, she went over to help. 'Which table are they for?' she asked. 'I'll carry some over for you,' but Greg declined.

'No, I'm fine,' he said, 'they're not actually for a table, I'm taking them upstairs to a bedroom.'

'Oh, I'm sorry,' she said, feeling silly and flustered. 'I didn't mean to interfere.'

Greg looked bemused until the meaning of her words became clear. 'Oh Marie,' he explained, 'you've got the wrong end of the stick; I'm taking them up to the brother of one of the rescued men. He's staying here for the night and probably very hungry, so I'm taking him a sandwich and I'm going to join him.'

'I don't understand,' Marie said, 'how does he come to be staying here?'

'I was with him for a while at the hospital and when he was advised to leave to get some rest I discovered he had nowhere to go. I arranged with Justin and Ralph for him to stay here. Now I must go before these get cold.'

'Of course, I won't keep you any longer.' Marie placed a hand on his arm. 'You're a good man, Greg.' Just as he was turning to go, she held him back. 'Just one thing before you go. What did you decide to do about Amelia?'

He glanced round and dropped his voice. 'I've gone along with what Bryony wanted, I suppose it's for the best really. We're leaving it until she gets back from her honeymoon.'

She felt sick with apprehension but said nothing. She was in no position to question peoples' judgement after what she'd done today, but she hoped with all her being that nothing would go wrong which would result in Amelia being hurt. At least the mystery of where Greg had disappeared to earlier had been answered. For a little while she'd wondered if he was with Katy but now she felt ashamed of her suspicions, after all he was perfectly entitled to go where and with whom he wanted.

Some of the older residents were already moving towards the lifts and stairs on their way to bed at the end of a very long and eventful day. Some were making observations about the differences between their own energy and the seemingly boundless stream which ran through the blood of the young people. Suddenly Marie felt emotionally and physically drained and she went in search of Stuart to see if he too was ready to call it a day. As so often happened their thoughts combined and he was already heading in her direction, just as eager as she was to head for home and the comfort of their own bed.

Despite the chill in the air several of the more hardy guests were sitting at the tables outside, but Marie pulled her coat closer and clasped her arms in front of her body to hold it in place. 'I just about managed with this summery outfit today,' she said, shivering slightly, 'but another couple of weeks and I'd have had to think again.'

'Well to be fair we haven't had to be outside very much. Sometimes guests are left hanging about for hours while the couple disappear having photographs taken miles away.'

'A slight exaggeration,' she said, 'but I know what you mean.'

On the beach below the promenade small groups of people had taken advantage of the Portland's firework display to arrange their own less spectacular shows, and some had started hastily assembled mini bonfires. 'Let's go across and see them,' Marie urged Stuart, much to his surprise.

'I thought you were cold and wanted to get home!' he exclaimed. 'I know I do.'

'Don't be such a fuddy-duddy; we'll only be a minute or two.' She was already turning to cross the road so he moved to her side and they walked to the promenade, where they stood leaning on the railings watching the young people enjoying themselves. 'This reminds me of when the children were small,' she said wistfully. 'We had such fun, didn't we?'

'Indeed we did.' Stuart bent his head backwards and gazed upwards. 'Look at that sky, it's so clear tonight. One of the good things about living here is we have such a wide expanse of sky day and night.' He pointed his finger. 'Can you see the Great Bear, just up there?' Marie wasn't impressed.

'You know I can never make out any of those things. If you ask me you could join up those stars and make it into anything you want it to be. No matter how hard I try I still can't see the shape of a bear or even a plough for that matter. They look pretty though, I'll grant you that.' She turned to go. 'I am getting an image of a mug of hot chocolate and that's without even looking at the stars.'

'At last, something we agree on. Let's get home.'

Marie's mood inexplicably changed when they reached home and she knew sleep wouldn't come easily to her. All the excitement and concerns the day had thrown up had to a certain extent kept the worry of what she'd done at bay, but now it resurfaced with a vengeance. There was no point trying to contact Debbie at this time but she could think of no other way to halt the consequences of her impulsive action. When Stuart handed her a hot drink she felt herself breaking down. 'What's the matter love?' he asked. 'Have I done something wrong?'

'No,' she replied, 'I have. Stuart I've got something I must tell you but I feel so ashamed. Actually there are a few things to tell you.' She couldn't bear to see the worry etched on his face but he had a right to know what she'd done.

'We'd better sit down then,' he said, 'this is sounding serious.'

'Do you remember that young couple in the café at lunch time?' she asked, and paused to wait as a frown creased his forehead in concentration. 'I seem to remember a few young couples,' he said. 'Which one in particular do you mean?'

She prompted his memory. 'The ones sitting next to us, they were behind me and I couldn't actually see them but I think they had two boys, and a little baby in a pram. Oh, and a little dog as well.'

'Ah yes, of course. They had a minor disaster when the dog charged into the waitress and sent everything flying.'

'Yes,' Marie said. 'Don't you think the father got very worked up about it? He seemed very angry.'

'No more than anyone else would do, I don't think.' He concentrated on the incident which had appeared fairly trivial at the time but which seemed to have affected Marie more than it warranted. 'He calmed down fairly quickly when Billy offered to replace everything free of charge.'

'That was only because his wife was getting upset.' Marie willed him to agree, to say the man had been totally out of order, but Stuart continued to shake his head.

'He wasn't the first and he certainly won't be the last man to be cross with his children and then calm down when his wife is getting upset, that's for sure. Marie, where's all this taking us? I don't understand.' He moved towards her but she gestured him away, leaving him floundering with indecision about what to do for the best.

'I reported him,' she blurted.

'What?'

Saying the words out loud made it more real and

she shook with the enormity of what she'd done. 'I reported him,' she repeated, and this time Stuart was left almost speechless, his head shaking from side to side.

'I don't understand what you're saying. A man gets cross with his children and you report him. What did you report and for God's sake who did you report him to? Marie, you're not making sense.' He sat looking incredulously at her stricken face, tears streaming down her cheeks.

'I can't believe I did it,' she said at last, 'but I was so worried about the children, and his wife. I reported him for abusive behaviour.'

'I think you'd better explain everything because I am totally flummoxed,' Stuart said. 'I've been with you all day and apart from the fact I never saw anything remotely bordering on abuse, you've never been anywhere or with anyone to report what you saw and heard, or more to the point, what you thought you heard.' Anxiety creased his face as she struggled to explain how it had all come about.

It had happened so quickly and although it had affected her badly at the time she couldn't quite recall the reasons why she'd been so sure she was right. How could she justify her actions when even she couldn't understand them? Impulsive behaviour wasn't her usual style and interfering in other people's lives was anathema to her, but here she was trying to work out why she'd done both in the space of a few moments. She did remember the distress in the young woman's voice when she'd pleaded with her husband, and it stirred up a feeling of concern once more. Maybe she hadn't been wrong after all.

Stuart listened impassively as the story unfolded, the snippets of conversation between the couple followed by the man's outburst of anger, and a flicker of understanding greeted her revelation about contacting Debbie while he was in the gents'.

'I think I can see how it must have seemed to you at the time, but it was most unlike you to act so hastily. I wish you'd talked with me first and we might have acted more rationally. Still, what's done is done so I don't think you should worry about it too much.' More tears followed with the relief of unburdening herself. 'I can't explain it,' she sobbed. 'I think it was a combination of everything, what with Bryony confiding in me about her and Greg and...' She stopped and held her breath but Stuart was deep in thought.

'There's still one thing I don't understand,' he said. 'What was the point of telling Debbie when you didn't even know where the family lived?'

'It was a sheer fluke,' she explained. 'Do you remember when the two boys started playing with those other children?' Stuart nodded, that at least was something he was aware of. 'Well the two youngest were showing off to each other about how they'd learned to say where they live in case they ever got lost. I recognised the little one's address because it's near where Debbie lives so it stuck in my mind. Afterwards it seemed as though it was meant to be, but now I know I was just being silly and I wish I knew how to put it right.'

Stuart put the mugs in the sink. 'I wouldn't lose any sleep over it; all you have to do is ring Debbie in the morning and tell her you were mistaken.'

'That's just the problem, I can't reach her. She's at a conference and contact isn't easy. I've been trying all day.'

'Well in that case there's nothing to worry about as she can't have taken any action, you can ring her on Monday morning.'

Marie nodded. 'Yes, I'll do that.'

Stuart turned and smiled. 'Now are you going to tell me about Bryony and Greg or is it top secret?'

Marie nodded. She thought he hadn't noticed her little slip-up but in a way she was glad of a diversion and he would learn all about it soon enough anyway. 'You'd better sit down,' she said. 'I'll tell you everything from the beginning.' It didn't take long but Stuart couldn't hide his amazement and disgust at Bryony's behaviour.

'I can't believe she's kept this from him for all these years,' he said. 'I shouldn't think he'll ever be able to trust her again.'

'Well it won't be easy, that's for sure, but I'm not worried about Bryony, it's Amelia I feel sorry for, and Ralph as well actually.'

'Oh of course, all this involves him too.'

Marie nodded. 'Yes it does. Bryony opened a can of worms and I've no idea how it's all going to be resolved.'

Stuart looked at her thoughtfully. 'You said it had been a burden keeping Bryony's secret all these years, did you never think to tell me?'

There was hurt in his voice and she knew he must be feeling upset to learn she'd been able to keep something from him for such a long time. As far as she could remember it had never been a conscious decision but the truth was she had kept it from him. 'I never thought you'd be interested, and anyway we were occupied with our own plans at the time. We were busy buying our home and starting our own family.'

'Two of our closest friends have an affair and a child together and you didn't think I'd be interested? I thought we told each other everything.' She knew he had a right to be disappointed in her, if the tables were turned she didn't think she could ever forgive him for keeping a secret like this for so long, but for the moment there were other things to worry about.

She leaned her elbow on the table and rested her head in her hand. 'I'm really sorry,' she said, 'but I hope you'll try to understand. I feel as though I'm damned if I keep a confidence and damned if I don't. I know one thing; I'm fed up with coping with other people's problems.'

'I do understand, love,' he said. 'I can see you had no choice and to be honest I agree with you, I would have had only a passing interest at the time when it happened.' He grinned. 'Well, well, our friend Greg is a dad after all. What a turn-up for the books.'

'It is, and I've no idea how it's all going to end.'

'If I was you, my love, I'd keep well out of anyone else's affairs after your experiences this weekend. Now let's get to bed where we should have been hours ago.'

'I think we'd better,' she agreed, 'before the dawn breaks completely.'

Chapter 27

The florists had almost finished unravelling the garlands from around the spindles, but they were under instructions to leave the large arrangements in reception in situ. The owner of the business had insisted the garlands could be left for at least another day but Bryony was determined to have them removed the morning after the wedding. She had no wish for an image of wilting blooms to be the last thing in anyone's memory of the big day, it was better for fresh flowers to be discarded than risk that. There had been no sign of either Greg or Ralph and when questioned Justin had shaken his head, saying only that both had been served breakfast in their rooms.

The wedding invitations to the guests staying at the hotel had clearly stated the time they would be expected to vacate their rooms, apart from the close friends and family who were invited to the luncheon with Amelia and Piers prior to their departure on the start of their honeymoon. The original idea had been to provide an opportunity for members of their closest circle of friends and family to get to know each other in a more relaxed environment, but Bryony was keeping her fingers crossed that no-one, especially Colin, would spill the beans on yesterday's mishap. Her heart was in her mouth every time she thought he'd made an appearance, but fortunately he seemed once again to be sleeping off the effects of the previous night's drinking. At least it was keeping him out of harm's way.

Some of the guests were still drifting about the hotel, as if reluctant to leave the luxury they'd enjoyed and the friends they'd made, and she'd hesitated before going down to face them. The celebrations had lasted much longer into the night than anyone could have imagined, and it had left her feeling drained and exhausted and unable to make any decisions, however small or insignificant. The moment when the lunch was over and everyone had left couldn't come soon enough for her.

Tradesmen were walking in and out of the door carrying boxes, and the musicians were struggling beneath the weight of their instruments and sound and lighting systems.

'Can't you speed some of these people up?' she asked Justin. 'They seem to be taking longer than necessary to take their leave. Talk about milking our hospitality.'

Justin shrugged with resignation. 'I don't suppose you can blame them; after all it isn't every day you get a complimentary stay in a five star hotel.' Watching a group wandering into the bistro bar, his shoulders lifted and fell in a sign of resignation and she detected a slightly defiant attitude which she was certain hadn't been noticeable in his manner towards her previously. She suspected he was feeling slightly superior since her showdown with Ralph, but he would have to watch himself before getting too cocksure of his position. She hadn't given up the fight yet and she was feeling increasingly sure of her powers of persuasion as far as Colin and Ralph were concerned.

She was confident of Greg's eagerness to share his life with her; it was simply a matter of timing and convincing him that there was no real need to wait before putting their plans into action. Even so, she was determined to keep more involvement in the business; if nothing else the mistakes of yesterday had taught her that nothing was certain and she needed to keep a grasp on her own independence. Marie's reaction had taken her by surprise but she was sticking by her own belief that telling Greg about Amelia wouldn't have served any useful purpose. It was just a pity that she'd lost control and blurted it out like she had. Trust Colin to bring her to breaking point with his stupid behaviour.

Watching a scruffy young man leaving the hotel, she asked Justin if he knew who it was. She didn't recognise him as a tradesman but neither was he a guest. Justin followed the direction of her eyes. 'Oh, that's the young chap whose brother and friend were rescued last night,' he told her. 'Tom, I think he's called.'

'What on earth is he doing here?' she demanded. 'Doesn't he know it's invited guests only?'

'I've no idea why he's here,' Justin said and with a look of satisfaction, added, 'but he was invited to stay the night apparently so I suppose he knows he's welcome.'

'Invited by whom? I certainly haven't invited him,' she blurted out, to the interest and amusement of several passers-by, making her drop her voice before fixing them with a smile and raised eyebrows.

'Greg was with him at the hospital last night I believe,' Justin informed her, 'and he rang to ask if we had a spare room. You weren't around but Mr Portland senior was and he gave me permission to say yes.' Looking for a reaction, he wasn't surprised to see a look of annoyance cross her face. 'I hope that was alright, I didn't know what else to do.'

Through gritted teeth, she replied, 'Of course you did the right thing, Justin. I'm pleased to see you're justifying my confidence in you to use your own initiative.' She swung on her heel and left him looking after her with a look of amused bemusement on his face.

*

Lunch had been designed for maximum effect and consisted of a cold collation with a small number of various warm dishes, followed by strawberry pavlova and traditional English trifle. When discussing the menu with the chef she'd been insistent that it must look impressive but be achievable with the absolute minimum of work. All the members of staff were to be rewarded with a substantial bonus for all their dedication to the success of the wedding, and unknown to anyone, she'd arranged for them all to be taken to a gala dinner at a country house later in the month. All the expenses and transport were to be paid for by the business. Satisfied that the dining table was looking its best, she went to the kitchen to check on the progress of the food preparation before finally going to sit in the wine bar with a large glass of white wine.

Sitting with her eyes momentarily closed, she was unaware of Greg approaching and she felt her heart literally skip a beat when he stood beside her.

'You look shattered,' he said. 'Still beautiful of course, but nevertheless shattered.' He remained standing but he placed his glass on the table. 'Do you mind if I join you or would you prefer to be alone?'

'Of course I want you to stay,' she told him as she patted the seat beside her. 'I've been hoping to see you all morning but you don't seem to have been around.'

'No, I've been a bit tied up; partly with the young chap involved in yesterday's drama as a matter of fact.'

Bryony nodded. 'Oh yes, I believe he stayed here last night, but I've no idea how that came about.'

'That was all my doing, I'm afraid. I hope you don't mind but I couldn't think of any other solution at the time, and given Ralph's response to welcoming everyone to share the celebrations, I thought it would be alright with you.' Bryony was desperate to talk about their future but Greg's distraction was obvious, so she feigned interest while he explained the situation which had brought him together with Tom. As much as she could summon up sympathy with what had happened, her own future was hanging in the balance and she longed for Greg to show even a modicum of interest in that. 'What a weekend this is turning out to be,' he commented at last. 'It's certainly been full of surprises.'

Tentatively sliding her hand over his where it was resting at her side and gazing nonchalantly around her, she whispered, 'Hopefully not all unpleasant ones.'

She stiffened when he edged away from her, saying, 'No, not *all* of them.'

'Greg, we need to talk.'

'Yes we do,' he replied, 'but not here.'

'I love you,' she whispered.

His voice sent a chill right through her. 'Do you? I wonder,' he said, standing up to walk away.

This would probably be the last chance to talk before she was caught up in other things and she thought desperately of a way to keep him there without sacrificing her pride by begging him, but her mind went blank. 'Please don't go,' she said. 'Every time I think we have an opportunity to talk you walk away from me.'

'I have to meet someone,' he replied, 'before they leave.' He glanced at his watch. 'I'll catch you later.' It was important to keep an outwardly calm appearance for the benefit of the people around but she watched him cross the room and leave without even a backward glance. A wave of disappointment and apprehension washed over her.

Chapter 28

Tom showered and dressed before tucking into the breakfast which had been delivered to his room by Tracy. He wondered how many hours the staff were being expected to work for this family wedding; more than they should, no doubt, and he hoped they were getting paid overtime rates for it. At least they were in jobs so they had something to be grateful for, which was more than he could say for himself. He tidied up the bathroom, following the instructions requesting guests to place used towels which they required changing into the bath, leaving the remaining ones on the pile. It was pointed out that this was primarily in the interest of climate change and water preservation but Tom thought it was most likely to be in the interests of the owner's bank balance.

Considering the cost of all the expensive toiletries and freebies provided for the guests, maybe he was being a bit too cynical. Sharon was always telling him off for being too much of a cynic but it was hard not to be sometimes. He looked at the fancy bottles of shampoo and bubble bath and decided he might take a couple for Sharon, they wouldn't be missed here and she would love them.

The bath which had been so much fun last night now just seemed plain silly, but he had to admit he'd quite enjoyed the experience while it lasted. Greg had phoned to say he had things to see to but Tom was welcome to keep the room until later in the day and they arranged to meet there mid-morning. 'Don't do a runner on me,' Greg said, 'I've got something I think you might be interested in.' Tom didn't have a clue what Greg could mean but he promised to be there as arranged.

'I'm going to the hospital,' he told Greg. 'I've already rung and they both seem to be recovering OK, but I want to see them. I don't have to keep to normal visiting hours, which is good so I'll be on my way soon.'

He struggled to remember the direction they'd taken to reach the room the previous night but he managed to find his way down the back stairs to the rear entrance without meeting too many people. The car park was busy with departing wedding guests but he didn't cause the kind of reaction he knew his appearance would attract at the main front entrance. He'd decided not to wear Greg's jacket despite him telling Tom he was welcome to it, but it was cooler today and he didn't know if he'd made the right decision. There was no way he was going back for it so he walked briskly in the direction of the place he'd left the car when he arrived yesterday. Memories flooded back but he put them out of his mind and concentrated on what he had to do today. Keeping well away from the promenade, he found the car, switched on the navigation system and headed off towards the hospital.

In the reception area a voluntary guide pointed out

the way to the zone Greg had told him he needed to be heading towards, and it took a few minutes of criss-crossing corridors before he found himself near to where he'd seen Danny a few hours ago. Because he was arriving outside of normal visiting times he had to report to a member of staff before entering the ward, but he was surprised when she told him that Danny already had a visitor. He had no idea who it could be but the staff nurse assured him that his brother had agreed to see the man in question and she was sure it would be alright for Tom to join them. After checking that this was acceptable she indicated for Tom to go in before leaving them with gentle instructions not to make the visit overlong.

Tom was surprised to see the bulky form of Geoff rising from the chair beside Danny's bed.

'Morning Tom,' he said, holding out his hand.

Tom found his fingers in the iron grip he remembered from yesterday and the gratitude he felt towards Geoff flooded his face. 'Good morning,' he replied, 'but this is a surprise, I didn't expect to see you here, not that I'm not pleased to see you because I am.' He pulled out a seat from near the wall and sat looking from Danny to Geoff with a quizzical look on his face.

'How are you?' he asked Danny.

'I'm fine,' Danny replied. 'I think I will be out today, it's amazing what they can do with nebulisers and drugs.' Tom nodded and said nothing but he could read him like a book and he knew his brother was feeling uncomfortable, and so he should after the trouble he'd caused, but there would be time for all that later. 'Have you spoken to Amy?' Danny asked.

'Yes, I rang Sharon before I came here and Amy was with her. They know you're both alright but they're waiting to find out what's happening here before any decisions are made. There's no point them coming over if you're going home soon, mainly because of the children. Mum's already tired out and it's not fair to ask her to look after them again.'

Danny grimaced. 'I'm not looking forward to seeing Mum, she'll kill me.'

'Only if I haven't done it first,' Tom told him.

'Look,' Geoff said, 'if I just clear up a few of the questions I've got I can leave you two alone. Are you still alright with that?' he asked Danny.

'Yes, it's fine,' Danny replied.

Geoff looked at Tom and raised his thick brows questioningly. 'Stay as long as you want,' Tom smiled back, 'you're more than welcome.'

'Thanks,' Geoff replied. 'I wanted to contact you this morning before I came but I had no idea where to find you. Did you have somewhere to sleep last night?' When Tom explained where he'd spent the night Geoff whistled. 'Wow, the illustrious Bryony Portland put you up, you are honoured.'

'Well actually it was Greg who arranged it, he's been a good mate even though we've only just met and he's...'

'He's a bit of a gent?'

'Well yes, I suppose so.'

'He is, you're right, but he's also a decent enough chap. Anyway the reason I'm here is to find out exactly what happened yesterday and I'm hoping your brother and his friend are going to clear up a few questions. If we can find out what went wrong it might help us in future rescue operations.' He positioned a memo pad on the locker at the side of Danny's bed and read from a few notes he'd already written there. 'The main thing that puzzles us is how you came to be rescued and brought to hospital without us being aware of it.' He lifted his head and looked at Danny who nodded.

'I'm not sure,' he replied. Tom and Geoff waited while different expressions passed over his face as he tried to make sense of what had happened. 'I think,' he said at last, 'it's probably because I wasn't actually rescued.'

'Go on,' Geoff prompted him.

'After we'd got stuck and we'd refused help to get us back...' He looked at Tom. 'They told us to throw a lot of cockles back and we didn't want to.' His eyes pleaded with his brother to understand. 'It was like throwing money away and we thought we'd be able to get back ourselves.' Tom and Geoff nodded sympathetically. 'Well anyway, soon after that I began to feel an asthma attack coming on and I was running out of my inhaler so when some other fishermen asked if we wanted to go back with them I agreed.' He paused and closed his eyes. 'I was scared,' he said quietly, 'really scared.'

There was silence in the room while they envisaged in their own way how vulnerable he'd been and the dangerous situation he'd found himself in. He opened his eyes and shuddered before leaning over to reach an inhaler and breathed in two puffs before continuing. 'Anyway, when we got back I realised we hadn't landed in the place we'd set off from and the men said they couldn't take me back there for some reason. They asked if I was going to be alright and then they left. By this time I was beginning to feel worse and I recognised the signs...' He looked at Tom who nodded, he was well aware of the danger Danny would be in if he didn't get treatment; hospital visits were not an unusual occurrence in his brother's life.

'I managed to get a taxi to come here and luckily I had money in my pocket because we'd already been paid.'

Geoff shifted in his seat and finished scribbling the notes he'd been making while Danny talked. 'That explains a lot,' he said. 'You were part of the operation as far as being missing was concerned but you were safely on shore by the time your friend was rescued. We weren't aware of that of course.' He turned to Tom. 'We were concerned how it could have happened but what Danny has told us makes it clearer.'

Tom was puzzled. 'But I don't understand why they didn't come back to the jetty and tell you what they'd done.'

Geoff pulled the side of his lips down. 'That's just it,' he said, 'they were obviously not licensed to go out to sea but they were probably locals who know the area well, so they were using another small landing bay out of the sight of officials.' He turned to Danny. 'I'm betting they didn't have any of their catch when they returned.'

'Not much,' Danny agreed. 'I was feeling grotty so I didn't take much notice but I think they were sharing some between them and they were definitely counting out a lot of money.'

'I don't get it,' Tom said, 'how do they come to have all that money?'

The big boys collect their catch from them,' Geoff explained. 'Some of them are legitimate and pay good money to get the cockles on board containers to make sure they are refrigerated and sold on as quickly as possible. Others do it for the same reason but with the added intention of avoiding the tax due on their profits. The ones who brought Danny in are insignificant in the larger scheme of things, but they put themselves in danger and that's where we come in. I'm not interested in the morals of it, just the safety aspect.'

'I wish I could get my hands on those men,' Tom exclaimed, 'they didn't even make sure Danny was alright before they left him.'

'They brought him back safely,' Geoff reminded him, 'and don't forget, they were trying to keep themselves out of sight and yet they still did it. You ought to be grateful for that.'

Tom sat back. 'I suppose you're right,' he said grudgingly before turning back to Danny. 'What I still don't understand,' he said, 'well, two things really, why you didn't call for help and you just said you were running out of inhaler, but Amy told Sharon you'd left it at home with your mobile.'

Danny nodded his head. 'Yeah, I did but that was a new one and when I realised I'd forgotten it I found an old one in the van. There wasn't much left but it was better than nothing. I'm taking part in a trial of a new drug and I did have that inhaler with me so it wasn't so bad.' He dropped his voice. 'Actually I'd have been in a real mess without it.'

'And what about Rick's phone, why didn't you use that to get help?'

'He kept it switched off for ages so Amy couldn't

contact him and find out where we were, and then when the engine packed in and we were trying to get it going he pulled his mobile out of his pocket and dropped it. We couldn't find it in the mud and that's when I started to get really scared.'

'I think that answers most of our questions,' Geoff said, 'now I think it's time you had some rest. I'll get on my way before the nurse comes to tell me off for overstaying my welcome.' He shook Danny's hand. 'It's been a pleasure to meet you, son,' he said. 'Take care of yourself and don't get into any more scrapes.'

'Don't worry I won't,' Danny replied, 'and thank you, sir.'

Geoff gave a wry smile. 'It's a pleasure.'

Tom wanted a few words with Geoff so he told Danny he'd be back later and promised he'd call in to see Rick. As they were passing the nurse's station he asked one of the staff what time Danny was likely to be discharged, but he received a puzzled expression by way of reply. 'What makes you think he's being discharged?' the nurse asked.

'He's just told me he is.'

'Well I don't know where he's got that idea from,' she told him. 'He's due to be seen by the doctor and as it's Sunday that isn't likely to happen today, so you're looking at tomorrow at the very earliest. Neither your brother nor his friend are going anywhere in a hurry, I can assure you.'

'Thanks,' Tom said before muttering under his breath to Geoff about his brother's way of getting things wrong. 'Are they in any kind of trouble?' he asked Geoff. 'I mean, is that why you're here?'

'No, of course not, we just needed the facts before

I can make a report out. One or two things didn't seem to add up but what your brother's told me has clarified it. Don't give it another thought, everything's fine.'

'Thanks a lot; I really appreciate what you did.'

'Don't mention it, now I'll get back and leave you to see your friend.' As he walked away he hesitated and turned back to face Tom. 'Don't be too hard on him, son. I expect he's already feeling bad enough as it is.'

Tom smiled. 'I'll try not to be, but I feel like throttling him.'

'That's understandable but a bit counterproductive after all our efforts to save him.' Geoff laughed and raised his hand in the air as he marched down the long corridor.

Chapter 29

Marie opened the French doors and stepped into the garden where she stood breathing the fresh air deep into her lungs. It was cooler than yesterday and there was an autumnal hint in the air; dew glistened on the tips of grass and shimmered like trembling crystals on the delicate sepals of arching fuchsia. A faint mist hung over the trees but the day held a promise of warmth.

The spring bulbs were sorted into groups in Stuart's shed ready for planting when they'd finished tidying up the borders, and already a sense of the familiar anticipation was building inside her. Experimenting with vibrant hybrid tulips was a particular joy and the best way she knew to liven up the garden in spring during an otherwise dull month of the year.

She made a mental note to lift the dahlia tubers and protect the sleeping hollyhocks from slugs to keep them as the backdrop for next year's bedding plants, but the dahlias were still good for another couple of weeks. Lethargic bees vainly foraged the late flowering honeysuckle sprawling the pebble-dashed wall, and a sparrow took refuge behind the resident blackbird, hopping between the plants searching for worms and the constantly busy ants. Instead of going back inside she sat at the white patio table and turned her face towards the warming rays of the sun, basking in the comfort of her own familiar and pleasant environment.

Stuart hesitated on the threshold, carefully weighing the balance of temperature before emerging with the breakfast-laden tray. 'Is it warm enough to eat outside?' he enquired. 'Or should I lay the table?'

'Oh let's eat here, it will probably be the last chance we get this year,' Marie replied. 'It's fairly warm in this little sun trap.'

'I'll get the croissants and yesterday's paper,' Stuart said after setting the tray on the table, 'we didn't get chance to read it yesterday with everything that was going on.'

'Yes, you're right. I only hope today proves to be a bit more relaxing, I've had enough excitement to last me a lifetime.' Glancing through the colour supplement her attention was drawn to a special offer of autumn shrubs suitable for coastal gardens when Stuart gave a mild exclamation before delving into his pocket. 'Sorry,' he said, passing her mobile across the table, 'this rang while you were out here, I think you've got a missed call or message.'

Marie took the phone from him but instead of looking at it she put it by the side of her plate and ignored it, preferring instead to watch the antics of the two birds daringly approaching the crumbs of croissant which had showered from their plates. The sparrow was still taking advantage of the safety provided by the larger bird by following closely behind as he sought out and pecked the tinier crumbs hidden in the grass. Reluctant to allow intrusion into the peace and quiet, she remained passive for a few minutes but Stuart was engrossed in his paper and oblivious to her reaction. Eventually she forced herself to access the message, dreading what she might see. 'Oh dear,' she said, 'it's from Debbie.'

Stuart was engrossed in his sporting supplement covering a far more interesting subject than a text from Debbie to Marie usually proved to be. Vaguely and without looking up, he asked, 'What does she want? Is she alright?'

'She doesn't want anything,' Marie said, 'but she's seen several missed calls from me and she's replying.' Scrolling down the text she felt all the serenity of the morning drain away and she was engulfed in a wave of apprehension. 'Oh dear,' she said again. 'Oh dear.'

The tone of her voice finally grabbed Stuart's attention. 'Whatever's wrong?' he asked.

'I left a message telling her to ignore what I'd said about that couple yesterday but she's replied to say it's too late, she'd already passed it onto a colleague who covers the area where the family live. Apparently she'd considered it serious enough to warrant instant action if a baby is involved.' Placing her elbows on the table, she dropped her head into her hands in despair. 'Oh dear, what have I done?'

'Well if you ask me you've done nothing wrong. Oh, I'm well aware...' he said when she lifted her face ready to interrupt him, 'that I thought you'd acted hastily, but if you were so convinced by what you heard and saw then you only did what you thought was right.'

'Oh, I wish I could do something!' she exclaimed.

'Anything to stop it going any further.'

Stuart folded his paper before placing it the table. 'Look love,' he said, 'let's get this into perspective. You thought a young family might be in danger and spoke to Debbie about it. She obviously believed it was serious enough to investigate and so did the colleague who she passed it to. They are both professionals who are dealing with these kinds of situations after all, and they wouldn't have pursued it if they thought you were simply overreacting. I suggest you just let matters take their course because if there's nothing wrong they won't take any further action.'

'You know that isn't always true, we saw that programme about some of the things that go on when people are wrongly suspected by social workers.'

'Yes,' said Stuart firmly, 'and we also know what sterling work people like Debbie are doing all the time.'

Marie sighed with relief. 'Yes we do,' she agreed, 'they are very sensible and caring. I think I'll try to switch off and leave them to get on with it.'

'Good,' said Stuart, picking up his paper again, 'now we can relax again and enjoy this lovely morning. Talking of relaxing,' he added hopefully, 'can we give the luncheon at The Portland a miss, do you think? Because one thing's for sure, with Bryony involved it will be anything but relaxing.'

Marie gave his suggestion some consideration and he did have a legitimate point, added to which there was still the possibility of some kind of fallout from Bryony's outburst yesterday. If that happened it would no doubt put her in the firing line of at least one person's anger. She wished she'd never become involved in Bryony's little schemes and secrets but unfortunately she'd had no choice. It was very tempting to give their apologies and say she was suffering from dancing at the wedding, which was in fact true; her back was very painful, but something held her back. If by any chance the truth came out it would be Amelia who suffered and she would need all the support and understanding she could get.

'Mmm. I know what you mean but I don't really think we can get out of it. Apart from incurring Bryony's wrath, which I admit doesn't worry me as much as it did, I have a peculiar feeling about everything that happened yesterday.'

Stuart reluctantly acquiesced. 'Yes, maybe you're right, but if we are going we'll set off a bit earlier than necessary and have a stroll on the prom. It seems a shame not to take advantage of this lovely weather.'

This sentiment coincided with that of many of the locals and visitors, who were filling up the town and promenade. The beach was alive with children and in the bay yachts moved slowly on the water, presenting a far more tranquil scene than the one visible the day previously. Frantic work had been undertaken overnight to put into operation a system preventing unlicensed vehicles from accessing the road leading to the promenade and the jetty. This had also been helped by the publicity caused by the previous day's drama which had emphasised the dangers facing inexperienced cockle pickers. Today's festive atmosphere was enhanced by the annual fun run which was taking place in aid of charity, and there were lots of runners and wheelchairs in fancy dress or festooned with balloons. Stuart laughed as he dodged two groups of young men racing each other pushing prams which carried a friend dressed as a baby wearing a towel for a nappy, a frilly sun bonnet, and waving a gigantic sugar dummy in their hand. They were throwing sweets to watching children and spectators reciprocated by putting money in the proffered collecting buckets. Marie fished in her handbag for as much change as she could find and Stuart emptied his pockets so they could share the money between as many people as possible.

'I'm so glad we came out,' Stuart declared when they'd spotted an empty bench to sit down and enjoy the spectacle. 'I wouldn't have missed this for anything.'

Marie agreed. 'I think this lunch is going to seem very sedate and boring after all this, but never mind, at least we know the food will be good.'

'That's true, I suppose we'd better be making our way there so we can have a drink before it gets going. Who did you say is going to be there?'

'Only family and close friends,' Marie told him, 'so it should be quite pleasant.'

Chapter 30

Tom was surprised to find most of the side streets were already packed with cars, forcing him to park further away from the centre of town than he'd set off from earlier in the morning. He walked to the hotel, avoiding the seafront, but everywhere was bustling with activity and he wished Sharon and the kids were here with him. The square he'd seen briefly when he'd been with Greg looking for somewhere to eat looked very different this morning, and outside all the cafés and pubs the staff were working at speed to pick up litter and clear up in anticipation of expected customers.

Reaching the chip shop where they'd eaten delicious fish and chips, even if they had turned to sawdust in his mouth because he was feeling so terrified, he saw it had become almost like a war zone. The litter bins were full to overflowing and while staff attempted to clear up they were becoming dangerously near to being attacked by two seagulls eager to carry off the easy pickings of fish lying nearby.

Stopping to help a young girl who was struggling to fill a black bin liner, he clapped his hands and threw the remnants of fish into the centre of the pedestrian walkway where the gulls fought over it before flying away with it in their beaks. The girl thanked him before rushing back into the safety of the shop and he stood and watched as the two birds were attacked from all sides by gulls who'd lacked the audacity to fly down into the square but were determined to have a share of the unexpected meal. Looking around, he envied all the people who were busy getting on with their jobs and it brought back to him the feeling of satisfaction when he'd been able to get up in the morning full of the prospect of a day's work ahead. He'd dreamed about and even started to plan starting his own business one day, but there was no chance of that now when even established builders had bitten the dust.

He fought the urge to get back in the car and drive home but Greg had asked him to stay, and after all he'd done to help him he at least owed him that. He had no idea what Greg wanted to see him about and all he could come up with was the thought that maybe he was a writer or journalist who was interested in the lives of working people. While they'd been together he'd shown an interest in Tom's situation and there was no doubt he was a professional man of some sort, his hands were a dead giveaway apart from his speech and clothes. He didn't have long before he found out and then he would be able to get home or at least arrange for Sharon and Amy to come over here. Danny seemed to have got hold of the wrong end of the stick about being discharged so he might be in for a longer stay than he thought. It was typical of Danny, he was always getting things wrong. Rick was improving but not about to be discharged and his wife was already on her way to visit him.

It had come as a bit of a surprise, Rick ending up worse than Danny after all his worry about his brother being in the biggest danger, but that Danny had at least had the sense to leave when he knew they were in real trouble. Rick had been an idiot and could have lost his life for the sake of a few hundred pounds. Then again, he reminded himself, it had been the lure of money which had caused him to come up with the idea originally. Danny's money had been carefully stored at the hospital but because Rick had ended up in the water his was in a bit of a soggy mess and a member of staff had told him it was locked in a store room waiting for a member of his family to collect it, and then they would have the problem of trying to separate the notes. He hoped for Rick's sake it would be salvageable otherwise it would have all been for nothing. He'd offered to go back and try and rescue as much of it as possible when it dried out a bit, but he had no idea when that would be. Danny had offered to share his takings with Tom but he'd refused, he hadn't put his life on the line but more to the point he couldn't bring himself to take advantage of what had happened.

He knew most of the guests were due to leave so he was able to get into the back entrance without attracting anybody's attention. He tried the card in the door to the room and held his breath; Greg had told him he could stay but he still thought there was a good chance he would be locked out. The light flashed and when he pushed the door he felt it move inwards and he was back in the room which had quickly become his base. The luxury of it didn't really impress him but having somewhere to stay while he sorted things out was really good.

The bed had been made, towels and toiletries replaced, and more tea and coffee sachets put in to replace the ones he'd used. 'I could get used to this life,' he told himself but he knew he couldn't. The room was on the front of the building so he had a good view of the bay and the promenade from the window, and he could see lots of people already out and about, walking or jogging along the prom. He was thirsty but he didn't know if he was allowed to use the tea and coffee when he would be leaving the room soon. He decided to risk it and made himself a cup of tea. He rearranged the tea bags until he was satisfied that no-one would notice one was missing, and then sat down to wait for Greg. It wasn't long before he heard a knock on the door and when he opened it Greg was standing there smiling.

'How are you?' he asked. 'And how are the patients?'

'I'm fine and Danny is pretty well. He thinks he's coming out today but he isn't and Rick isn't brilliant but he's getting better.'

'That must be a relief,' Greg replied, 'no harm done in the end.'

'No, but it could have been a disaster,' Tom said. 'It was more good luck than good management, I can tell you.'

'That applies to most things in life I suppose,' Greg said. 'I do believe you can make your own luck sometimes but then at other times you get things thrown at you that you never expected.'

'You can say that again,' Tom replied with feeling. He had no idea what Greg wanted to talk to him about but after he'd offered him a cup of tea they both sat down in the easy chairs. Greg's first words took him by surprise but he tried to hide it; he was proud of his trade and not afraid to show it.

'You're a builder, aren't you?' Greg asked.

'Yes, and a bloody good one, he replied. 'I've got all my certificates, and testimonials from customers by the dozen, but what good does it do you when there's no work?'

'I think I can help you there.'

Tom lifted his head and looked at Greg. 'Is this a wind-up?' Tom asked.

'No, it's the real thing. I can put you in touch with a man who'll give you some work.' His voice rose with enthusiasm. 'I've been involved in a new development in Benton and when it starts they're going to be looking for men in the building trade, men who are good at their trade, especially bricklayers.'

Tom stared back, hesitant and scared to build his hopes up. 'I've heard that rumour but I didn't believe it. There aren't any developments being started now, and in any case if it were true there are plenty of out-of-work builders and even more labourers living nearer than me.' He failed to keep the frustration and anger out of his voice. 'What bit of work there's been has gone to the men who'll do it for next to nothing, and in a way I don't blame them, but although you might argue that something is better than nothing I won't do it because then it affects my benefits. By the time you've finished the job you have to start the process of claiming all over again with no money coming in, in the meantime.'

'It sounds pretty grim,' Greg said.

'It is when you've got a wife and family to keep.'

He looked at Greg and a flicker of hope burned inside him. Somehow he knew instinctively he was genuinely trying to help, but he'd had his hopes built up before and he was scared of it happening again. 'You aren't a builder yourself,' he said, looking pointedly at Greg's hands. 'Just exactly what is your involvement in the development?'

Greg smiled at Tom's forthright approach. 'No, you're right, I'm not a builder but I am an architect and I helped to design and plan it. There were a lot of other people involved in the project obviously but I did a lot of the plans.'

'And is it definitely going to happen?'

'It is, and very soon. I hope you'll be interested.'

Tom was still wary. 'How can you be sure you can help me get work? You didn't know me before yesterday.'

'I think I know you well enough to believe you when you say you're good at your job, and that's all that matters. I can arrange for you to have a meeting with the foreman in charge and all you have to do is turn up and produce anything you have that's relevant to your application.' He grinned. 'Don't look so shocked, judging from what you've told me you're a good bricklayer and if so they'll snap you up. The people backing the project have stipulated it must be built by experienced builders using the best materials.' Sitting back in his seat, he turned thoughtful for a moment. 'Any recommendation from me will be acted on, so I have to be sure of my facts before I do anything, so I want you to be straight with me.' He leaned forward and Tom, who didn't have a clue what he was talking about simply nodded. 'How about

Danny and your friend?' Greg asked. 'Aren't they in the same position as you?'

Tom's interest perked up, he was almost daring to believe something good was about to happen.

'Yes,' he replied, 'they are. Danny's younger than me but he followed in my footsteps and he's now a trained bricklayer and Rick is a plumber.'

'Is he a good one?'

'The best, he's got his Corgi registration so he does central heating as well.'

Greg went to the mini bar, opened two small bottles of lager, and handed one to Tom who shook his head. 'I'll be driving home soon, I can't drink.'

'You won't be going back until after lunch so one small drink won't matter. Here, take it. With a bit of luck you'll all have work for the foreseeable future.' He lifted his bottle and Tom slowly followed suit.

'I'm sorry Greg,' he said, 'but this is all a bit sudden. I don't want to seem ungrateful but I don't want to get excited about it until I know something more concrete.' They both burst out laughing and Tom shook his head, almost daring to believe what Greg was telling him. 'I'd love to give Sharon the news but what if nothing comes of it?'

'I tell you what,' Greg said, 'I'll believe you about being qualified as a master builder if you'll believe me I can secure you a job. Look,' he added, putting his beer on the table before pulling out his phone, 'I've already texted the man in charge of building to let him know I've found some men he might be interested in. He'd asked me to keep my eyes open for experienced builders because although he's got his own men lined up he still needs more.' He handed it over for Tom to read. 'Obviously he may not read it before tomorrow morning but now my reputation is on the line, so you've got to trust me and you'd better not let me down. By the way, it's expected to take a few years to build; it's a big project so it'll keep you in work for quite a long time. I know the inside-outs of this development and its financing, and it's rock solid.'

Tom began to feel a shred of hope. 'This is turning into quite a weekend,' he said, 'but I'm still frightened of being let down.'

'You won't be,' Greg replied, 'if you're half as good as I think you are.'

'Wow,' was the only thing Tom could say.

After a short discussion about the proposed complex at Benton, Tom gradually began to be convinced that what Greg was saying was real and he grew more enthusiastic by the minute. For the first time in ages he suddenly felt optimistic and although it was too much to take in all at once he couldn't stop grinning. 'I can't believe it,' he said.

'You'd better believe it,' Greg told him, 'because it's about to happen.'

Tom put his head back and swallowed the last of his beer. 'All this is making me hungry, can you recommend somewhere for a cheap lunch?'

'Oh, didn't I tell you?' Greg said with a smile. 'You're invited to lunch here and of course it won't cost you a penny.'

'Oh no,' Tom said with alarm, 'I can't eat here, look at my clothes.' He swept his hands over his body and watching him, Greg admitted his appearance did leave a lot to be desired.

'Look,' he said, 'you're about the same size as me and I've got a spare shirt in my room you can have. If you wear that with the jacket I lent you, you'll be very presentable.'

Tom shook his head. 'No, I'm sorry I can't do it, I'll just go and get a bite somewhere.'

Greg pulled his mouth down and nodded his head slowly. 'Well, if you insist but you'll let people down and,' he looked straight at Tom, 'you might even appear a bit ungrateful.'

'Ungrateful,' Tom exclaimed, 'what the hell are you talking about?'

'You are a bit of a minor celebrity and there are some people wanting to meet you, Damian's a member of the lifeboat crew and his mother Marie is a good friend of mine. I'm sure you'll get on really well. Bryony of course has let you stay here, and she's the one who's invited you, so she may feel a bit let down too.' He smiled encouragingly.

'No pressure then,' Tom said. 'I suppose I don't have much choice. I can understand it might not go down well if I refuse but what's all this celebrity thing? Where's that come from?'

'Well you could say you're basking in reflected glory.'

Tom shook his head. 'I don't know what the hell you're talking about. Tell me again but in simple English.'

'It's your brother and friend who are getting all the press but you are the next best thing, and as a guest in the hotel you are also available.'

'OK then, I'll stay,' he said reluctantly. 'I wouldn't mind meeting the chap you said helped in the rescue.'

'I think that can be arranged as he's already expressed an interest in meeting you.'

'What were the names of the others again?'

'Bryony, who owns the hotel...'

'Is she the one you told me about, your girlfriend?' Tom asked.

Greg nodded but continued without pause, 'But the one most interested in meeting you is the crewman's mother, Marie.'

'Well I suppose I should thank them all, but I'd planned to do it in private.'

'Just relax and enjoy yourself, you'll be fine. Now I'll just go and get that shirt and then you can start to get ready. At least you've got something to celebrate now, your brother and friend are safe and soon you'll all have work to go to.'

When Greg had closed the door behind him, Tom fell onto the chair and took a deep breath. What a weekend this was turning out to be and it wasn't even over yet.

*

Tom stood in front of the full-length mirror and grinned like a Cheshire cat at his new image and the thought of how his mother would react if she could see him now. 'You've scrubbed up quite well, Tom,' she would say with pride. He was very pleased with his appearance considering he'd spent almost two days without a change of clothes, but to be fair he was wearing other people's cast-offs as well as some of his own. Wanting to kill time before meeting Greg, he'd wandered into town where he'd seen charity shops done up like designer outlets, and when curiosity made him explore further he'd found a pair of jeans he couldn't resist. He jangled the few pounds he had left in his pocket and before he knew it he was leaving the shop with the jeans neatly folded in a bag. They went pretty well with Greg's shirt and jacket, and although his shoes were well worn at least they were polished, thanks to the cleaning kit he'd discovered in his room.

Feeling more like his old self than he had done for ages, he decided to experiment by going down to the hotel reception area to leave by the front entrance. He was fed up with the feeling of failure even when it wasn't his fault, and for a short time at least he was going to enjoy himself. He made his way through the guests who were already taking advantage of the drinks on offer as they passed their time until food was served. No-one stared or looked surprised to see him, but he was a bit embarrassed when a couple of girls looked him up and down from under their very long, curly lashes. This was definitely an improvement on sneaking out by the back entrance.

The breeze was getting stronger and kites were filling the sky with colour as kids ran up and down, laughing and squealing as they tried to keep them in the air. Tom became determined to buy Sam and Ben a kite each before their next visit to Merebank, when hopefully he would be earning again and treats would be a matter of course and not just a memory.

He was desperate to get home again but he'd promised Greg he'd stay for lunch and he owed him, so it was the least he could do, but he still wasn't so sure the mother of the bride was too keen on him being there. Every time their paths had crossed she'd looked at him with suspicion, as if wondering what he was up to, but he had to admit she was pretty good-looking for her age and he understood what Greg saw in her. Pity she was already married to someone else but what did that matter these days? He couldn't imagine being with anyone but Sharon and the thought of her made him want to run to the car and go straight home. Being realistic, he knew what kind of welcome he'd probably get from her and his mother, so he decided to make the best of the situation and enjoy himself first before having to face them.

Looking at his watch, he decided to walk a bit further but soon he saw the shelter where he'd tried to rest and where Greg had found him. It felt weird sitting in the same spot but this time everything was so different, and he leaned back and felt himself really relaxing for the first time in ages. Things were going to be better from now on, he just knew it.

In the distance he could see a lot of sudden activity and when he stood up he could see the outline of the lifeboat being pulled out across the sand in the direction of the sea. Some other idiots must have got themselves in trouble and thanks to people like Geoff and the crew, they would have the help they needed. He wondered if the man Greg had mentioned would be involved this time, but thought not as he was intending to introduce them today. He was looking forward to meeting him and his mother Marie, who Greg was so sure Tom would get on with.

It was soon time to be heading back, Greg had said something about going to see a friend before she left for home but he didn't expect to be long, so Tom decided to enjoy a leisurely walk back along the promenade.

Chapter 31

The chef had excelled himself despite her instructions to keep things simple. Two enormous dressed salmon lay on a sea of glistening blue ice surrounded by fresh prawns, oysters, and every seafood imaginable. She noticed with amusement he'd even included some of the cockles freshly harvested from the bay. The array of homemade raised pies and cold meats were displayed amongst a mouth-watering selection of salads and freshly baked bread, and the whole thing looked delicious. She would make sure he was in line for a pay rise before she made Justin the manager of the hotel, even though hopefully she would still be in overall charge of the business.

The uncertainty of Ralph and Greg's reactions meant she'd lost the focus of where her future lay, blurring the lines of her role. She had to keep reminding herself that she could still remain in charge of the financial side of the business and decisions like that would fall within her remit anyway. She intended to introduce the new position of events manager once she was firmly back in control. All she had to do now was persuade Greg to forgive her and Ralph to recognise how indispensable she was.

All the guests who were due to leave before lunch had finally gone. Amelia and Piers had made a point of speaking to them all before they left, leaving both sets of parents to guide them smoothly on their way. It wasn't proving easy to keep tabs on Colin, who seemed to be wallowing in self-pity and as usual had found himself another excuse to drink more than he should. Her nerves were getting more and more on edge in case he let something slip or even deliberately said something, and for once she didn't know what to do. If she acted as though nothing had happened he just might let things lie, but if she warned him to be careful there was a possibility he might be provoked into doing something out of spite. She wouldn't put it past him to deliberately go out of his way to cause her trouble but she was relying on his better judgement to avoid upsetting Amelia. In his more rational moments he'd never deliberately hurt anyone, but drink seemed to change his personality and he seemed to be relying more and more on alcohol.

She'd tried to contact Marie to find out if she'd spoken to Greg but for some reason she seemed to be avoiding her calls, so Bryony still had no idea if she'd had any success or not, and Greg was still proving impossible to pin down. How on earth he'd become involved with the scruffy young man connected to the rescue operation she had no idea, but all his concern seemed to be directed towards him to the detriment of herself. Partly out of desperation to please him she'd agreed to his preposterous request to allow the man to stay for lunch, but it still hadn't made any difference to his attitude towards her. She would be glad when the day was over and she had the place to herself again, and then they could finally sit down together and discuss things in a rational manner.

Closing the dining room door behind her, she was surprised to see Justin replace the telephone and look round anxiously. 'Oh Bryony,' he exclaimed, uncharacteristically reverting to her Christian name, 'thank goodness you're here.'

'Whatever's happened?' she asked him. 'What's wrong?'

'It's Mr Portland, he's ill.'

'Oh, not again,' she replied irritably. 'Where is he this time? Calm down Justin, it can't be that bad and we don't want everyone knowing, so please keep your voice down.'

Justin's agitation grew. 'No, not your husband, it's Mr Portland senior.'

Bryony's throat constricted with fear. 'Ralph!' she breathed. 'Why didn't you say? Where is he? What's wrong?'

Vigorously rubbing his cheeks, Justin could barely speak. 'I have no idea; he rang from his room, but I could hardly hear what he was saying.' Bryony was already running towards the lift.

'Come up with me in case I need help.'

'But there's no-one on the desk,' he said.

'Sod the desk, get in.'

Ralph was lying on the bed fully dressed, but his face was ashen when he turned to look at them with a weary smile. 'Don't panic,' he said gently. 'I'm sure it's nothing serious I just had a funny turn.' Bryony rushed to his side and knelt by the bed. Taking his hand between hers, she stroked it gently. 'What kind of a funny turn? What happened? Take your time, there's no rush.'

'I just felt a bit dizzy, no not dizzy exactly, more faint than anything. The room started spinning and I had to lie down.' He tightened his grip on her hand. 'I'm sorry Bryony,' he said, 'the last thing you need today is me being ill. I'll just rest for a little while and then I'll probably be alright.'

It took all her willpower to hold back the tears which were blurring her vision. 'I'm sending for Dr Swales, and you must not move until he comes.' When he started to object she raised her hand. 'There is nothing you can do to stop me so just do as you are told.'

Ralph reluctantly gave in, he had no strength to do otherwise. 'You're the boss,' he said, 'and I haven't got a choice have I?'

Struggling to keep her voice steady, she leaned over and kissed his clammy forehead. 'Not a chance.'

Outside the room she told Justin to return to the desk and say nothing about what had happened. 'I'm going to ring the doctor and I'll come down as soon as I know what's happening.'

Justin turned to go and she went along the corridor to her bedroom. Although it was Sunday she knew Dr Swales would at least advise what action to take, but on hearing the news he insisted on visiting the patient himself. She leaned against the wall in shock. This was something she was totally unprepared for and it hit her like a bullet. Whatever she'd been planning to do, even though it would hurt him, she'd always hoped that once he recovered from the shock she'd still have his love and support. Something was suddenly shifting under her feet and it scared her.

Reluctant to leave Ralph, she tried Colin's phone but it was conveniently turned off. She breathed a big sigh of relief when Greg answered his and without a moment's hesitation told her he was already on his way up. 'What happened?' he asked, striding along the corridor from the top of the stairs. His face was full of concern and once again Bryony was aware of the esteem and love that Ralph generated in everyone who knew or came into contact with him. She briefly explained what had happened before slowly opening the door to check if Ralph was awake and agreeable for them to go in the room together. He was propped up on pillows and waved them both into the room.

'What a thing to happen today of all days,' he said as they sat side by side next to his bed. 'I think it's indigestion after all that lovely but very rich food yesterday. I think the hot sandwiches so late in the day may have finished me off. Unfortunately the older you get the more careful you have to be about what you eat.'

Greg's face was creasing into a frown. 'What do you mean, you think it's indigestion? I thought you'd simply started to feel a bit faint.'

'That's right, I did but...'

Bryony caught a brief but telling glance fly from Ralph to Greg, who nodded his understanding. Instantly she knew there was more to this than a mere dizzy spell and she felt utterly helpless and petrified. Fighting off her instincts to throw her arms round both of them, she remained outwardly calm, feigning ignorance of what had passed between them and trying with all her might to ignore the implications of what might be happening.

'Whatever happens,' Ralph was saying when she pulled herself together to listen, 'this must not be allowed to spoil Amelia's wedding. I'm an old man so it should be possible to convince her that the excitement and food have proved too much for me.'

'Rubbish,' Greg declared, 'you are not old and in any case, you're as fit as a flea. It probably is as you said, just a touch of indigestion due to having too much rich food and excitement.' He smiled reassuringly. 'I'm pretty sure you won't be the only one nursing a bad head or stomach this morning.'

'Talking of which,' Ralph said with a wry look, 'how's Colin holding up this morning?'

'I think he's fine,' Bryony said, 'Greg's here simply because he was around when I went downstairs after I'd seen you. Do you want me to go and get Colin?'

Ralph leaned back on the pillow. 'No, don't tell him yet, I don't want any fuss especially before I've seen the doctor. You two must go and join the other guests before your absence is noticed.' He closed his eyes and Bryony was reluctant to leave him, but in order to carry out his wishes she was left with no choice, so she patted the pillow and laid her hand gently on his shoulder.

'Are you sure you'll be alright?'

'Yes, I'm sure, and I'll relax more easily if I know that everything is going as planned for Amelia and Piers. It needs you there for that to happen, so run along and enjoy yourselves.'

Together they left to go and join the others but in the privacy of the private corridor Bryony turned to Greg hoping for a sign of forgiveness. When he ignored her and carried on walking, she hurried after him and grabbed his arm. 'Greg please, we've got to talk.' The frown of worry between his eyes deepened and she knew he found her words distasteful, but she was desperate to find a resolution to their problem. They could only achieve that by talking, but he turned away and she struggled to hear what he was saying.

'I don't think now is the time. Anyway, I'm not sure there is anything to discuss.'

She wanted to hold him back and force the issue but they had already reached the stairs and were in full view of all the people gathering in reception. She had a quick word with Justin, telling him the doctor was going to Ralph's room via the back entrance and would inform Justin when he was ready to leave. Justin was to ring her mobile once to alert her and she would go up to see him. On no account was anyone else to be told what was happening. When Justin pointed out that Ralph's absence would be very obvious she assured him she would deal with that and if questioned he would simply have to plead ignorance of the whole thing.

Luckily the call came while the aperitifs were being served, enabling her to slip away without being noticed. Apprehensively, she approached Ralph's suite and stood for a moment before going in. She could hear their low voices and the occasional ripple of laughter which she hoped was a signal of good news. She knocked on the door before entering and was relieved to see Ralph sitting in the chair looking almost back to normal. 'Well I must say you seem to be recovering well,' she exclaimed before turning to Dr Swales. 'Is he as good as he looks?'

The doctor stood up and placed his hand on

Ralph's arm. 'He certainly is, I'm pleased to say. I thought at first the symptoms might indicate a heart problem but his self-diagnosis was spot on.'

Bryony sighed with relief. 'Was it simply indigestion?' she asked. 'Like Ralph said it was?'

'Well it's not quite as simple as that, I'm arranging for tests to be done.' He looked at Ralph. 'Is it alright for us to discuss this?'

Ralph nodded his assent. 'Of course it is, the family need to know what's going on.'

Bryony's heart gave a lurch; Ralph was still treating her as part of the family after all that had happened. She turned back to the doctor. 'What kind of tests?' she asked.

'I suspect my friend may have an ulcer,' he replied, 'so we'll investigate that first but we do have to rule out heart problems so I'm making arrangements for a few of those tests as a precautionary measure. He is under strict instructions,' he said firmly, 'to take things easy, as well as watching his diet until we know for sure what the problem is. Yesterday's excitement and food were probably the final straw.' Gathering his things together, he smiled at Bryony before walking towards the door. 'I believe the wedding went off well yesterday and that Amelia was a beautiful bride.'

'Yes, it was lovely, thanks. I'll come and see you out.'

'There's absolutely no need,' he insisted, 'I know my way.'

Bryony sat beside Ralph and took his hand in hers. 'You gave me a bit of a fright,' she told him. 'I was scared.'

'There's no need to be,' he assured her, 'it was all a bit of a fuss about nothing, although I have to admit it had me worried for a while. The doctor has advised me to give lunch a miss and rest for a while but I don't want everyone thinking I'm ill.'

'Don't worry, I'll simply say you've got a bit of an upset tummy. I think I'll wait until it's time for them to leave before I say anything; that should send them scurrying through the door quicker than anything.'

Ralph laughed but his expression quickly changed and his face suddenly became serious. 'If nothing else I think I should take this as a wake-up call.' Bryony tried to interrupt but he held her hand tightly and shook his head. 'I'm quite sure this is nothing serious but I am getting older, not old, I hasten to add, but older, and I certainly don't want to be more involved in the business than I already am. I'm afraid I was a little hasty yesterday and I'm sorry.'

'I'm the one who should be apologising,' Bryony protested. 'I don't know what came over me, blurting it all out like that, but I shouldn't have done it.' She didn't know what to say to ease his pain but nothing could take away the shock of learning about his granddaughter. 'I'm truly sorry you found out about Amelia like that, it was unforgivable.'

'I'm not denying I was upset, but I can't lie and say it was a complete shock because deep down I think I've suspected it for a long time. Anyway, what I really wanted to discuss was to ask if you'll still play a part in the business. I'm not asking you stay as Colin's wife, this is purely a business proposition, but we do need you.'

Bryony was stunned. She'd hoped to persuade him

to let her have a role but she wasn't prepared for this. 'What would you want me to do?' she asked.

'Well I appreciate how you've trained Justin and Ellie and I share your hope that they are ready to take over the management of the hotel, so I thought you could remain in control of finances and help to promote the business. No-one else here has your flair as you well know.'

'I'd be delighted,' she said. 'Thank you Ralph.' Glancing at her watch, she stood up to leave. 'There is just one thing.' She hesitated. 'I'm due to leave on Wednesday, for three weeks' holiday. Is that alright with you?'

He nodded with understanding. 'Yes, I know. Now you must get back to your guests.' He laid his head on the back of the chair and she left the room quietly.

Chapter 32

The foyer and reception area were already filled with people when Marie and Stuart entered the hotel. 'I thought you said it was lunch for a few close friends and family,' Stuart said as he looked around for a familiar face. Marie nodded, 'I suppose we shouldn't be surprised that Bryony's idea of a small number of people isn't quite the same as ours, but I must say I didn't expect so many to be here.' Returning the smiling welcome from several of the guests, she acknowledged to herself the problem Bryony had been faced with in her attempt to keep it limited to a favoured few. The Portland family was well represented, and of course Piers' relations had all travelled from various parts of the country and even different countries, so with the addition of close friends like her and Stuart it was easy to see how it had grown.

'It's a bit like the wedding itself,' she told Stuart, 'it's more a case of who dare you leave out more than who you really want to invite.'

Stuart grimaced. 'If I'd known that I'd have gladly given up my place for someone more deserving than me.' Marie refused to be drawn into his mood and taking his arm, began to walk in the direction of the long table holding a tempting array of drinks.

'Come on, you grumpy old man, I can see a lovely cocktail with my name on it and I don't mean one of the non-alcoholic variety, we'll leave those for the people who'll be driving home.'

Slightly mollified, Stuart helped himself to a drink before going over to join Colin and a number of other men who'd congregated in a corner, where the main topic of conversation was football and the previous day's results, which they'd all caught up with on the television. Having been deprived of their normal Saturday recreation there was plenty to talk about and the discussion was soon centred on the league table, about which there were several differing views. Colin and Stuart had supported opposing teams all their lives and enjoyed the banter, but nothing would shift them from believing their own team was superior in every way.

After chatting with various members of both sides of the wedding parties Marie found herself momentarily alone, but she was quickly joined by a very flustered-looking Bryony.

Still smarting from the way Bryony had tried to use her to influence Greg without giving her the whole picture, she was reluctant to engage in conversation, but she knew she had no choice with so many people around. Despite that, she was determined not to get involved in any more of Bryony's antics so she braced herself against whatever was coming.

'I've just had a terrible shock,' Bryony whispered.

'Oh dear,' Marie sarcastically wondered aloud, 'now why doesn't that surprise me?'

'You don't understand,' Bryony replied, 'it's

something serious but you mustn't tell anyone.'

'Oh spare me your secrets,' Marie said, 'I have no wish to hear any more,' but Bryony wasn't listening.

'It's Ralph,' she said, 'he's ill.'

Marie was expecting another of Bryony's personal dramas but this was seriously shocking and she reacted without thinking. 'What do you mean Ralph's ill? Is it serious?' Bryony gripped her arm and glared at her, glancing round to make sure no-one had heard.

'I honestly don't know. I think Dr Swales thought it might be his heart, but then he seemed to change his mind and agree with Ralph that it was indigestion and too much excitement yesterday. When has Ralph ever suffered from the effects of food or excitement? It's ridiculous and I'm sure they were only saying it to stop me from worrying.'

Marie wondered if Bryony was exaggerating the situation but she did seem genuinely frightened and it could be genuine if the doctor had been called.

'We don't know what Ralph suffers from, he might be prone to things you are not aware of, and don't forget he is getting older.'

Bryony's voice rose with indignation. 'He's in his seventies for God's sake, he isn't old. That's what I told him and Greg agreed.'

Marie was puzzled. 'Greg? Was Greg there?'

'Luckily he was, yes. As usual I couldn't find Colin when I needed him but I managed to contact Greg, who was a lot more use anyway. He was upset, I know, and I'm not sure if he believed what the doctor said either.'

'I hope he's going to be feeling better soon, it's

quite possible the doctor is right and it is simply a result of excitement of the occasion.' She glanced across the room to where Amelia and Piers were involved in an animated conversation with some of the younger members of his family. Amelia looked as carefree as a newly married woman deserved to be, but as yet she was unaware of the shocks waiting on the horizon. Marie sent up a silent prayer for her to be safely on route to her honeymoon before the bubble burst.

Looking around the room trying to locate Colin, she relaxed when she saw him still under the watchful eye of Stuart. With a bit of luck there would be no immediate mishaps from that quarter. She was so deep in thought it took a few seconds for her to realise Bryony was waiting for her to respond to a question she hadn't even heard. 'I'm sorry,' she said, 'I was miles away.'

'You can say that again,' Bryony retorted, 'I was asking if you managed to have a word with Greg and if so how he reacted?'

Marie made no attempt to hide the feelings which had been simmering since she'd realised how devious Bryony's actions had been. 'No,' she replied, 'fortunately I didn't make a fool of myself, but it was no thanks to you.' Bryony looked genuinely baffled but Marie was in no mood to play games. 'Look at you,' she said, 'you'll almost convince me you really don't know what I'm talking about.'

Bryony shook her head. 'I don't know what you're talking about,' she replied.

'Well let me spell it out to you. You asked me to speak to Greg on your behalf but what you conveniently forgot to mention was that you'd already let slip about your plans and also about...' she glanced around to make sure there were no eavesdroppers, 'Amelia.'

Bryony's face paled. 'Oh God, I'm sorry. How did you find out?' Marie silently looked over to the group where Colin was enjoying a joke with Stuart and some friends and Bryony nodded. 'I might have known,' she said quietly.

'Why didn't you tell me?' asked Marie. 'I didn't want to interfere anyway but if I'd known that there is no way I'd have said anything. I could have looked such an idiot.'

'You know Greg would never think badly of you, he always thinks you're wonderful.'

'I doubt it. Anyway, where is Greg? I haven't seen him today.'

'Your guess is as good as mine, he's either fawning over Katy Sheridan or he's with that...' Suddenly Bryony's expression softened and she looked intently towards the door. 'Talk of the devil,' she said, 'here is the man himself.' Greg had entered the room with a young man who looked vaguely familiar but for the moment Marie couldn't quite place him.

'Who's that with him?' she asked.

'Oh, him,' Bryony said, 'he's the man he's taken under his wing for some reason. It's the brother of the man rescued from the bay last night, but why Greg is taking such an interest in him is beyond me.'

'Oh, I remember where I've seen him before; it was on the promenade yesterday when his dog ran off. Oh what a shame; they seemed like a lovely family and their day must have been completely ruined by what happened to his brother.'

Bryony's interest was already centred elsewhere. 'Unfortunately I've got to go, I must introduce myself to Greg's friend but I'll catch up with you later,' she said before hurrying away.

'Not if I can help it,' Marie muttered to herself, watching her walk straight over to Greg with absolutely no attempt at disguising her intentions.

When Stuart joined her she couldn't help worrying about Colin being left to his own devices, if only because of the harm he could inflict on others, but Stuart assured her the friends he'd left him with had agreed to take over. 'On pain of incurring Bryony's wrath,' he said with a smile. Marie nodded absent-mindedly; she was watching Bryony's performance very closely.

'Just look,' she added, and Stuart scanned the room, trying to see what had caught Marie's attention. 'She can't stand that young man, not that she knows him of course, but she's jealous of the attention Greg's giving him.'

'And your point is?' Stuart asked.

'My point is,' Marie said, giving herself a mental shake, 'she left me to go and ingratiate herself with Greg by pretending to be interested in his friend.'

'I wouldn't upset yourself, love, you know what she's like. Who is the chap with Greg anyway?' he asked.

'His brother and best friend are the two who were rescued last night.'

Stuart was staring at them, trying to puzzle out where he'd seen the man before. 'I know him from somewhere,' he said.

'That's exactly what I thought,' she replied, 'but then I remembered...' She turned in response to Stuart's groan of recognition. 'Whatever's the matter?' she asked him. 'You're as white as a sheet.'

'I'm pretty certain it's the man in the café, the one you reported to Debbie.'

'Oh my god,' Marie moaned. 'Are you sure?'

'Yes,' said Stuart, 'I am.'

Chapter 33

Luke was sending warnings about the imminent danger of the salmon floating away on melting ice if lunch wasn't served immediately; the guests were getting restless and Amelia was worried about setting off on her honeymoon suffering from malnutrition if she didn't eat something soon. Bryony was reluctant to start without Greg so she decided to delay for just a little longer and went over to ask Marie if she knew where he was.

Marie was strangely dismissive, showing no sign of interest in Greg's whereabouts or Bryony's dilemma, so after engaging with her for a few moments of small talk she turned to leave.

The rush of relief when she saw Greg enter the room was followed by a sense of frustration at the sight of the man by his side. Despite his rather unconventional mode of dress she had to admit his appearance was a big improvement on when she'd seen him last, helped enormously by the shirt and jacket which she was convinced belonged to Greg. His bearing was different and he walked in a self-confident and assured manner which hadn't been evident earlier.

She seemed to be doomed in her attempts to make plans for her future and once she again, she was regretting the decision to prolong the wedding celebrations this way. There were still so many ways for it to go wrong and she simply wanted it to be over.

She'd managed to fob off the few people who'd enquired about Ralph and up to now Amelia had accepted the explanation of her grandfather's indisposition. Colin seemed to be behaving himself but she knew him well enough to recognise the effort needed to maintain his performance of bravado. From somewhere deep inside her came an overwhelming sense of compassion and regret for what she was inflicting on him, and on impulse she went over and asked him to announce that lunch was now about to be served. Delighted to agree, he performed this unexpected duty with such aplomb it was accompanied by laughter and cheers, and the guests moved as one into the dining room.

Taking advantage of the general preoccupation with food, she hurried upstairs to see Ralph and check he was still feeling better. He was sitting in a chair in front of the wide window which gave him an uninterrupted view of the bay. On a table nearby was a tastefully laid tray with a small selection of tempting portions of food chosen by Bryony and brought up earlier by Ellie. A small carafe of his favourite white wine stood beside a crystal bud vase holding a cream rose taken from Amelia's bouquet.

'You're spoiling me,' he said, 'and there's really no need because I'm feeling fine.'

Bryony felt a surge of relief but somehow there was a sense of vulnerability about him which she'd never known before, and she wanted to take him in her arms and hug him. Knowing that under the circumstances he might find such a demonstration of affection inappropriate, she allowed herself the customary kiss on the cheek and kept her own emotions under control.

'It looks as if the weather might be changing,' she said, 'we were so lucky to have such a beautiful day for the wedding.' She moved closer to the window to get a better view of the promenade and the grassy downs where families were still engaged in all kinds of games and sports, while teenagers defied the strengthening breeze to top up their tan.

Her voice when she spoke was deliberately casual, but she knew Ralph wouldn't be fooled. 'I wanted to have a word with you about what happened yesterday,' she said. 'It must have been a terrible shock, especially the way I did it.' She turned to look at him. 'I'm so sorry; I'll never forgive myself for what happened.'

'I'm not denying it was a shock at the time, not just for me but Greg and Colin as well, but it's done now and we have to move on. It will never affect my feelings towards Amelia but of course I can't speak for my son.' His face clouded over and Bryony wished she could live that time over again and protect him from the hurt she'd inflicted.

Dreading what his reply might be, she forced herself to ask him, 'Do you think it might have contributed to your attack this morning?'

Ralph shrugged his shoulders. 'Who knows?' he replied. 'Maybe I am getting too old for surprises, but I do know I'm almost back to normal and that includes feeling a little hungry, so I suggest you return to your family and friends and leave me to enjoy this delicious food.'

Bryony moved reluctantly towards the door and hesitated before leaving, there was something else she was anxious to know. 'Earlier you said you wanted me to continue working here, but if you feel differently now that you've had time to reconsider I'll understand,' she said, but he dismissed her feelings of concern with a smile.

'No, I haven't changed my mind, after all it's important to keep the hotel running smoothly for the benefit of the town and the staff, not to mention Amelia and Hugh and their children when they come along.'

'Thank you,' Bryony said before turning away. She didn't want Ralph seeing the tears she was once again struggling to hold back. She gently closed the door behind her.

Chapter 34

Tom approached the dining room with apprehension but for some reason Greg seemed keen for him to be there, and more than once he'd said he'd like him to meet Amelia. 'Is it still top secret?' Tom asked and Greg nodded.

'Very,' he replied, and Tom told him he had nothing to worry about, he wasn't going to say anything.

He'd checked that Danny and Rick were still improving, Amy and Beth were already on the way to the hospital and he'd promised his mother he would visit the hospital before he set off for home so he could tell her exactly how Danny was. Sharon was very upbeat and told him to thank everyone who'd been involved when he met them at the meal, and not to forget to pass her thanks onto Greg who she couldn't wait to meet one day soon. He'd been expecting a telling off but for some reason she seemed to have decided against it, at least until she had him in her sights when she would probably let rip.

To his surprise he found he was enjoying himself immensely; everybody he'd met here had been friendly and seemed pleased to see him. They weren't a bit stuck up like he'd imagined they would be.

Amelia was full of fun and obviously having the time of her life, but he was surprised when she came over and introduced him to some of her friends. Greg looked at her as if he would burst with pride and after she'd moved on Tom couldn't help wondering how it was all going to end. No wonder Greg was upset to find out so late in the day that she was actually his daughter; he'd missed out on so much of her life.

He settled down to make a mental note of everything so he'd be able to tell Sharon all about it when he got home. All this reminded him a bit of their own wedding, which had been great, but he couldn't help thinking about how things had gone downhill since this recession hit the building trade. He had to keep pinching himself in an effort to believe what Greg had promised him.

Damian's mum Marie seemed really nice, but she seemed a bit on edge when they were first introduced. At first he wondered if it was because she resented the people who put her son's life in danger, but when he tried to apologise she simply smiled and told him that was what the lifeboat crew were there for. She completely wrong-footed him when she told him they'd met before the previous day but try as he might he couldn't recall where.

'It was when your dog ran off and he wrapped himself round my legs,' she told him. Suddenly an image shot into his mind; Rusty winding the lead around her legs as she twirled around trying not to fall while he did his best to grab the dog and unravel the lead. He felt mortified and began to apologise but she laughed it off and assured him no apology was necessary.

'You had other things to think about so don't worry about it,' she said, 'but isn't it a strange coincidence that we should meet again like this?'

Tom nodded. He was beginning to feel like he'd fallen into a strange land where things just got weirder and weirder. Marie invited them to join the group at her table and after accepting, he and Greg went to the buffet. There was an astonishing array of food and Tom took his lead from Greg and picked out a selection of finger food from one end of the table. 'We can always come back for more,' Greg said. 'Eat as much as you want because there's more than enough for everyone. If you want my advice though, I do suggest you don't fill yourself up on savouries before trying the dessert; the chef's pavlova and trifle are out of this world.'

'Have you known Marie long?' Tom asked as they walked back to the table.

'All my life,' Greg said, 'and she's one of the nicest people I've ever met.'

Tom had no reason to doubt Greg's opinion of Marie but he felt oddly aware of her darting strange looks at him while they were eating, and he couldn't help wondering if she really was as laid back about what had happened or if it was all a pretence. Her husband was really friendly but he was genuinely interested in cockling and kept asking Tom questions which he couldn't answer, and it showed up how ignorant he was about it all. Heaving a sigh of relief when someone changed the topic of conversation, he was just about to sink his teeth into a piece of delicious pie when his phone rang. A quick glance told him it was from Sharon so he apologised before leaving the room to take the call.

Her voice was unnaturally low and hesitant. 'I can't talk long,' she said, 'because she's just gone into the other room to make a phone call.'

'Who's gone into the other room?' he asked.

'A social worker,' she replied, 'she says someone's made a complaint.'

'What kind of complaint?' he demanded. 'What are we supposed to have done?'

'Not us,' she replied. 'You, someone reported you for abusing me and the children.'

He stood rigid with shock. 'I can't believe it, there must be some mistake. Who would do such a thing?'

Sharon's voice was quivering, almost fading away. 'I don't know, she wouldn't tell me. Oh Tom, I'm so scared.'

Tom's mind went blank and he cursed himself for staying on here when he should have been at home. 'Look, don't worry, there's obviously been some mistake; I'll sort it out when I get back,' he told her. 'I'll come home straight away; they can't do anything before I get there.'

Unwilling to draw attention to himself, he took his time walking back to the table but every muscle in his body was straining to get him back to Sharon's side. An awful feeling of doom swept over him. Just when things seemed to be getting better something else had to go wrong; surely they deserved a bit of good luck for once. He was going to make this quick but Greg deserved some sort of explanation about why he was rushing away. Not only was this a disaster in itself but it would probably mean the end of the promise of a job. Nobody would want to employ a man accused of domestic violence. The injustice of it all fired him up and by the time he reached his empty seat he was quivering with anger. He returned Greg's questioning look with a shake of the head, unable to put into words what he'd just heard.

'Was it the hospital?' Greg asked. 'Has something gone wrong?'

'No,' he replied through his teeth, 'it wasn't the hospital but something has gone wrong. That was Sharon, there's a social worker with her because someone's reported me for abusing her and the children.' There was a fraction of a second's silence before Greg responded.

'Then you must get back to her immediately and clear up the misunderstanding. Go and get your things from the room and I'll meet you at the door, I want to make sure we have the right contact details.'

Tom stared at him. 'Do you mean the offer of a job still stands?'

'Of course,' Greg assured him. 'I don't know exactly what you're being accused of but you don't seem like a person who would do anything to harm your family in any way.'

Tom couldn't stop shaking. 'Whatever's been said, there is no truth in it whatsoever. I hope you believe that.' Greg nodded and they left the room together. In the foyer they halted at the sound of Marie calling Tom's name.

'I need to tell you something,' she said.

'Is it important, Marie? Because Tom's had some bad news and needs to get on his way quickly,' Greg said.

'I know, but I'm fairly certain what I'm going to say has a bearing on what you've just heard.' She glanced around the room. 'It isn't easy to do this,' she began. 'Do you mind if we go and sit in that corner where we'll be able to have a bit of privacy?'

Tom took a deep breath to contain his impatience but something told him he would regret it if he didn't listen to what she had to say. This was proved in an instant with her first few words. 'I'm afraid I was the one who told them,' she said simply. 'I reported you to social services.'

He stared at her, absolutely speechless, and Greg was the first to find his voice. 'I don't understand, you don't even know Tom,' he said.

'That's right, I don't, but I do know I've made a terrible mistake.' She turned to face Tom. 'I can't begin to apologise enough.'

Tom was outraged. How could this person, who'd been a stranger until today, do such a thing?

'This doesn't make sense,' he said. 'What are you talking about?'

'I was in the café at the same time as you yesterday,' Marie began, 'and I couldn't help hearing snippets of the conversation you were having with your wife.' She paused to take a deep breath. 'I'm afraid I misinterpreted it and thought...'

'Go on Marie,' Greg urged her gently.

'Well you both know what I thought; I put two and two together and made a hundred.'

Greg turned to him. 'I don't understand,' he said, 'what you possibly said to put such an idea into Marie's head. Have you any idea?'

He tried to remember what he and Sharon had been talking about in the café but all he could think about was Rusty and the flying food. He shook his head. 'You'll have to remind me,' he said to Marie, 'but make it quick because I haven't got time for this, I need to go.'

He listened while she recounted the odd words she'd picked up and when she'd finished he nodded his head as it all came flooding back.

'Yes,' he said, 'you're right, we did say all those things but you only heard a part of it. When I agreed with Sharon that I was angry when she told me she was pregnant with Lily, I meant angry with the situation we were in when I couldn't provide for our family, not because we were having another baby.' He explained briefly about Sharon's accident at work and as he talked he saw a sense of understanding in Marie's worried eyes. A sense of relief flooded his own body when she told him she was prepared to give her side of the affair to the people in charge and she would make sure no action was taken.

'I'm so sorry,' she repeated, as they all stood up.

'Don't worry,' Tom replied, 'I suppose you meant well.'

He couldn't help feeling sorry for her as she walked back towards the dining room and Greg hesitated before following her. 'I'll be in touch,' he said, 'now go and get your things and be on your way.'

Tom took the stairs two at a time to the dismay of some of the guests who were coming towards him but he didn't care, the sooner he got home the better.

He was just handing in his card at reception when his phone rang and he could hear Sharon's garbled voice, but it was impossible to make out what she was saying. 'Calm down,' he said 'and speak slowly so I can understand you.' He was bursting to tell her his good news but he'd decided to wait until he was outside the hotel, and now here she was with her own good news. When he finished the call he felt a big grin splitting his face, and without thinking he found himself walking back into the dining room to re-join his new friends.

Chapter 35

Marie kept her eye on the door, waiting for Greg to come back and join them. She couldn't imagine what he must think about her but she'd had no choice; she'd had to tell Tom what she'd done before it was too late. Stuart had practically pinned her down to the seat to stop her from running after them.

'You must just let it run its course,' he told her, 'nothing you can say or do will make any difference so let it be.'

But it did make a difference to her, she couldn't live with herself if Tom had been left wondering who had been so spiteful and reported him. She'd briefly finished explaining to Stuart how the confusion about what she'd overheard had happened, when she saw Greg returning to join them again. He made no comment concerning Tom's departure but to her immense relief he sent her a reassuring smile.

Claire made no attempt to hide her frustration at being left out of what she obviously saw as a conspiracy going on around her, and Marie was relieved to see how she perked up at the arrival of Damian and Louisa. The unexpected sight of Tom walking towards them filled her with trepidation, but he was beaming broadly which went a long way to calm her shattered nerves.

Greg was the first to react as he stood up to greet him. 'Are you joining us again?' he asked.

Tom threw his smile round the table. 'If it's alright with you,' he replied, and everyone wholeheartedly welcomed him back.

Claire seized her opportunity. 'You look happy,' she said, 'have you had some good news?'

Marie cringed but Stuart gripped her hand under the table.

'You could say that,' Tom replied, but before he could say any more Greg stood up.

'Come on Tom,' he urged him, 'let's get you some food before it's all gone.'

'Thanks, I will if you don't mind, I've built up quite an appetite with all the excitement.'

'Oh, what excitement's that?' Claire asked, but to her annoyance they were already halfway across the room. 'Are you ever going to tell me what all this secrecy is about?' she asked Marie.

Marie was watching the two men who were engrossed in conversation, at least Tom was doing most of the talking and Greg was listening, and at one point they both glanced over in her direction, obviously discussing her. She took comfort in their relaxed posture and turned her attention to Claire, who looked as if she was going to burst with curiosity.

'I can't say anything at the moment because it's Tom's personal affair,' she explained, 'but when the weekend is over I'll explain my part in it.'

'But...' Claire began, a very pained expression clouding her face. Marie held her hand up.

'No buts,' she said. 'I've told you I'll explain everything later.' Claire's face fell but she had to be satisfied for the time being.

Marie didn't know whether to leave immediately or stick it out and leave at the first possible opportunity. She knew Stuart would be willing to go; he hadn't particularly wanted to come in the first place and she'd only persuaded him to do so because he knew she was worried about Amelia. Although she'd spotted Amelia and Piers leave the room together, obviously making their final preparations before leaving, she wouldn't relax until she'd seen them safely on their way.

Tom was making the rounds of the people he'd met, he looked far more assured than when she'd first met him and he carried an air of confidence which had been missing earlier. He approached her with a smile and she opened her bag and took out the place setting from the previous day and handed it to him. 'I've written our address and contact details on the back,' she told him. 'I hope you'll visit us when you come to Merebank again; I'd love to meet your wife and children in happier circumstances.'

He hugged her tightly and whispered, 'Do you know, you've actually done us a favour?'

'How on earth do you work that out?' she exclaimed.

'The social worker quickly decided there was no problem, apparently helped by Sharon's workmate who called by chance while she was there. As they were working together on the night Sharon hurt herself she'd called to check she was alright, and,' he added ruefully, 'because she'd heard about Danny and Rick.'

Marie waited for him to continue. 'I still don't understand.'

'While she was there the social worker went in the other room to make a phone call, that's when Sharon phoned me. She was checking the benefits we get and apparently we haven't been claiming enough since Lily was born and we'll be getting an increase and some back pay. It will help until I start working again in a few weeks and that wouldn't have happened without you interfering.' His triumphant expression turned into embarrassment at his gaffe, but Marie gaily laughed it off, after all he was quite right; she had interfered, but she was so relieved that something good had come out of it.

'I'm so glad you're not too angry with me,' she said with relief, 'because you have every right to be, but what did you mean about starting work in a few weeks? Have you got a job?'

'I have,' Tom told her, 'and it's all down to this man here.' He turned to Greg. 'I'm still trying to take it in. Go on Greg, you tell Marie.'

Greg briefly explained about the job offer on his latest project and Marie looked from his face to the continuously grinning Tom. They made an unlikely duo but the bond between them was obvious, and she had a feeling it would last way beyond this extraordinary weekend.

She sank back into her seat and Stuart affectionately took hold of her hand and whispered to her, 'All's well that ends well.'

'Indeed it is,' she replied with relief.

'Now it is time I was going,' Tom said. 'I've got to

go to the hospital for visiting and then I'll be on my way home at last.'

With a few bounds he was off, and they watched him pass the window, striding along the promenade with a spring in his step. Last night he'd vowed never to set foot in the place again but today he felt his old enthusiasm returning. The nightmare was over and he felt the same as he'd always done about his favourite resort. Checking he had enough left for the hospital car park, he spent the last bit of money he had to buy himself an ice cream cornet, a treat he hadn't allowed himself in months, and licking it with enjoyment, he hurried back to the car. He couldn't believe he would soon be working again and all because of a chance meeting with a stranger. He hoped Greg's daughter and her husband ended up being as happy together as he and Sharon were. He couldn't help feeling a bit sorry for her as there was still the small problem of finding out about her real dad; he wondered how she would cope with that.

Chapter 36

The lunch was finally coming to end in a flurry of goodbyes, and even the closest family and friends of the bride and groom were preparing to leave after wishing them bon voyage. Marie would have been happy to slip away unnoticed but Bryony had made a point of coming over and pleading with her to stay until everyone else had left, so she had no choice but to remain. She sincerely hoped she wasn't going to be asked to speak to Greg or anyone else for that matter; she had no desire whatsoever to become tangled once again in their or anyone else's lives. She'd already had enough of that.

When Damian came over with Louisa to tell them Louisa was leaving with her friends, Marie hugged her affectionately. 'It's been lovely meeting you, and I hope we see you again soon,' she said and Damian laughed.

'Don't worry Mum, you'll be seeing quite a lot of her in the future.' Louisa smiled affectionately at him and nodded.

Greg watched them go. 'They look very happy,' he said, 'I hope it all works out for them.'

'Yes, she seems to be a lovely girl; I'm just a bit...'

'What's wrong? Have you got reservations about

her?'

'No, not really. I suppose I'm just being silly but I can't help feeling sorry for Katy Sheridan and that Louisa might have contributed to her marriage breaking up.'

'I can put your mind at rest on that score,' Greg replied. 'Apparently that wasn't the first affair or even the second, and Katy's been miserable for years. She's already given him plenty of opportunities to change, but this public display was the last straw and it's given her the push she needed to finally leave him.'

'My goodness,' Marie exclaimed, 'did Katy tell you all that?'

'No, actually it was her friend who's come to take her back. I went along this morning to check if she'd managed to arrange a lift and her friend arrived while I was there. When Katy went to get her bag Lucy filled me in with the details of what had been happening. She's been trying to get her to leave for years and she's determined that this time she'll go through with it.'

'Oh, well in that case...'

'So you see, there's nothing to worry about, in fact you could say that Louisa has done Katy a favour.'

'Well I wouldn't go as far as that but I do feel a bit better about it.' She turned to him and gave a knowing smile. 'Are you by any chance intending to see Katy again?'

Greg shrugged. 'Now that would be telling.'

'Come on Greg, you can tell me,' she urged.

'I've said I'll ring her when I get back from holiday, just to check she's alright.'

'Have you indeed?' Marie replied, and wondered where that would leave Bryony, but deep down she hoped Greg would find happiness with someone new. 'Well whatever happens I wish you luck.' All at once it was quiet in the room and looking round, she saw they were the only people left. 'I wish we could go but Bryony wants to see me for some reason.'

'Well I'm not hanging around when I've said goodbye to Amelia and Piers. See you in a minute.'

Damian passed Greg as he came back to sit next to his mother. 'Well Mum,' he said, 'what a wedding that was.'

'It certainly was,' she agreed, 'and you've got yourself a lovely new girlfriend.'

His face was beaming. 'I have indeed. It's an old cliché isn't it, getting off with the bridesmaid?'

Stuart laughed at Damian's choice of words. 'I don't think you'd better use the phrase 'getting off with' when Louisa's around,' he advised his son. 'There must be a more romantic way to describe it, although at the moment I can't think of one.'

'When you do, Dad, let me know,' Damian said. Suddenly the sound of raised voices stopped him mid-sentence and they all sat very still as they tried to make out what was happening. 'That's Amelia's voice,' he said anxiously. 'Whatever can be happening?' He jumped up and started moving towards the door but Marie shot out of her chair and tried to hold him back.

'No!' she cried. 'Don't get involved, there's nothing you can do to help.'

'Mum, she's my oldest friend; at least I've got to try.' Gently but firmly he lifted her hand off his arm. As the voices penetrated the wall he looked at her closely. 'Do you know what this is about?' She nodded sadly.

'Unfortunately I think I do, but there's nothing we can do to help. You are right though, she may need a friend, so go and see if you can at least give her some support.'

Damian hurried away and Marie sank into Stuart's arms. 'Oh dear,' she wept. 'I've been dreading this for years.'

Chapter 37

Bryony and Colin stood together, presenting a united front as Piers' family set off on their journey home. At last she could breathe again instead of the constricting feeling in her chest as she'd counted down the minutes to the final departures. Colin had been throwing her odd glances since he'd noticed Ralph's absence, despite her assurances that he was simply feeling a little tired. She'd managed to distract him from going to discover for himself what was happening, primarily because she suspected he'd broach the subject of the previous day's revelations and she didn't want Ralph exposed to more upset than was absolutely necessary.

Thankfully he'd kept a brake on his drinking for most of the day, but he was gradually getting past the gregarious stage and was now showing the inevitable confrontational side of his character. Passing the dining room, she glanced in and saw Marie and Stuart talking to Damian and she remembered she'd asked Marie to stay behind. She hadn't considered Stuart being there as well which was silly of her, but none of them looked up as she passed so she couldn't tell them it was alright for them to leave. It wouldn't take long to sort Colin out and then she'd go in to speak to them.

Amelia announced she and Piers would pop in to see her grandfather before they left and to Bryony's consternation Colin said he would join them. This was a situation she hadn't predicted and it could have dire consequences. 'No,' she said too quickly, 'let them have a few minutes alone with him, they're not going to see him for ages and you can spend as much time with him as you like when they've gone.'

Scornfully Colin dismissed her. 'Do you think I don't know what you're up to? I'm not that stupid.' Angrily pushing her away, he moved forward and almost fell, but holding onto a chair he righted himself and stood taunting her. 'You're frightened I might say something but you don't need to worry, your secret's safe with me.'

Amelia voice broke with nervous laughter. 'Dad, what are you talking about? What secret?'

Bryony saw Greg crossing the foyer to join Marie and Stuart in the dining room and willed him to keep out of view, but Colin followed the direction of her eyes and called out to him. 'There you are,' he said scornfully. 'I wondered where you'd got to.'

Greg turned and hesitated but Amelia ran over to pull him into the group. 'Greg, come and join us before Mum and Dad have another bust-up. I can't be coping with that just before we leave.'

'What's going on?' he asked. 'I thought I heard raised voices but I couldn't believe it.'

Colin had lost his belligerence and was feeling increasingly sorry for himself, but he seemed determined to make himself heard. 'I'll tell you what's going on,' he said, slowly and deliberately, 'my wife is trying to prevent me from seeing my own father.'

Greg raised a questioning eyebrow. 'Why?' he asked.

Shrugging her shoulders, Bryony gave up trying to persuade Colin, who she knew from experience was past accepting any kind of explanation. With a feeling of resignation she tried to explain that she thought Ralph was resting, and although he would welcome Amelia and Piers visiting him to say goodbye he probably didn't feel like having too many visitors.

Greg nodded. 'That sounds reasonable enough to me, you'll have plenty of time to see him when everyone's gone,' he suggested reasonably, but Colin was beyond reason.

'Oh well you would side with her,' he said sarcastically, 'and now of course we all know why.'

Amelia looked from one to the other and her voice trembled nervously. 'Dad, you're drunk. Stop talking in riddles.'

Greg moved swiftly towards Colin and locked his eyes into his. 'I think we should discuss this another time,' he said, and something in his voice pierced Colin's fuddled mind.

Reluctantly he gave in. 'Okay,' he mumbled, 'I'm going to get myself a drink.' There was a collective sigh of relief as they watched him go towards the bar, but Bryony couldn't stop herself from shaking, and when Amelia came to stand close to her she gripped her hands so tightly she could feel her nails biting into her flesh.

'Mum, what did Dad mean?' Amelia asked.

'Try to forget it,' Bryony said. 'You know what he's like when he's had too much to drink.' Taking Amelia's hand, she led her towards where Piers was standing.

'Come on you two, go and say your goodbyes to Grandpa, it nearly time for you to be leaving.'

They were almost out of earshot when Colin muttered audibly to himself. 'That is if he still considers you to be his granddaughter.'

Amelia stood stock still and everyone else held their breath. Spinning round, she faced them, her eyes glistening. 'Will someone please explain what is happening,' she asked, because I'm not going anywhere until they do.'

Bryony stood rigid with fear as she watched Piers moved closer to put a protective arm around his unresponsive wife. 'Please,' she begged, looking now at her mother, 'I feel scared and I don't know why.' Bryony started to go to her but Amelia's hand shot up. 'No, Mum,' she said, 'I want to know what Dad meant. Why would Grandpa not consider me to be his granddaughter?'

Bryony could feel her heart thumping against her ribs and her mouth was dry. 'Let's go in the bar and sit down,' she suggested, but Amelia refused to move.

'I'm going nowhere,' she said, her voice rising, 'until you tell me what's going on.' She looked over to where Colin was standing in the doorway to the bar. 'Dad,' she said, 'what did you mean when you said Granddad might not think of me as his granddaughter?'

Colin was floundering and Bryony panicked when Greg said to him, 'No Colin, I think Bryony should be the one to explain.'

Amelia was losing control and began shouting to raise her voice above them all. 'If somebody doesn't tell me soon I'll go mad!'

Bryony wanted to whisk Amelia away to protect

her from what was happening, but she was helpless and knew it. She'd never expected this to happen and she didn't know what to do but she was left with no choice, she had to tell Amelia the truth. Taking a deep breath and using all her courage she said simply, 'Your dad... I mean Colin, he isn't actually your biological father.' An eerie silence filled the room before Amelia's pitiful cry split it in two.

'I can't believe this!' she cried. 'So who is my dad, do I even know him?'

'It's Greg,' Colin said. 'I'm surprised you haven't already guessed.' He disappeared from the room.

'Is it true?' Amelia asked Greg, who nodded. 'I don't understand!' she cried. 'Why have you never told me? Were you ashamed?'

Greg shook his head slowly from side to side and Bryony's heart now went out to him as the realisation of what she'd done finally hit her. Before he could reply she said, 'No Amelia, I have to take full responsibility, Greg only learned of this yesterday.'

Amelia swayed and Piers held her up and demanded a chair. He was just helping her into it when Damian approached. 'What's going on?' he asked. 'I thought I heard Amelia crying.' He looked at them all before resting his eyes on Piers, glaring hard. 'Have you done something to hurt her?' he demanded. 'Because if you have, I'll...'

Greg moved swiftly to put a restraining hand on Damian who was coiled like a spring. 'No, Damian,' he said, 'Piers has done nothing wrong.'

'Well someone's upset her,' Damian said, 'so you'd better tell me what's going on.'

Amelia turned her tearstained face to him. 'If you

can make any sense of it will you explain it to me? Because I don't understand at all.'

This time it was Greg who explained as briefly as he could, and by the time he'd finished Amelia was sobbing uncontrollably. Damian went to her and took her hand and she stood up and told them she was going to her room. Holding Damian's hand, she asked him to go with her and for a moment Piers stood indecisively, wondering what to do, but slipping her arm through his she walked unsteadily between them towards the stairs.

Bryony was distraught as she stood helplessly watching them support Amelia as she stumbled on the staircase, which only the day before she'd descended so happily on her way to be married. Wanting nothing more than to be allowed to go somewhere and hide, she prepared herself for the inevitable backlash. Everyone would blame her and rightly so, but surely they could understand she'd been left with very little choice from the start.

Greg walked away and went into the dining room where Marie and Stuart were still waiting, and no doubt more than willing to commiserate with him, which left her feeling even more alienated. Colin had gone into the bar to help himself to a drink and for once she sympathised and decided to join him. She didn't hear Justin's tentative approach until he gave a little cough to let her know he was there. She was just about to dismiss him when he told her there was a man who wished to speak to her.

'I can't speak to anyone,' she told him, 'send him away.'

'It's a Mr Ethan Denning,' he persisted. 'He said

it's a personal matter.'

'What does he want?' she asked.

'I'm sorry, he didn't say, but I'll tell him you can't see him at the moment?'

Bryony thought for a moment, there would be no harm finding out what he wanted and anyway it would be rude to shun a member of Amelia's new family. 'No, I'll see him,' she said.

He was waiting by the front entrance and she registered again the good looks and a certain savoir faire despite his more casual gear. He was immediately apologetic. 'I'm so sorry, I seemed to have rudely intruded on a family crisis. Please forgive me, I'll leave immediately.'

She knew her appearance must shock him; her eyes were red and her hair was all over the place, but something inside her wanted to hear what he said.

'No, don't go, at least not until you've told me what you came to say.'

He hesitated before pulling a card from his pocket and handing it to her. 'I just wanted to give you this,' he said, 'and tell you that you and your husband are welcome to use it if ever you fancy a trip. It's beautiful at any time of the year, not just for the skiing season.'

She read the card and when she turned it over saw there was a mobile number written on the back. 'That's my private number,' he explained, 'so if you decide to go ring me to check when it's free.' Smiling broadly he added, 'There are a few of us going next week and you and your husband are welcome to join us if you like.'

'My husband and I are splitting up,' she told him frankly, 'so I will be on my own after this weekend.'

There was no hint of surprise or sympathy on his face. 'Then you could still come if you wish,' he said.

'I don't think so,' she replied, 'I wouldn't know anyone.'

'I can assure you that is no reason to refuse; the group isn't made up exclusively of couples.'

He was disarmingly persistent and she could feel herself weakening as a tremor of excitement filled her body, and without thinking she asked, 'What about your wife? Doesn't she mind you inviting unknown women?'

'Oh, I thought you knew,' he replied. 'There is no Mrs Denning. Well there is, I suppose, but she's an ex-wife. Look, I'll leave you with the details, please get in touch whenever it's suitable.' He shook her hand and walked steadily down the steps but at the bottom he turned and waved and she hoped they would meet again soon.

She'd lost all track of time when Amelia returned with Piers and Damian. Amelia seemed composed but very pale, and looked lovely in the outfit she'd chosen to wear for travelling. Her hair was fastened back but damp tendrils escaped around her face and only her eyes gave away her sadness. Her voice was calm and measured. 'There are a couple of things I want to ask,' she said, turning to Greg. 'Is it true what Mum said, that you only found out about this yesterday?'

Greg nodded. 'Absolutely,' he replied, 'your mother will vouch for that.'

Bryony struggled to hold herself together. Somehow Amelia's calmness unnerved her more than her earlier understandable distress, and when Amelia turned to her she dreaded what she was going to say.

'Mum, how could you do this to me? How could you let me live my whole life based on a lie?'

Bryony's eyes pooled and brimmed with tears. She was lost; there were no words to adequately explain her actions all those years ago and she didn't know what to say. 'Please try to understand,' she pleaded, 'I couldn't say anything when you were born, it just wouldn't have been acceptable. There were your grandparents to consider, apart from anyone else.'

'Humph.' Colin grunted, 'I suppose I didn't count.'

Bryony glanced at him before continuing, 'Then as you got older it didn't seem appropriate.' She clasped her hands together in frustration and looked around for a single sign of understanding, but no help was forthcoming from any of them. 'It wasn't a conscious decision, you must understand that. I was waiting for the right time and the right time just never seemed to come.' Her voice faded away. 'It wasn't easy to live with.'

'Do you think this is easy for me now?' Amelia cried.

Bryony broke down and wept. 'No,' she said, 'I would have given anything to prevent this from happening.'

'Unfortunately Mum, you mean anything but the truth.' She looked at her watch. 'I know it's bad timing but we really do have to leave otherwise we'll be too late for check-in.' Going over to where Colin was sitting forlornly nursing an empty glass, she bent down to kiss him. 'Bye Dad,' she said. 'Thanks for a lovely wedding, and don't forget, you'll always be my dad.'

Pulling himself up, he took her in his arms and embraced her. Bryony shrivelled inside as she watched her daughter turn to walk towards the dining room, where she kissed Marie and Stuart goodbye before assuring them that she and Piers would visit them the next time they came home. 'Wherever home is,' she said, and Marie flinched. She hugged Damian tightly. 'Thanks for your support and especially those wise words,' she whispered, and he gripped her back.

Bryony held her breath and waited, hoping against hope that her daughter wouldn't shun her in front of them all. Amelia turned and the smile she gave her was weak and full of sadness as she remained standing, considering what to do. Bryony's heart twisted when she saw her turn and walk away.

Greg was watching and his eyes brightened when Amelia went to him and drew him towards the door. 'I don't know what to say to make it easier for you,' he said, 'but I am so proud to have you as my daughter, even if I'm not allowed to acknowledge you.'

'What are you talking about?' Amelia asked gently. 'We're not living in Victorian times. You're my father and the time for hiding it is over.' She turned to face him. 'You will understand, won't you? Dad will always have to be my dad, like he's always been.'

'Of course he will be, there's no other way. He's done a very good job of bringing you up and you can't take that away from him.' Greg took her arm. 'You never cease to amaze me,' he said. 'You went upstairs with your heart broken but when you returned you were much calmer. What happened?'

'Two things happened actually,' she told him. 'The

first was when Damian reminded me that I'd always said you were as good as a second father to me. He told me I should simply view it that I'd been right all along and I'm very lucky to have two dads who love me. He pointed out I've gained a father, not lost one, and I believe he's right.'

Bryony glanced at Marie, who was beaming with pride at Damian.

'Damian is very wise, I think,' Greg said, 'and the other thing that happened, what was that?'

'I went in to see Granddad. I was afraid that this would make a difference to how he felt about me, especially after what Dad had said, but he told me he was upset I could even think it. As far as he's concerned I'm his granddaughter and that's the end of it. So you see everything is back to normal, except it's even better because now I have you as well.'

They'd all reached the top of the steps and Piers was waiting with the car which he'd brought round from the car park. Bryony hoped against hope that Amelia would at least single her out for a brief embrace but she was overcome with disappointment to see her blow them all a kiss before running down the steps towards her waiting husband. Just as she reached the bottom she quickly turned round and ran back. 'I nearly forgot,' she said to Greg, 'didn't you say you are visiting St. Lucia on your cruise?'

'I am,' he replied, 'and I'm really looking forward to it as it's one of the places where we dock for a couple of days. Why are you asking?'

'Because,' she replied mischievously, 'that's where we're going for our honeymoon. Can we meet up while you're there?'

Greg hesitated, looking towards the car. 'I'm not sure, I think you should check with Piers first. It is your honeymoon, after all.'

'Oh it's fine!' she cried. 'It was Piers who suggested it. Will you please say yes before I go?'

'I'd be delighted,' he said. 'I'll be in touch once I'm on the way.'

'Fantastic,' she said.

Bryony's heart was breaking for what she knew she'd lost, and although she tried to hide it she knew Amelia had seen the look of hurt on her face. 'Bye Mum,' she said. 'I'll ring you from the airport.'

Bryony nodded before turning wordlessly to go back into the hotel, where she sank onto a chair and finally gave way to her feelings. Greg went to sit in an adjoining chair, but made no attempt to comfort her.

'I suppose there's no future for us now,' she sobbed, and Greg shook his head. 'I think I could have accepted what you'd done if it had only affected me,' he said, 'but there was only one possible outcome and it was Amelia who was always going to be the main one to suffer.'

'Couldn't we just try?'

'No, I'm sorry.'

She watched him walk away and leave.

*

Ralph was much brighter when she went in to see him but she was surprised to find no sign of Colin, who she'd expected to be there.

'Are you alright, Father-in-law? Is there anything you need?

'No thanks,' he replied, 'you've made sure I'm

being very well looked after. I presume Amelia and Piers got off alright.'

'Yes, she seemed to have taken things better than I could have hoped for but I'm really sorry it happened like it did.'

'Things often don't go according to plan, I'm sorry to say. I suppose you'll be glad when you can get away from all this and enjoy your cruise. I take it that's where you're going.'

'It was, but not now. I'm not going; it's over between us.' She saw the sign of hope enter his eyes and reluctantly she disappointed him. 'I'm sorry Ralph but it doesn't mean I'll be staying with Colin. That is definitely not going to happen.'

Ralph nodded. 'I suppose I didn't expect it really,' he said.

'I am going to be taking a holiday in a couple of weeks,' she told him. 'I feel the need for a break but I'll make sure everything is in order before I go.'

'That's fine with me; you need to get away for a while. Now I think I'll have a little rest if you don't mind.' He didn't say what he was thinking but he didn't need to. She knew exactly what he meant, she would need to go away to escape the inevitable backlash of gossip and criticism.

*

Outside the hotel Damian told his parents he was meeting up with some of his mates from university before they all went their separate ways. Marie couldn't resist telling him how proud they were of the way he'd helped Amelia, which brought a modest but appreciative grin to his face. 'We've been mates all our lives,' he said, 'all I did was point out the facts and the truth.'

'Nevertheless, it worked,' Stuart beamed, as he held his hand out to his son. Damian shook it before turning to lope his way down the side street to the old pub where his friends were waiting. 'He's a good lad,' Stuart said with feeling. 'I hope that lass he's taken a shine to doesn't let him down.'

Marie thrust her hand into the bend of Stuart's arm and he laid his hand affectionately over hers. 'I've got a good feeling about that,' Marie said, and Stuart feigned a groaning response.

'Oh heaven preserve me from match-making women with feelings,' he declared. 'Come on, let's get home to a bit of peace and quiet.'

'Amen to that,' Marie agreed, 'I really have had enough excitement this weekend to last me a lifetime.

*

Bryony went to her room and poured herself a gin and tonic. There was a lot be said for being single and fancy free, and Greg didn't hold the only key to her freedom and happiness after all. Taking the card from her handbag, she Googled the ski resort and found Ethan's chalet, which was everything he'd described and more. The virtual walk through breath-taking scenery to surrounding areas and restaurants filled her with excitement, as an image of herself and Ethan Denning suddenly transposed itself onto the screen. She knew it would take some time to gain Amelia's forgiveness and understanding, but in the meantime she still had her own life to live, and although it had taken an unexpected turn it was looking very promising.